C000156921

DARK DREAM'S TRAP

THE CHILDREN OF THE GODS BOOK 28

I. T. LUCAS

Copyright © 2019 by I. T. Lucas
Dark Dream's Trap

All rights reserved.
No part of this book may be reproduced in any form or by any electronic or
mechanical means, including information storage and retrieval systems,
without written permission from the author, except for the use of brief
quotations in a book review.

NOTE FROM THE AUTHOR:
Dark Dream's Trap is a work of fiction!
Names, characters, places and incidents are products of the author's
imagination or are used fictitiously and are not to be construed as real. Any
similarity to actual persons, organizations and/or events is purely
coincidental.

JULIAN

"Good morning, my love." Julian walked into the bedroom with a tray.

The breakfast he'd prepared consisted of coffee and chocolates, because as far as food went all he'd found in the kitchen was a half-empty box of cereal and a couple of frozen pizzas. The chocolates were a lifesaver.

Even though Ella had feasted on them last night, he still had plenty left over in the box she'd given him for safekeeping. She loved those little treats, but it was a shame that this was all he could come up with the morning after the most monumental night of their relationship.

Not only had they confessed their love for each other, but Ella had promised to give the therapist a chance, and that was almost as big a deal as the I love you's.

"What time is it?" Ella mumbled, opening just one eye a crack.

"Around ten." He put the tray on the nightstand and leaned to kiss her soft lips.

She looked so adorable with her cheeks rosy from sleep, her pink hair sticking out in all directions, and her expression open and trusting and full of love.

For him.

"Would you like me to pour you some coffee?" He lifted the carafe.

"Breakfast in bed?" She stretched her arms over her head and yawned. "You're spoiling me, Julian. I might come to expect this every morning."

He dipped his head. "It would be my pleasure to serve."

"Aren't you sweet." Ella reached for his cheek. "I won the lottery with you." She planted a quick closed-mouthed kiss on his lips and then flung the comforter off. "I need to use the facilities, but in the meantime, I would love it if you poured me some coffee."

"It shall be done, my lady."

Chuckling, she rushed into the bathroom.

The sunlight from the open window made the plain white T-shirt he'd given her nearly see-through, outlining the contours of her curvy tight body as if she were wearing a sheer nightgown.

Sexy and adorable. What a killer combination.

As his shaft rose to attention, pressing painfully against his fly and accusing him of self-inflicted torture, Julian had no defense to offer his suffering member. He would be lying if he claimed that giving Ella his most worn-out T-shirt hadn't been a calculated move.

Shaking his head at his teenage antics, Julian was reminded of what his mother said about men. They were forever boys at heart, and that included immortals as old as Kian. There were exceptions, of course, like her mate.

Turner must have been born with an ancient brain. Julian could imagine him as a boy, somber and serious, dedicated to learning as much as possible and as quickly as his huge brain could absorb it. He probably had never taken part in the shenanigans ordinary boys amused themselves with.

Was that why Bridget had chosen him?

Every couple was different, and so was every relationship.

There was something magical about that connection, though, something Julian hadn't expected.

Surprisingly, the incredible closeness and the feeling of being a unit had little to do with physical intimacy. It was more about the mental fusing, about the breaking down of barriers, and about laying one's soul bare for the other person and trusting that they wouldn't stomp all over it.

After Ella's meltdown last night, Julian felt closer than ever to her, and her confession about the attraction to Lokan hadn't diminished the effect in the least.

Her misguided feelings toward the Doomer mattered much less to him than the cleansing of her guilt over it and the obliteration of the wedge it had put between them.

There was a perfectly logical explanation for why Ella had reacted like that to Lokan. The affinity that Dormants and immortals felt toward each other had made her feel close to the Doomer, and because she had no way of knowing that he was an immortal and she was a Dormant, and what that meant, Ella had interpreted it as sexual attraction.

Or at least that had been the initial impetus.

Later, when he'd started intruding on her dreams, Navuh's son had used his good looks, his intelligence, and his charm to reinforce those feelings, and possibly compulsion as well.

As Julian had suspected from the moment he'd learned about Ella's dream visitor, Lokan was playing Ella and not the other way around. Despite all that had happened to her, she was still a naive eighteen-year-old, while the Doomer was an immortal with centuries of experience plotting and manipulating. She was no match for him.

Damn, she was so young and had gone through so much already.

It wasn't fair.

He wanted to hold Ella in the safety of his arms and

3

shield her from the world twenty-four seven, but he would settle for the nights.

Having her curled against his body, his arms wrapped securely around her, had felt so right. It hadn't mattered to Julian that that was as far as it had gone. Well, the primitive side of him didn't like it one bit, but, fortunately, the savage occupied a very small part of his psyche and he'd beaten it into submission.

For now, he was satisfied with just being close. The rest would come later, after Ella had several sessions with Vanessa.

How did the saying go, "All good things come to those who wait"? It was a simple way to state a well-known fact. Those who were adept at delaying gratification got ahead of the crowd, and Julian was a master of that.

When Ella came out of the bathroom, he had the two cups of coffee ready, hers with cream and sugar and his with just sugar.

"I'm hopping right back." She crawled into the bed, stacked four pillows up against the headboard, got comfortable sitting up, and pulled the duvet up to her chest, covering everything up.

What a shame.

He handed her the mug. "Just as you like it. Cream and two sugars."

"Thank you." Cupping it between her hands, she took a sip and smacked her lips. "Perfect."

"Yes, you are." He bent and kissed the very tip of her nose. "I love you."

"I love you too." She shook her head. "Why does it feel so awkward to hear you say that?"

Because Ella still didn't believe that she deserved love, but that was going to change. Firstly, because she would be hearing him say it fifty times a day, and secondly, because

Vanessa was going to clean up the trash that Ella had allowed to accumulate in her head.

All that nonsense about being tainted and about having some darkness inside her had to be disposed of as soon as possible. The longer it lingered, the more it festered, diminishing the brightness of Ella's incredible spirit.

"I'm going to say it a lot, so you'd better get used to it."

"Ditto."

"Nah-ah, young lady, ditto isn't going to cut it. I want to hear the words, preferably accompanied by a hot kiss." He was hoping for more than that, but for now it would do.

For some reason, Ella's smile turned into a grimace. "About that. I don't think we should hang out together until the mission is over."

Talk about driving a dagger into his unsuspecting heart. "What are you talking about?" Things were going so well, and now she was throwing this at him?

Grabbing another pillow from his side of the bed, she hugged it to her. "I don't want us to be apart either. But catching Mr. D is more important than us. We can wait a little longer, but every dream encounter I have with him, I'm running the risk of letting something slip, getting him suspicious, and sabotaging this opportunity for the clan."

"We've been hanging out together every day, and you did just fine."

She brought her knees up, curling her arms around the pillow as if it was a shield. "That was before we deciphered the combination to unlocking my passion. Now it will be so much harder to refrain from doing more. And I know it's going to rock my world, and then I won't be able to continue pretending with Mr. D."

Ella thought that making love to him was going to rock her world? At least he could take solace in that.

Julian let out a breath. "Do you trust me?"

Ella rolled her eyes. "Of course, I trust you. I don't trust myself."

"Until the mission of entrapping the Doomer is over, we will keep our relationship strictly platonic, and I'm going to be in charge of that, so you have nothing to worry about." He took her hand. "I might not look it, but I'm a stubborn guy. When I decide on something, it's very difficult to sway me away from that decision. I won't let you seduce me even if you try."

Smiling, she lifted a brow. "Are you sure about that? I'm stubborn too. You said so yourself."

"That you are. But remember, you made me a promise, and I expect you to keep it. I want you to make an appointment with Vanessa for Monday."

"I can't do it on Monday. I'm filming."

"So?"

"I can't get myself all worked up before it, and I scheduled the taping for after dinner."

"Fine. Then Tuesday."

Letting out a resigned breath, she nodded. "Okay, but just so we are clear on that. I'm going to have one session with her, and if I don't like it, I will not have another."

"Three. You can't decide if she's helpful or not based on one meeting." Remembering how Ella visualized everything, he added, "You can't clean all of your kitchen cabinets in one go, let alone your brain. All kinds of nasty things are lurking in there, and they need to get trashed. And after that is done, the interior needs a good scrubbing with soap. You can't start filling those cabinets with beautiful new china until all of this is done and they are sparkling clean."

2

ELLA

*I*t was really clever of Julian to come up with something Ella could visualize. It worked. Those cabinets up in her brain definitely needed spring cleaning. She just wasn't sure that Vanessa was the right tool for the job. Talking to a shrink was like using a cloth to clean up caked-on grime. It just smeared it around but didn't get rid of it.

"I hope that Mr. D can expedite my interview. I want this over and done with, so I can focus on us and our relationship."

"You don't have to wait." When she opened her mouth to argue, Julian lifted his hand. "I'm not talking about sex. We can get closer in other ways."

"What do you mean?"

"We can be together, just not alone with each other. We can hang out with family and friends."

It was much better than not seeing him at all, which Ella wasn't sure she could actually do. Maybe with plenty of phone calls, but even those had the potential of sliding into sexual territory. For now, complete abstinence was best.

Hanging out with her mother, Magnus and Parker could

actually be fun and bring the entire family closer. "You're always welcome in my house."

"I know. And I like your mother and brother, and Magnus too. When I come over, instead of going to your room or out for a walk, we can spend time with your family. And the same goes for you. So far, you've only gotten to know my mother and Turner in their professional capacity. I think it would be nice to meet for dinner as a family. My mom doesn't cook much, but Turner can bring takeout on his way back from the office, or we can all go out to a restaurant."

That sounded wonderful. Growing up in a tiny family, Ella had envied her friends who had uncles and aunts and cousins and grandparents. Their birthdays had seemed so much happier than hers. Secretly, she'd hoped to one day marry a guy with a large family or a clan.

"I love it, and not only because of the obvious. Hanging around a lot of people will fill my head with more than just you, which is good for the dream encounters."

He arched a brow. "What do you mean by obvious?"

"You know, we are kind of engaged, right? So, it makes sense for us to get close to each other's families and friends."

Embarrassed, Ella put her mug on the nightstand and popped a chocolate into her big mouth. She should've done that five seconds ago instead of blurting nonsense about a nonexistent engagement.

When Julian sighed, her gut clenched. Now he was going to give her a speech about rushing to conclusions and tell her that they were not getting married anytime soon.

Not that she wanted to, not yet anyway. She was too young, for one, and then there was the issue of her education. Ella hadn't given up on that. Couldn't even if she wanted to. Since she was a little girl, her mother had been drilling the importance of college education into her head. She couldn't disappoint Vivian like that.

Except, college and marriage were not mutually exclusive.

8

Kids were another thing, though. Getting pregnant with Ella was the reason her mother hadn't gotten the education she'd wanted.

Not that pregnancy had anything to do with marriage.

Because she and Julian couldn't use contraceptives while working on the activation of her immortal genes, there was a slight chance Ella could get pregnant during the process. But maybe the prohibition was only on condoms?

She needed to ask Bridget if oral contraceptives were okay.

Once she turned immortal, her fertility would drop to almost nothing, and that was regardless of whether she and Julian wanted to wait with starting a family or not.

At the thought, a wave of sadness washed over Ella. It wasn't that she wanted kids right away, but she didn't want to wait centuries to have them either.

Julian was going to make such a great father. He was warm, patient, smart...

Crap, way to get carried away. There was plenty of time before any of that became relevant, and she was pretty sure Julian was about to tell her precisely that.

Instead, he said, "This idea is growing on me, and the more I think of it, the more I like it."

Ella let out a breath and cast a sidelong glance at the three remaining chocolates on the little plate. She really shouldn't eat any more, but the thing about being addicted to the sweet goodness was that she treated it as a reward or a pick-me-up, whether she was stressed or relieved, happy or sad, celebrating or mourning. Right now it was stress.

Julian reached for one and handed it to her. "It's going to be like an old-fashioned courtship, when couples weren't allowed to be alone before the big day, and all their meetings were done with family members present. I think that when sex is not on the table, it eliminates a lot of pressure. It becomes a non-issue."

"Except for the blue balls," she murmured.

"Don't worry about that." He chuckled. "I'll survive."

Hopefully, not by using a substitute other than his own hand. Suddenly, it occurred to her that it was strange for Julian to be so understanding about her dream encounters with Logan, and about her other issues. Perhaps it was because he was slaking his needs elsewhere?

But as soon as the thought flitted through her head, she cast it aside. Julian was just an angel of a man. That was all. And, apparently, he liked a challenge, even if it was about withstanding torment. It hadn't escaped her notice that he was a highly competitive overachiever, and as such he must be very good at handling delayed gratification.

They had that in common.

Well, except for the freaking chocolates. She had no self-control with those.

Still, she had to ask, "How?"

"I'll buy a tool belt."

She arched a brow. "What does that have to do with anything?"

"Manual labor. I'll get Yamanu to teach me construction and work till I drop. It will be a double whammy. The halfway house will get done faster and for less money, and I'll come home too exhausted to think about anything other than getting in the shower and then bed."

He chuckled. "To sleep."

"Poor baby." She cupped his cheek.

"Not at all. I'm actually looking forward to it. It will keep me distracted while you clean your cabinets." He put his hand over hers on his cheek. "Going platonic will get rid of a source of tension between us and allow us to focus on getting to know each other instead."

Reaching for the coffee mug, Ella took a sip to wash down the chocolate and then put it aside and spread her arms. "Can I give you a hug? Because you are the best guy on the planet, and I'm the luckiest girl."

He leaned into her arms, put his cheek on her shoulder, and sighed. "You know, there is a medical explanation for why it feels so good to hug and cuddle."

"Go ahead. Geek out on me," she teased, but the truth was that she loved learning new things.

"Hugging stimulates the pressure receptors under the skin, which increases the activity of the vagus nerve, which in turn triggers an increase in oxytocin levels. Oxytocin can decrease heart rate and cause a drop in the stress hormones cortisol and norepinephrine. It can also improve immune function, promote faster healing from wounds and diseases. It also increases the levels of good hormones, like serotonin and dopamine, which in turn reduce anxiety and depression."

"Oh, wow. Doctors should prescribe hugs in addition to medication."

"I agree."

Stroking his soft hair, she chuckled. "I found the solution to your midlife crisis at twenty-six. You should become a proponent of hugs and cuddles as a cure-all. I can visualize you running a hugging clinic with volunteer huggers, preferably old grandmas with soft bosoms. Those are the best, but you wouldn't know since everyone here is young."

3

BRIDGET

"That's a beauty," Sandoval said as he took the ring from Turner. "But it pales in comparison to your lovely lady, my friend."

Bridget waved a dismissive hand. "You're such a charmer, Arturo."

His eyes twinkled as he spread his arms in an exaggerated gesture. "Please tell me that this marvelous, fiery red hair is done by a gifted stylist. I'll send my wife to him."

"Sorry to disappoint you, but this is my natural color."

"*Dios mío*! What a lucky man Turner is. I can just imagine the fire burning inside a natural red-head like you." He then shook his head. "But the temper, that must be very hot too."

It was good that Turner wasn't the jealous type, not overtly anyway, because Bridget was having fun flirting with the guy. It was harmless, he wasn't aroused, and it had been ages since she'd engaged in teasing banter like that.

The one downside of having a brainiac like Turner for a mate was the absence of easy, lighthearted banter. He was always serious, rarely smiled, and avoided nonsensical conversations like the plague.

"You have no idea. I go from zero to one hundred in a split second." She snapped her fingers.

"I believe that." Sandoval glanced at Turner. "But my friend here looks better than ever, so you must be good for him. All this new beautiful blond hair, and that unlined skin." He smoothed his hand over his thinning hair. "I want the name of that transplant place."

The story they had told him to explain Turner's youthful appearance was that he'd gotten a hair transplant and laser work on his face.

It always amazed Bridget how easy it was to sell people an unlikely story just because there was no other more reasonable explanation they could conceive of.

For most Dormants, the transformation didn't bring much change, but it had for Turner. He looked fifteen years younger and better than he had in his early twenties.

He'd also lost some of the hardness, the edginess she'd found so sexy when they'd first met. But even though it had been part of why she'd fallen for him, Bridget didn't miss it. He was happier now than he'd ever been, and knowing that she was the reason for it was priceless.

"When we get back to Los Angeles, I'll look for the brochure and email you the name of the place," Turner said. "The revolutionary technology was developed in Switzerland, and that's where their only location is. In a couple of years, they might open a branch in the States."

Sandoval grimaced. "Never mind. I'm not going to travel all the way there for a hair transplant. There are enough reputable establishments here."

Turner's expression remained as impassive as ever, but Bridget knew him well enough to imagine a ghost of a smirk lifting the corners of his lips. He must've known about Arturo's inability to visit Switzerland, and that was why he'd made up the story about the clinic being there.

Following a knock on the door, one of Sandoval's many security guards entered. "The appraiser is here."

Arturo waved a hand. "Let him in."

So that was what the flirting had been all about. While waiting for the expert to arrive, Arturo had been stalling.

"Is he trustworthy?" Turner asked. "I mean as far as spreading the rumor about the ring."

"You intend to sell it, yes?" Sandoval asked. "Then you need the word to spread."

"I was hoping you'd buy it from me and then sell it. I'm doing this as a favor for a friend, and it's already taking too much of my time."

Training his gaze on Bridget, Sandoval grinned. "I'm thankful to your friend. If not for the ring, I would not have the excuse to finally meet your beautiful wife and offer you both my hospitality."

As the guard escorted the appraiser into the room, Arturo got up and greeted the guy as if he were an old friend.

"Yasha, thank you for coming. Please meet my good friends, Victor and Bridget Turner."

As they shook hands, she exchanged glances with Turner. He'd asked Sandoval not to sell the ring in Russia, but he hadn't said anything about the nationality of the appraiser.

Not that Yasha was necessarily a Russian.

It was a common name, and he could've been from any country in the Eastern Bloc. Nevertheless, Bridget's good mood had taken a nosedive. Sandoval had just introduced an unknown variable.

It took Yasha five minutes to examine the ring. "Would you like me to email you the estimate?"

Arturo clapped him on the back. "Sure. But I need a ball-park figure. How much do you think it could bring on the black market?"

"Twenty-five to thirty."

"Millions, I assume?"

The guy snorted. "Dollars, not rubles."

Bridget's gut churned with unease. She had a feeling that the guy had not only recognized the ring, but that he also knew who'd originally bought it.

It was to be expected, though. Not many diamonds of this size changed hands in the world, and someone like Yasha would be familiar with each one of them.

After the appraiser collected his tools, Sandoval escorted him to the door. "Thank you. Can you do me a favor, my friend?"

"Anything, for you."

"Please don't tell anyone I have the ring." He leaned to whisper in Yasha's ear. "I'm considering buying it for my wife, and I want it to be a surprise."

"Of course." The guy dipped his head before leaving.

Obviously, Sandoval didn't intend to buy the ring for himself or his wife, but he liked to maintain the appearance of a legitimate businessman who didn't deal in anything illegal.

After closing the door, he walked back to his armchair and sat down. "I'll give you twenty for it."

Turner shook his head. "That's much less than its lowest appraised value."

Sandoval grinned. "Yes, but since you are doing this as a favor for a friend and want to be done with this as soon as possible, I'm offering to take it off your hands. Instead of waiting for me to find you a buyer, you can get the money to your friend right away."

"Twenty-three," Turner said.

Sandoval shook his head. "Twenty-one, and that's my final offer. Take it or leave it, my friend. And just so you know, I'm being very generous because of our friendship and because of what you have done for my family."

Reminded of what Sandoval's nephew had done to Turner, Bridget's temper flared hot, and before she could put a muzzle on it, she blurted, "Your relation, the one Turner spared and then convinced you not to kill, had ordered a hit on him. I think you can do better than twenty-one."

Sandoval laughed. "And here is that famous temper. But you are right, my dear Bridget. Twenty-two, and that's my final offer."

Bridget offered him her hand. "You're an honorable man, Arturo."

Twenty-two million was going to buy several halfway houses, not just one.

"Indeed, I am." He looked at Turner. "So, are we even now? My debt of honor to you is paid?"

"There was no debt, Arturo." Turner offered him his hand for a handshake. "Just old friends helping each other out."

4

LOSHAM

*A*s his cell phone rang, the last name Losham expected to appear on the screen was his brother's.

He let it go to voicemail.

Lokan was a smart son of a bitch, and talking with him before he knew what the call was about was not a good strategy. The thing was, Losham's island sources hadn't reported any unusual activity or another shift of power among the half-brothers. Navuh liked to switch things around and reassign his sons to different leadership roles, so that none would get too comfortable or entrenched in their positions.

Another benefit of this system was that each knew the other's job.

Except for Losham, who until recently had been his father's right-hand man and advisor. Not anymore, though. He'd been demoted from his lofty position to leading the Brotherhood's drug dealing and pimping operations.

Except, Navuh hadn't replaced him with anyone else yet. Was that what Lokan wanted?

Was he sniffing around about the possibility of taking Losham's place?

It wasn't as if he would call to ask after his brother's

wellbeing.

The half-brothers weren't close. To the contrary. The constant rivalry over leadership positions in the Brotherhood didn't encourage familial loyalty, and neither did their father's favoritism, which was a moving target.

The favorite son today could become the least favored tomorrow, and Losham was a prime example of that. He'd thought himself indispensable, his strategic mind and good advice vital to Navuh and the Brotherhood, but he'd been wrong.

He was still unsure what had brought it about. It could've been punishment for a series of minor blunders or the result of shifting priorities. But since he'd covered up his mishaps well, it was most likely the latter.

With major contributors leaving the Brotherhood's protective umbrella, funding had dried up, and a new source of income was needed.

Regrettably, hot spots around the world were cooling at a rapid rate, and there was little demand for the Brotherhood's army of mercenaries. Their entire business model was collapsing or, rather, leaning heavily on two spindly legs that at the moment couldn't carry its weight.

That was why Navuh had assigned his best man to the job of shoring them up.

What had been a fringe source of income that was used mostly to bribe and blackmail high-ranking public figures around the world had become the core that had to sustain them until a new source was found.

It was all about technology now, and the Brotherhood wasn't equipped to compete in this new world. At least not until Losham's new breeding program started bearing fruit, producing offspring with mighty brains rather than brawn.

When his phone announced that he had a new voicemail, Losham clicked on the recording and listened attentively, trying to pick up subtle nuances in his brother's tone.

"Hello, Losham. I'm in the Bay Area, and I thought it was a good opportunity for us to meet. How about dinner later today? I'm waiting to hear from you before making other plans, so please let me know as soon as you can."

Damn. Lokan hadn't hinted at what he wanted to talk about, and the way he'd phrased his request, Losham had no choice but to answer him promptly.

Any delay would be interpreted as fear, and that was even worse than meeting his half-brother unprepared.

On his laptop, Losham closed the news broadcast he hadn't been paying attention to anyway and straightened his shoulders.

The damn demotion must have eroded his self-confidence.

There was no real reason for him to be wary of Lokan.

The guy was younger, less experienced, and had done nothing overly daring in recent years, unless schmoozing with Washington's movers and shakers could be considered hazardous.

Well, for a human it could be, but not for Lokan.

The guy was charming, he had to give him that, and his ability to compel was nothing to sneer at. It was a rare and coveted talent, extremely handy when dealing with humans. But neither compulsion nor his brother's fake charm had any effect on Losham. It was absurd for him to get anxious over a friendly talk.

Instead of calling back, he shot a quick text with the name of a restaurant he wanted to hold the meeting at. At least he had the advantage of the home court. The location of the hotel he'd chosen was perfect for bringing in a team of warriors and stationing them all around the big place without Lokan being any the wiser.

As cunning and underhanded as his younger half-brother was, he was still no match for Losham.

5

ELLA

"Good morning, sweetheart," Vivian said as Ella came in, then looked her up and down and then up again. "You look happy. Good news?"

Ella knew precisely what her mother was asking, but she wasn't going to indulge her curiosity. Besides, there was nothing to tell on that front.

Instead, she opted to share her other good news.

"Mr. D is arranging an expedited interview for me at Georgetown. All I have to do is fill out the application and send them my transcripts, which is why I'm going to Roni. I don't know what kind of grades poor Kelly Rubinstein had before her premature death, and if he needs to give them a makeover."

Vivian's face fell. "Oh."

Remembering what Julian had told her about hugs, Ella pulled her mother into a tight embrace. "This is good news, Mom. The faster it happens, the faster it ends, right?"

Vivian sighed. "I know. What can I do that I'm such a scaredy-cat? Facing that Doomer terrifies me."

Ella let go of her mom. "He's actually not that bad once you get to know him. I bet most people think he is charming.

But enough about him. I have to shower and change. Julian is picking me up in twenty minutes, and we are going to a barbecue at Roni's."

That brought the smile back to Vivian's face. "I'm so glad that you're making new friends. Roni is about your age, and his fiancée is very nice. You are going to have a good time."

Ella certainly hoped so. According to Julian, Roni wasn't the most charming of guys, but he was an amazing hacker and, more importantly, he was willing to help. She could handle some surly attitude as long as he helped her out.

As she stepped into the shower, Ella was thankful for the short haircut and the time it shaved off her bathroom routine. Most days she didn't even bother to blow dry it, letting it air dry instead. It seemed like the messier it was, the nicer it looked.

But today she was pressed for time, and two minutes with the blow dryer took care of that.

A little mascara, lip gloss, and she was ready with minutes to spare.

Julian was already waiting for her when she came out, chatting with her mother about the halfway house and how much easier it would be for her to run her classes there instead of schlepping all the way to the sanctuary and back.

"I would love not having to make that drive, but the girls in the sanctuary need me. Once they are in the halfway house, they are already on the road to recovery."

Ella leaned and kissed her cheek. "We'll talk about this later. Right now Julian and I have to skedaddle."

"Have fun, kids."

When they got to Roni's, the backyard party was already in full swing, with Roni flipping steaks over the weirdest looking barbecue Ella had ever seen.

It was egg-shaped.

"Let me introduce you to everyone," Julian said as he walked her over to Roni.

"Hi." Roni waved with a pair of tongs that were dripping steak juices. "Grab a plate. They're almost ready."

"Thank you. And thank you for helping me with the college application stuff."

"Pfft." He waved with the tongs again. "It's child's play for me."

"Nevertheless, I'm grateful."

He nodded, looking embarrassed.

That was cute. After Julian's warning, she'd expected the guy to be full of himself, and he kind of was, but he still felt awkward when thanked. She had a feeling that Roni's crusty attitude was a shield, and under it he was a nice guy.

"Hi, Ella." Sylvia came out into the backyard, holding a big salad bowl. "Come meet my mother." She put the bowl down and took Ella's hand. "She's in the kitchen."

Casting an apologetic glance at Julian, Ella let Sylvia drag her away.

"Tessa and Jackson are coming too, and so are Sharon and Robert. Do you know them?"

Ella shook her head. "I know Eva and Tessa, so naturally I've heard about Sharon and Robert, but I've never met them."

She was curious to meet Carol's ex and, also, the one he'd found true love with.

Sharon must be special to fill Carol's shoes, so to speak. Although small in size, Carol cast a big shadow.

In the kitchen, a short brunette was tossing a rice pilaf that smelled delicious.

"Mom, I want you to meet Ella."

She turned around, smiling shyly as she offered Ella her hand. "I'm Ruth, but I guess everyone knows me as Sylvia's mom."

There weren't many families in the village, and the only two with grown children that Ella had known about were Bridget and Eva, and now Ruth. But even though she should've been prepared, it was still hard to reconcile Ruth's youthful looks with her being Sylvia's mother.

In fact, the woman looked younger than her daughter. Perhaps because she was so shy while Sylvia was so outgoing, or maybe because the daughter was taller.

"Nice to meet you." Ella shook her hand. "Have you met my mother, Vivian?"

"I work outside the village and I come home late. So, I don't get to hang around much."

"Oh yeah? What do you do?"

"I run a café."

"Cool, so you're an independent businesswoman."

Ruth blushed. "I'm just the manager. The café belongs to Nathalie, Eva's daughter."

"Oh, right, the one Jackson manages..." Ella scratched her head. "I'm confused. Jackson manages the café here and Carol and Wonder work for him. You manage the one in the city, right? And both of you answer to Nathalie?"

"The original café where I work belongs to Nathalie, and this one and the one in the keep are partially hers as well. Jackson is in charge of the entire operation, and shares in the profits. I run the old café, and Carol runs the new one here. The keep has only vending machines."

"Are you talking about Jackson's sandwiches and pastries empire?" Tessa came into the kitchen.

Sylvia arched a brow. "I wouldn't call it an empire, but it's quite impressive for a guy his age. How old is he, nineteen?"

"Almost twenty."

"For someone so young to achieve so much is incredible," Ella said. "It gives me hope."

"Hope for what?" Sylvia asked.

"My charity. The idea is great, and I know it's going to work, but then I also have doubts because I'm thinking that an eighteen-year-old can't possibly know what she's doing. That's why hearing about Jackson's success is so inspiring."

Tessa wrapped her arm around Ella's shoulders. "It's going to work. I have a good feeling about it. And you, girl, have killer instincts."

Ella had no idea what Tessa was talking about. "What do you mean?"

"You know how to put the right spin on things. Like calling the filming tomorrow a presentation and not a lecture. It would've never crossed my mind that it might make a difference, but it would. And your decision to go first is not only brave but also smart. Your brain is just wired right for this. It's like you know what you're doing even though you've never done it before."

"What do you mean by going first?" Sylvia asked. "Doing what?"

"My story is going to be the first we tape, and I'm going to do it in front of all the girls currently residing in the sanctuary. Lead by example so to speak."

Sylvia whistled. "That takes guts. Doesn't it bother you that everyone will know your story?

Ella shrugged. "We are filming in silhouette, and I'm thinking about manipulating the voice recording too. No one will know who did which video."

"Still, it takes immense courage to tell a crowd of people what happened to you, and then release it to the world," Tessa said.

"You know what Eva would say to that?" Ella put her arm around Tessa's tiny waist.

"What?"

"No guts, no glory."

6

LOSHAM

*L*osham arrived at the meeting place well ahead of time.

After verifying that his warriors were strategically stationed throughout the hotel's lobby and the restaurant itself, he ordered the most expensive bottle of whiskey the restaurant had to offer and an appetizer that was aromatic enough to mask any subtle scents he might emit.

As someone who had to hobnob with politicians, Lokan probably wasn't under the same monetary restrictions as the rest of the Brotherhood's leadership, and Losham planned on having him foot the bill.

After all, the meeting was Lokan's idea so he should pay for it.

What Losham wondered, though, was whether his brother would bring a team of warriors with him or flaunt his confidence by showing up by himself.

The only companion Losham was going to admit to was Rami, who was outside, waiting in the car.

As the host escorted Lokan to the private enclave Losham had reserved, Losham got up and opened his arms to embrace his brother. "It has been too long," he said as they slapped each other's backs.

"Indeed." Lokan smiled. "With both of us stationed in the States, we should make an effort to meet more often."

When the host left, Losham switched to their native tongue. "How have you been? Things going well for you?"

"As well as can be expected. I'm dealing and wheeling, but the thing about dirty politicians is that you can't trust their word. Not even with the hefty contribution we are making to their campaigns. Without the proper personal bribe and a nasty secret to threaten them with, nothing gets done. Which means even more time and money spent on digging out the skeletons buried in their backyards. I was lucky to find an excellent detective agency. If you ever have a need for that kind of work, I'll gladly share the contact information with you."

Was that an olive branch?

Losham chuckled. "With what I'm tasked with, I have no need for those types of services. But I'm surprised you do. With your compulsion ability it shouldn't be a problem for you. You could just force them to do your bidding."

"Regrettably, it doesn't work on everyone, and as I discovered, the more corrupt a human is, the harder it is to compel him or her. They are suspicious of everyone and everything and are not open to suggestion."

Losham was surprised at Lokan's admission. He was confessing to a weakness, which was like exposing his soft underbelly to an opponent armed with sharp teeth. Or fangs, as was the case.

Since Lokan was too smart to just let it slip, this must be his way of reaching out to Losham.

Interesting.

What did he have in mind?

Deciding to play along, Losham sighed. "Frankly, I envy your position. From my elevated station as our father's top

26

advisor, I've been relegated to dealing with humanity's muck. I can't say that I enjoy what I'm doing." He smiled. "If you are willing to switch, I'll gladly take those corrupt politicians off your hands. In fact, you are much better suited for my job than I am. With your compulsion ability, you could order the girls to take themselves to the island. You could save us a lot of money and manpower."

Reaching for the whiskey, Lokan poured himself a shot and downed it. "I would love a change of pace, but I can't see myself doing what you do. The drugs I could manage. If stupid humans want to numb themselves and destroy their own brains, who am I to deny them that choice? But the women are a different story. I'm not a proponent of slavery, especially sexual slavery. There are enough women out there who would do it for the money."

That was a very odd sentiment for a Doomer. "Why do you care? Humans are like sheep, and they need an iron-fisted shepherd to guide them."

Lokan tilted his head and pinned Losham with a hard stare. "Do you really believe that, or are you parroting our father?"

Apparently, Lokan was not as smart as he seemed. He was talking treason and trusting Losham not to use that against him?

Perhaps it was a trap?

Yes, that made much more sense. Navuh had sent Lokan to check up on him, and his brother was goading him into admitting dissent.

This was bad. It meant that Losham was a suspect and everything he said was going to be used against him.

"Are you questioning my loyalty, Lokan? Because I can promise you that it is absolute. Our goal is to one day rule the entire world. If we leave it up to the humans, they are going to destroy themselves and this planet."

That was a line Navuh often used in his propaganda

speeches to justify his world-domination ambitions. Whether it was true or not was irrelevant. The only thing that mattered was that the warriors believed in it and fought for the supposed cause.

Lokan regarded him for a long moment, as if trying to decide whether he was telling the truth, but Losham was careful to keep his expression impassive.

Next, his brother made a failed attempt at discreetly sniffing for emotions and grimaced. The Brussels sprouts in parmesan crust and garlic butter were delicious, but the same couldn't be said about their smell.

"I'm not here on behalf of our father, if that's what you're worried about."

Losham waved a dismissive hand. "Why should I be worried? I have nothing to hide."

Letting out an exasperated breath, Lokan poured himself another shot of whiskey and downed it. "So, you are happy with the status quo, you have no ambitions whatsoever, and you don't think it's time for a change?"

"What kind of change?"

"Our father's ideas are outdated, and he is too stubborn and set in his ways to change. If we don't do something, and by 'we' I mean the sons, the Brotherhood is doomed. It will become obsolete."

It was all true, but Losham couldn't decide whether Lokan was suggesting a revolt or just stating the facts as they were. In either case, he wasn't going to play into the cunning son of a bitch's hands.

"It is true that the world is changing around us and the Brotherhood cannot continue as it is, but our father is well aware of that. I suggested several changes to address the issue, and he accepted them all. We need to work with him, not against him."

Losham leaned closer to his brother. "You are still relatively young, Lokan, and somewhat naive despite your smarts. Navuh is irreplaceable, and his charisma is what holds the brotherhood together. Without him, infighting would have decimated our forces a long time ago, and we would have really become obsolete. We are strong just as long as we stick together and work as a team."

Lokan chuckled. "Only you would call a nearly one-thousand-year-old immortal young. Or naive." He poured himself and Losham another shot. "So, tell me, what are the changes that you suggested?"

"We need brains. That's the number one priority. Well, actually it's number two. First priority is to establish a reliable inflow of cash. We can't do anything about the level of intelligence of the Dormants we have, they are a given, but we can bring in smart humans to breed with them, which I've already started working on. The next generation of Doomers is going to be all about the brains and not the brawn, and the new generation of dormant females is going to be better quality too. We are going to keep improving the stock."

Lokan nodded. "That's a long-term plan."

"It is, but then we have time."

"Where are you getting the smart humans from?"

Spreading his arms, Losham snorted. "We are in San Francisco, the hub of new technology and the brains that come up with it. Most of these geeks can't get laid without paying for it, and they find a sex vacation to a mysterious island very appealing."

7

E L L A

*E*lla had been in dreamland for a while when the scenery suddenly changed.

"Logan? Is it you?" She looked around.

It wasn't the beach and it wasn't sunny. She was standing on a bridge with a canal passing under it, but it wasn't Venice. She'd seen enough pictures of it to know that.

"Where am I?" She crossed her arms over her chest to keep herself warm. Even though it was only a dream, the wet breeze was freezing cold and it was seeping through her clothes as if she was actually there.

Materializing behind her, Logan wrapped his arms around her and pulled her against his warm body. "We are in Hamburg. You wanted me to show you the world."

His hold was gentle, and his body was throwing off heat like a furnace. Leaning against him, Ella was thankful for the warmth.

"Did you bring me here on purpose because it's so bloody cold and I would have to let you hug me?"

Nuzzling her neck, he chuckled. "I did not. It's just a beautiful city, and you wanted me to show you the nicer places around the world. It's located in the northern part of

Germany, so it gets really cold here even in the summer. But I can solve that problem for you."

With a snap of his fingers, she was encased in a long puffer coat. A bright pink coat that was the same color as her hair. Panicking, she reached for a strand and looked at it, but in the dream it was still shoulder length and light brown.

Thank God.

"Are you all warm and toasty now?" Logan asked.

"Yes, thank you. Can you also give me gloves?"

He snapped his fingers again. "Done."

"Thank you." She lifted her hands with the pink fingerless gloves. "They are cute."

He kissed the top of her head. "As are you. Do you want to go for a walk along the canal? There are fancy shops a few blocks away."

"I don't care about stores, but I would love a walk. I want to see more of this gorgeous city. It's like Venice, just in the north."

As they started walking and Logan wrapped his arm around her waist, she leaned her head against his arm. "Is Hamburg one of your favorite cities?"

He nodded. "I like the north. I come from a very hot place, so I appreciate cooler climates."

"I like warm weather. I don't like to be cold."

"I'll remember it for our next shared dream. I was thinking of taking you to Scotland. The Isle of Skye is one of the most beautiful places in the world."

"Then take me there. Just dress me up appropriately." She lifted her foot. "Can you give me warm boots too?"

He snapped his fingers. "Done."

"Thank you." Lifting her foot again to examine the boots he'd conjured for her, Ella admired Logan's taste. They looked like Eskimo moccasins, made from soft brown leather and with an intricate pattern in pinks and purples sewn on top. She wished she could take them with her into the real

31

world, and wondered where he'd taken the idea from. Was he actually in Hamburg at the moment or some other northern country?

"You are visiting me more often lately. Are you less busy?"

He chuckled. "Not really. I just can't stay away. You've enchanted me, my Ella. I now understand Gorchenco's obsession with you. You're special."

Crap, why did he have to be so nice all of a sudden? Where was the devil she knew?

Except, he might be thinking of her telepathy and not her feminine charms.

Yeah, that was probably it.

"You're also not as wary of me as you were in the beginning," he added. "I enjoy spending time with you."

"You've learned to behave. And you should not be surprised that I was so scared of you after that kissing attack you launched. What the hell was that about?"

"I'm sorry about that. It's just that I'm not used to women refusing me. And sometimes a woman says no when she means yes. She just needs a little convincing. It's a very old game that males and females have been playing for ages."

Ella rolled her eyes. "That's such bullshit, Logan. Nowadays, if a girl wants to hook up with someone, she's not playing games and pretending that she needs convincing. That might have been true fifty years ago."

He cocked a brow. "Do you do that? Just hook up with some random guy and go for it?"

"Well, no. But that's because of what I've been through. I don't want to hook up with anyone. Not yet, anyway. But when I'm ready, I'm not going to pretend that I don't want to when I do. A no is a no. And a yes is a yes."

"That's because you are an American. Where I come from, women are not so progressive and things are very old fashioned."

"Why is that?"

He shrugged. "My country is very religious, and modesty is enforced."

Ella widened her eyes, affecting innocence. "Are you from Iran? I would never have guessed. You have no foreign accent."

Logan laughed. "Why Iran?"

"Hot climate, very religious, and bent on world domination. It all fits."

"I'm not from Iran."

"So where are you from? Pakistan? Afghanistan?"

He shook his head. "None of those. I come from a very small nation that you've never heard of, and I can't tell you which one it is."

Ella wondered if her eye trick would work on him. Probably not, and she didn't really need him to confess where he was from because she knew, but she was curious.

"Tell me something about yourself. I know that you like being mysterious and all that, and you think that it makes you sexy, but how can I develop feelings for you when I know nothing about you? Do you have brothers or sisters? Are you close to any of them?"

He sighed. "I have many brothers, but we are not close. We share a father, but each of us has a different mother."

She arched a brow. "Your father has a harem?"

Ella knew the answer to that, but she had to pretend surprise. Besides, she was curious to find out how Logan felt about it, and whether the focused gaze that had other people open up to her was working on him.

He nodded. "Yes."

Wow, it seemed that it did. Either that or Logan was in the right mood for revealing stuff about himself.

"Oh, boy. That's horrible. Is your mother okay with that?"

He grimaced. "I don't know."

"You never asked?"

"I couldn't."

Ella stopped and took his hand. "Did she die?"

"Probably. But I have no way of knowing because my father doesn't let his sons grow up in his harem. We were raised by caregivers."

"Why?"

He shook his head. "I don't want to talk about it. Let's move to more pleasant subjects. Did you email your application to Georgetown?"

It seemed that she'd discovered Logan's Achilles heel. The guy was angry at his father for getting rid of his mother or just separating them.

Why would Navuh do that, though? He was such a monster, even to his own children.

Taking his hand, she smiled at Logan in an effort to restore his good mood. He was scary when angry. "I'm waiting for my transcripts to arrive."

"The fake ones, I presume."

She nodded. "I don't like having to do a deceitful thing like that. My real grades were probably good enough to get in, but I can't use them because I'm supposed to be dead."

He gave her hand a little squeeze that reminded her of Julian.

Crap, don't think about him! Ella tried to visualize Jim, but it was no use. Instead, she wrapped her other hand around Logan's wrist to enhance the contact.

He smiled down at her. "I'm glad you are alive. And don't worry about the fake grades. It happens all the time and in various ways. Those academic echelons are just as corrupt as any other organization where people can get bribed or blackmailed."

"How do you know that?"

He shrugged. "All of humanity is like that, even those who purport themselves as saints."

"I'm not like that. My mother is not like that. And I know

34

a lot of good people who are not like that. You have a very warped perception of humanity."

He arched a brow. "Do I? Perhaps you can find good people among the common folks who are powerless. But once given power, people abuse it. It's just human nature."

"So what are you saying? That there is no hope for us?"

He sighed. "Don't mind me, Ella. I'm just an old, jaded warlord."

Her heart aching for him, Ella forced a snort. "Logan, are you having a mid-life crisis at twenty-eight? Because you can't be a day older than that."

8

BRIDGET

"*I*'m glad to be rid of that ring,'" Bridget said as Sandoval's driver eased into traffic. "I didn't feel safe carrying it around."

Turner clasped her hand. "I don't know why. Okidu drove us to the airstrip, we took the clan's private jet, and Sandoval's men picked us up from the airport. At no time were we exposed to danger."

"I know. Still, I feel lighter without it."

"That's because it is no longer on your finger. That thing was massive."

For some reason, Turner had decided that the ring was safer on her finger than hidden within a purse. Bridget hadn't been happy about wearing it, and not for security concerns alone. The ring had a bad juju.

Shaking her head, she berated herself for believing in superstitious nonsense. She was supposed to be a scientist and stick to the facts. Nothing had happened on the way, and the trip was a success.

Both parties were happy with the deal they'd struck, and after Turner had verified that the twenty-two million had been wired into the clan's Swiss account, they had parted with hugs and kisses and promises of meeting again in Los Angeles for dinner.

Right. As if Bridget was going to allow that. The last time Turner had gone to a dinner meeting with Sandoval, it had been a trap set up by the guy's nephew who'd hired hitmen to assassinate her man.

"Are you sure that you want to waste the rest of the day at a quilting convention?" Turner asked. "Instead, we can play tourists in Miami, getting driven around in Sandoval's limo."

Knowing her mate, Bridget had come up with a productive twist for their sightseeing. She hadn't expected him to complain about it.

"There isn't much we can see in half a day. I'd rather check out the convention."

"I'm sure it's going to be a waste of time. What are the chances of Roni's grandmother being one of the finalists?"

Bridget shrugged. "Statistically, probably none. I know that you are going to scoff at this, but I've come to believe that the Fates play a much larger part in us finding suitable partners than anything we do intentionally. But if we sit around the village and do not get out there, they can't put us in their path. Like Julian and that psychic convention. If he hadn't gone there, he would've not met Vivian."

The partition was up, and the driver couldn't hear their conversation, but there was always a chance that Sandoval had listening devices in his limo, and it wasn't as if Turner could search the vehicle. Which meant that they had to communicate in code and not use terms like Dormants and immortals.

"There is a big difference between that and a quilting competition. It made sense to search for special people in a psychic convention."

She smirked. "And it makes sense to search for a talented quilter in a quilting competition."

"They have them all over. It's not like this is the only one."

"True." Bridget crossed her arms over her chest. "But this one is the biggest and most prestigious." She smiled. "Besides, I want to buy a quilt for Julian and Ella. I have a feeling she is going to move in with him soon, and his place needs a feminine touch. Nothing like a beautiful quilt to brighten up a bedroom."

Wrapping his arm around her shoulders, Turner kissed the top of her head. "Under that no-nonsense façade of yours, you are a closet romantic. Isn't it too soon for buying quilts?"

"I'm not going to give it to them until they move in together. I don't want to be the pushy mother who sticks her nose where it doesn't belong."

"Did Julian tell you about them having plans to do that?"

"No, but they are so in love. Everyone can see that. It's only a matter of time."

Turner shook his head. "She is too young. If I were her father, I would not be happy about this. She needs to go to college and experience life before committing to a life-long relationship."

"Right." Bridget snorted. "Would you have listened to anyone telling you to do that after you met me?"

"You can't compare us to them. We weren't kids when we met."

She leaned and kissed his cheek. "Consider them luckier. They don't have to spend years looking for that special someone. They've already found each other. And as I said many times before, eighteen is not too young. If she can be drafted into the army and trusted with a rifle, she can be trusted to know her heart and choose who she wants to spend the rest of her life with."

Pulling up to the building where the quilt competition was taking place, the driver stopped at the curb and lowered the partition. "Call me when you are ready to leave."

"Thank you," Bridget said.

"We won't be long," Turner added. "I have better things to do than spend the day looking at quilts," he murmured under his breath.

9

TURNER

*A*s Turner and Bridget went from room to room, he scanned the audience while Bridget oohed and aahed at the quilts.

Come to think of it, there was no reason for them to be there. Most large venues like this convention center had surveillance cameras, and he doubted they were closed circuit. He should have Roni check on that. If the kid could hack into them and then run the recordings through William's facial recognition software, that would increase the chances of them catching Roni's grandmother.

Normally, Turner wouldn't have diverted resources to such a long-shot pursuit, but since Roni had a vested interest in it, he could do that in his spare time. If he had any.

The kid was suffering from the same affliction Turner and Kian had been cursed with. Not knowing when to quit. Luckily for the three of them, they had mates to force some time off on them.

"Look at this one," Bridget said. "Isn't it gorgeous?"

"It is. And so is the price. Five thousand dollars for a quilt?"

Not all the rooms were dedicated to competition pieces.

Some had been rented by quilting artists to put their work up for sale.

The prices were extravagant. Not that they weren't justified. He could imagine how many work hours went into each quilt, but there were cheaper ways to produce them. An artist could make a computer rendering and have the quilt sewn in India or some other country with low wages. In fact, he was pretty sure some of them had done it. After all, even artists had to make a living.

She waved a dismissive hand. "It's a one of a kind work of art, not a quilt mass produced in China."

"Then it should hang on the wall instead of covering the bed."

"They can do with it whatever they please. I'm getting it."

He glanced at the other quilts hanging on the walls. All of them were beautiful, but the one Bridget had chosen was indeed unique.

"Fine with me."

As she whipped out her credit card and approached the artist, Turner was struck by a thought. What if Roni's grandmother was selling quilts as a way to support herself?

This was another avenue to investigate.

What if she'd done it in other venues like this one? There couldn't be too many quilting artists selling their creations in conventions, and they all probably knew each other. At least by sight.

Walking over to where Bridget was chatting with the woman, he pulled out his phone and showed her the grandmother's picture. "I was wondering if you've seen this quilter around."

She shook her head. "I'm sorry." She handed him the phone back.

"Are you sure?"

"I would've remembered a young woman like that

because quilters tend to be much older. But you should ask Cheryl. She knows everyone."

"Who's Cheryl?"

"She's one of the organizers." The woman pushed to her feet. "Let me get her for you."

Before either of them had a chance to say anything, the quilter ran out of the room, leaving them alone with her creation.

"Isn't she afraid someone might steal one of her works?" Bridget asked.

"They probably have them tagged."

"True. But I can't see any."

A few moments later their quilter returned with a woman who he assumed was Cheryl. A ball of energy with a mountain of white hair piled up high on top of her head.

"I heard that you're looking for someone?" she asked.

"Yes." He pulled out his phone and brought up the picture again. "Have you seen her?"

As Cheryl took the phone, her pupils dilated momentarily, indicating recognition. "Why are you looking for her?"

"A good friend of mine is looking for his cousin who he has lost track of. He said she's a gifted quilter, and if I see her while I'm here to tell her to call him. Do you know where I can find her?"

She looked at the picture again. "I only met her once, and it was five years ago, I think. I'm not sure. I think her name is Melinda. Is that right?" She quirked a brow.

"The truth is that I don't know what name she uses." Turner went with the truth. "She's gotten in some trouble and changed her name. That's why my friend lost track of her."

Cheryl narrowed her eyes at him. "That friend of yours, is he really her cousin? And if he is, why is it so important for him to find her?"

"He is estranged from his parents, and she is the only other family he has."

The woman didn't look convinced. "I can't really tell you where you can find her, but I remember her talking about selling her quilts online. She told me the name of her website, and I even checked it out, but I can't remember the name of it for the life of me."

"What kind of quilts did she make?" Bridget asked.

"Mandalas. All of her quilts were gorgeous mandalas. But that's not uncommon. It's a popular motif."

"Did she win any prizes?"

"Not that I know of. If she did, it was probably in some small-town competition."

Bridget cast Turner a questioning look. "I think that's enough to go on."

"Perhaps."

10

ELLA

*E*lla adjusted the camera's angle and returned to the chair she'd put in front of the white backdrop.

"Try it now," she told Tessa.

"Looks good." The girl gave her a thumbs up.

The dining hall was getting transformed into a theater, with girls pushing tables aside and stacking them one on top of the other.

They were making room for the extra chairs that were being collected from all of the classrooms. Altogether, nearly a hundred girls resided currently in the sanctuary, and all of them were going to attend Ella's presentation.

The only speech she'd prepared was a warning about what she was about to do, so whoever was not up to hearing her story could leave. Newcomers were especially vulnerable, and it might be too much for them to be exposed to a retelling so soon after their rescue.

When her phone rang, she knew who it was before looking at the screen.

"Hi, Julian."

"How are you holding up?"

She got up and started pacing. "I'm nervous."

"I have good news for you that will cheer you up."

"Shoot. I need an infusion of positive before I plunge into the abyss."

"Turner called me. He sold the ring."

"For how much?"

"Are you sitting down? Twenty-two million."

That was a hell of a lot more than she'd expected. Ella let out a whistle. "How many halfway houses will that much money buy us?"

"Maybe two."

"Are you kidding me? That should be enough for thirty."

"Real estate prices in the Los Angeles area are insane, and then you need to factor in the cost of remodeling and furnishing and hiring staff and all that."

"What if we move the houses somewhere else? I'm sure we can buy double that in Nevada or Arizona. And if we go to places like Kentucky, we can build a small town for that much money."

He chuckled. "I'm not sure about that, but in principle you're right. The problem is that the clan is here."

She glanced around and whispered, "Kian should've built the village somewhere else."

"We need a large metropolis to hide in plain sight. And New York prices aren't any better."

"Right. Well, at least we can have two. Is it in addition to the one you're remodeling now?"

"I hope so. But I'm not an expert. I'll have to pay a visit to our accounting department and have a professional go over the numbers."

"I didn't know we had an accounting department."

"It's only four people. The rest is done by outside firms."

Ella still had so much to learn about the village and the business empire the clan owned, and how it was all managed. Heck, she'd learned that there was an entire rulebook of clan-specific laws. She wanted to take a look at that too. It should be fascinating to find out how the organization functioned, and she was sure it wasn't as difficult to understand as the medical research papers she'd tried to tackle for Merlin.

Perhaps she shouldn't pursue nursing as her profession. It seemed as if her natural talents were better suited for something else.

Ella Takala, Director of Save the Girls was a much more appealing title than Ella Takala, Nurse Practitioner.

"One day I want to sit down with you and have you explain how the entire thing works. But I have to go now."

"Good luck. I wish I could be there to support you."

"I know. I love you so much."

"I love you too."

The truth was that she preferred it that way and was thankful for the excuse of males not being allowed in the sanctuary. Regrettably, the same didn't apply to Vivian, and asking her not to come had been difficult. Her mother had shed a few tears, then nodded, saying that she understood.

Ella was going to bare her soul, but it was in front of others who'd gone through similar experiences.

There was no way she could have her mother or Julian present. Having them listening to her story would have influenced how she told it. Not because she wanted to hide things from them or make it less embarrassing for herself, but because she would have known how difficult it was for them to hear it, and instinctively she would have modified her story to make it more palatable.

That would have been counterproductive to say the least. The girls needed to hear her talk about her feelings and identify with her. Only then would they consider following her example and telling their own stories on camera.

Julian was still going to hear it when they worked on the editing, but maybe it wouldn't be as bad for him if she held his hand through it.

When the dining hall was full and everyone was seated, Ella addressed her audience.

"Many of you already know what this is about, but for those who don't I'm going to explain. Just like you, I was lured into a trap, sold, and violated. My story is not as horrific as some I've heard here. In fact, it's pretty mild in comparison."

She motioned to the camera and the white backdrop. "I'm going to talk about it on camera, and my friend Tessa is going to record it. The recording is going to be in silhouette, so no one can recognize me, and I'm even going to change my voice. Later, we are going to edit it so it's impactful enough to put on YouTube."

When murmurs started, she lifted a hand and waited until everyone hushed down. "It will serve two purposes. One is for the fundraiser that is going to provide money for more centers like this one and for transition places that are going to ease your re-entrance into society. The second purpose of these videos is to serve as a warning to all the unsuspecting girls out there and their families. We will tell them what to watch out for, and how to recognize the warning signs."

Ella paused, took in a breath, and then continued. "If any of you feel like this is too much for you, please don't feel bad about leaving. I know that I would not have been able to sit and listen to a story like mine right after being rescued. All I wanted to do was to forget. But then I realized that by hiding my head in the sand I was helping out the monsters. As long as this is swept under the rug of society, as long as people believe that this cannot happen to them, the monsters are going to keep winning."

She glanced at Vanessa, who nodded her approval. "We can make it harder for them. By telling our stories, we will warn others, raise public awareness to the atrocities being committed under their noses, and hopefully raise shitloads of money so we can help rescue and rehabilitate more girls."

When Ella was done, one of the queen bees started clapping, and a moment later the entire room erupted in applause.

Only one girl slunk out of the room.

Sucking in a long breath, Ella let it out through pursed lips. It was show time.

Raising her hands, she waited until the applause died out. "I need to ask you a favor. This is going to be as hard as chomping on broken glass, and I would hate to do it twice. Please try to be as quiet as possible until I'm done."

11

JULIAN

*A*s Julian knocked on Ella's front door, he clutched the brand new box of Godiva chocolates he'd bought on the way home as if it were a precious miracle elixir for curing heavy hearts.

Not that he knew for a fact that her heart was heavy, but he assumed it was. It must've been so difficult for her to tell her story in front of a room full of people, despite all of them except for Vanessa being sisters in pain.

She'd sounded tired when he'd called her, not depressed, but Ella was very good at fronting strength she didn't possess. Hopefully, he knew her well enough by now to see through that façade.

Opening the door, she smiled at him, and then she saw the box. "Oh, Julian. This is exactly what I need." She reached for the chocolates. "Give it."

When he'd bought the box, he'd envisioned asking Ella for a kiss before handing them over, but her feral expression convinced him to reconsider. Ella didn't seem in the mood to tolerate teasing.

She was tearing the wrapping while closing the door behind him.

"Hi, Julian," Vivian said. "Would you like to eat something? I can warm up a plate for you."

"No, thanks. I've eaten."

"Coffee?"

"Yes, please."

"For me too," Ella mumbled around a chocolate.

Magnus chuckled. "That girl has a serious problem."

There was a moment of silence as everyone in the room stared at him.

Raising his hands in the air, Magnus shook his head. "I meant your addiction to chocolate. You're not an immortal yet, Ella. Those can't be good for you."

Julian cleared his throat. "Actually, chocolate has many health benefits if eaten in moderation. It has a positive influence on cognitive function, lowers bad cholesterol, and reduces the risk of irregular heartbeat."

"I just love it when you geek out like that." Ella wrapped her arm around his waist. "At least you say those things in a language people can understand."

"You didn't pay attention to the moderation clause," Magnus said.

Ella waved a dismissive hand. "Overindulgence is okay in emergencies."

That shut the Guardian up as if someone had stuck a shoe in his mouth. Turning on his heel, he beat feet after Vivian to the kitchen.

"Come on." Ella led Julian to the dining room table. "I brought my laptop out here so we'll have plenty of room." She winked at him.

He sat down and waited for her to join him. "How did the presentation go?" When he'd called earlier, she'd only said that it had gone fine without giving him any details.

"It was as good as can be expected from an unscripted and unrehearsed telling of a traumatic experience. It needs a lot of editing work, but it had the effect I anticipated. I have four volunteers for tomorrow. But I'll probably only manage two. I was surprised at how long it took me to tell my story. By the time I was done, my mouth was all dried out. I didn't think about bringing a water bottle with me. And I cried a few times and had to compose myself."

His heart felt like it was about to crack, but all he could do was clasp her hand. "You are so brave, baby."

She waved a hand. "The crying was good too. It made the whole thing more convincing."

Right, as if she'd done it on purpose.

"What did you do? Did you ask for volunteers after you were done?"

"Not right away. I could see the indecision on their faces, so I added that they will be able to edit their stories after the filming and cut out things they were uncomfortable with. And that after that we will edit them further. Naturally, I didn't elaborate that my editing assistant was a guy. Anyway, that seemed to reassure them, and that was when I asked for volunteers."

"Good thinking. What did Vanessa have to say?"

Ella grinned. "She was all over herself about how wonderful I did and how proud she was of me. She said I was an inspiration."

He narrowed his eyes at her. "I hope you didn't cancel your appointment with her tomorrow."

She huffed. "I did not. Only because of you, though. You should have seen Vanessa's face when I admitted to having been violated. She had tears in her eyes, and they weren't the sad kind. She looked so happy that I finally saw reason that I didn't want to spoil it for her and tell her that it was your doing."

Even though Ella was making it sound as if she was going to therapy just to please him, the vise around Julian's heart was starting to ease. Mainly because it seemed that telling her story had been therapeutic for her, and not traumatic like he'd feared.

As Vivian put the tray on the table, she seemed surprised that they were still there. "You can take the cups with you if you want."

Ella looked up at her mother. "We are going to work here, if you don't mind. I only have one chair in my room."

As Magnus and Vivian exchanged glances, the Guardian shrugged. "We can watch a movie in our bedroom so you can work in peace. Are you filling out the application for Georgetown?"

"Yes, and several other places in case Mr. D checks." Ella looked at Julian and smirked. "Roni gave me a stellar transcript. I feel so much smarter all of a sudden."

"You are smart," her mother said.

"I concur." Julian pulled out the folded printouts he'd brought along. "I saved my application essays. You can use them as a sample for yours."

"That's good. I had no idea where to start."

"Good night, kids," Vivian said. "And good luck with the applications."

"Thanks." Ella sent her an air kiss.

When they were alone, Julian chuckled. "So much for our plan. They couldn't get out of here fast enough."

"It's still a good plan. Parker comes out every twenty minutes or so to get a snack or something to drink."

Julian waggled his brows. "A lot of things can happen in twenty minutes."

"Yeah, we can fill out half of an application."

12

BRIDGET

*a*fter stowing the quilt in the overhead compartment, Bridget got comfy in her seat and glanced at the curtain separating the cabin from the bathroom area. She had fond memories from the last time she and Turner had flown first class.

"Not as nice as the clan's jet," Turner said. "I wish Charlie could have waited for us."

"I disagree. We needed the jet to deliver the artifact safely. The one we are taking back is not worth nearly as much, but it's dear to me and valuable in other ways."

The quilt was pricey, but the information they'd gotten while purchasing it was priceless. With Turner's resources, Bridget had no doubt he would locate Roni's grandmother, or Melinda as she'd been calling herself five years ago.

The only problem was that the information was old, and the woman might have changed her name again, or she might have stopped selling her mandala quilts online. The first was likely, the second not so much. First of all because it seemed to be a passion of hers, and secondly, she probably supported herself selling the quilts. The beauty of it was that she could do it from anywhere in the world, using the internet to promote her creations.

Unless something spooked her, she was going to keep on doing it.

"Would you like a drink, Ms?" the stewardess asked.

"Yes, I would. A Bloody Mary, please."

"And for you, sir?"

"Scotch, please."

"On the rocks?"

"Neat, thank you."

Leaning over the bulky armrests, Bridget whispered in Turner's ear. "There are advantages to flying first class commercial. Unlike the jet, you get a stewardess to serve you drinks and meals, and the facilities are roomier."

Her guy was bright, and it didn't take much for him to catch her drift.

With a sly smirk, his eyes darted to the half-closed curtain. "You have a point. Is that why you booked the redeye?"

"It didn't even cross my mind. I just wanted us to have the entire day to enjoy in Miami. The curtain brought back pleasant memories."

"Do you want me to perform reconnaissance?"

"Of course. Each model of aircraft is different."

Releasing his safety belt, Turner jumped up to his feet. "I'll be right back."

Bridget wondered how different it would be this time around. Turner was an immortal now, stronger and more nimble. Not that he hadn't been so as a human. He'd kept himself in excellent shape. Still, nothing could beat the fountain of youth that came with immortality.

Coming out, he smiled at the stewardess as he passed by her and then took his seat next to Bridget. "It's tight, but we can manage just as we did before."

"I can't wait," she whispered in his ear.

"Patience, love. We need to wait for the meal to be served and then for the lights to be turned down."

She was patient as a doctor, somewhat less as an administrator, and not at all as a woman. Especially when vivid memories of their initiation into the mile-high club were flashing through her mind. Just thinking about what they were about to do had her nipples contract painfully and her core tingle.

She used to hate moments like that, when her arousal flared in response to some trigger and she had to find a random hookup to sate her hunger. It had felt like a chore, like having to grab something to eat while pressed for time. She needed the sustenance, couldn't go on without it, but hated to take a break for it, and hadn't enjoyed it.

Now, with Turner in her life, she welcomed the random flares. Each one was an opportunity for something wonderful, and each time felt like they were connecting anew.

When the lights went down, Bridget walked over to the bathroom and cast a shroud around the immediate area, imbuing it with a light sense of dread. Whoever wanted to use the restroom wasn't going to stand right there and wait. They were either going to return to their seat and wait for the green light to come on or trudge to the crowded coach and use one of its bathrooms with the rest of the plebs.

A moment later the door pushed open and Turner squeezed in behind her, pulling it closed.

"Take off your dress, love."

He wanted her to get naked? Bridget had planned on pulling her skirt up and her panties down, not the full Monty.

But what the heck. It wasn't a hardship.

Her dress was the pull-on type, and it only took a second to yank it over her head, but trying to hang it on the hook was another story. Especially with Victor cupping her breasts from behind and his erection pressing into her ass as she was fumbling with the thing.

"I can't concentrate when you do that." She tried again.

Taking the garment from her hands, Turner reached over her and completed the task in a split second.

"Show-off."

"You like it." He pinched a nipple through her bra.

Yes, she did. Her mate was a one of a kind super brainiac who could do anything he put his mind to, and that wasn't limited to his genius. He'd also built a barbecue from scratch with his own two hands, which had impressed the heck out of her.

Standing in her high heels and her matching bra and panty set, she let her head fall back on his shoulder. "You'll have to take the rest off me."

Nuzzling and nipping her neck, he snapped the bra clasp and slid the straps down her arms. "Put your hands on the door and lean forward," he commanded.

Bridget liked where this was going.

With deft fingers, Turner hung the bra on the same hook that was barely holding the dress, but even the freaking inanimate object knew better than to try to best him.

In the end, Turner always won.

Crouching behind her, he hooked his thumbs in her panties and pulled them down. "Lift your foot. Now the other one."

She heard him stuffing them into his pocket. Was he saving them for her, or did he want her to spend the rest of the flight panty-less?

Kinky.

A moment later his warm hands cupped her ass, and he licked into her.

Her mate was talented in so many ways, and Bridget applauded his penchant for striving to be the best at everything he did, especially when it was pleasuring her into oblivion.

As she pushed back against his tongue, he circled his arm around her and pressed his finger to the top of her slit.

The dual sensations were like twin torpedoes, shooting her up toward an orgasm in seconds. Except, she needed a little more to break through the barrier, and Victor was taking his time, slowly licking and sucking and gently massaging that tight bundle of nerves.

Frustrated, she groaned and swiveled her hips, urging him to give her what she needed.

That earned her a hard slap on her ass-cheek.

The slight sting managed to help her stretch the barrier, but not break through it.

"I need to come now, Victor," she hissed through clenched teeth.

Obliging her, he retracted his tongue and replaced it with two thick fingers. Pumping in and out of her, he pressed the thumb of his other hand to her clit.

That was what she'd needed. Breaking through the barrier, Bridget rocketed into a climax that had her eyes roll back in her head and her legs turn into noodles.

Holding her up, Victor purred his approval and kissed her moist lips before pushing up.

As she heard him release his buckle and then lower his zipper, Bridget braced for the penetration that was coming, but after his gentle foreplay, the ferocity of that first thrust took her by surprise.

"Victor," she breathed.

Holding on to her hips, he pulled back and slammed into her again, and again. Oblivious to the door's rattling and to his own growls, Turner unleashed the beast living inside his immortal body.

Dimly, she was aware that her shroud might not hold up while her concentration was shot all to hell, and that the noise they were making would be overheard over the engines' noise.

Still, she somehow managed to maintain it almost to the very end. But when Victor bit into her and she was flooded with euphoria, there was no way she could hold on to it and she let it go.

Long moments passed until Bridget regained enough control to recast the shroud. Behind her, Victor was breathing heavily, his shaft still twitching inside her.

She chuckled. "Are you ready for round number two?"

"You know me. I'm always happy to rise to the challenge." He nuzzled her neck.

ELLA

"*I*'m so glad that you've decided to come to talk to me." Vanessa smiled and pointed to one of the two armchairs in her office, then sat in the other.

This time there was no desk between them, only a small side table with a box of tissue and a couple of water bottles on top of it.

Made sense. A lot of crying must go on in the therapist's office, and from experience Ella knew that confessions tended to dry out the throat.

Shifting in the wide armchair, she crossed one leg over the other. "To be frank, there are two reasons I'm here. One is that I promised Julian I'd talk to you, and the other one is the affinity thing that I want you to explain to me. Julian said something about immortals and Dormants feeling affinity for each other."

Vanessa nodded. "Amanda believes that, and there might be something to it, but we didn't have a large enough sample to test this hypothesis. Unfortunately, I don't think it's a good method for identifying Dormants. People feel an affinity for each other for a variety of reasons, and it's next to impossible to isolate one particular cause."

That wasn't what Ella wanted to hear. It sounded wishy-washy. "My mother says that she felt an immediate affinity for Magnus, but then he is a hunk, so it might have been infatuation and not affinity. But she also says that she feels at home in the village like she never felt anywhere else."

"What about you, Ella?"

"You mean if I feel at home here?"

Vanessa nodded.

"I do. But I didn't feel like I didn't belong in my old life." She waved a hand. "Naturally, there was some teenage angst, and this face made me feel different." She pointed. "But that was because people always stared at me. It wasn't like that with my friends, though, or even my classmates. After they got used to me, they kind of forgot about my looks and treated me like everyone else."

That wasn't entirely true. Ella remembered feeling like an alien from time to time, but talking with Maddie and her other friends, she'd realized that it was like that for almost everyone. They'd all been trying to find their place in the world.

"What about Julian? Did you feel an immediate affinity toward him? I understand that you guys are dating."

That was a mild way to put it, and Ella appreciated the therapist not jumping on that whole fated one and only wagon.

On the one hand, the promise of undying love and unbreakable commitment was alluring and hard to resist. But on the other hand there was too much pressure attached to that. Maybe that was something Vanessa could help her with.

"Julian is an amazing guy and so easy to love, but I still have trouble believing in the fated true-love mate thing. Any girl would have fallen for him, so it's not a big surprise that I did. But how do I know the difference between just loving him because he's great and accepting that he is my destined mate? Would I know for sure if I were an immortal?"

"Not really. Again, we don't have enough couples to base a theory on, and none of them came to talk to me, but from what I've heard, everyone had doubts at one point or another."

Letting out an exasperated breath, Ella slumped in the armchair. Expecting answers from Vanessa had been an act of pure optimism. Just like any other shrink, she had none to give, and only posed more questions.

"Eventually they know, though, right?"

"It would seem so."

"I have another question for you. Is it possible to confuse that affinity thing with sexual attraction?"

"What exactly are you asking?"

Ella rolled her eyes. "Let's say that an immortal guy meets a dormant girl and he feels an affinity for her but thinks that it's attraction, and vice versa. A dormant girl meets an immortal guy, feels an affinity, and mistakenly thinks that she's attracted to him."

"I think that affinity can reinforce attraction, but I don't think it can cause it or be mistaken for it. I might feel an affinity toward a dormant woman, but since I'm heterosexual it will not translate into desire. If I meet a dormant guy, without knowing what he is, I might or might not feel attracted to him. Other factors need to be present too."

"Like what?"

Vanessa smiled. "The obvious ones. We are each drawn to a particular type. And then there are pheromones, which may be a factor too, not a very significant one and not well understood yet, but we know they exist."

That was interesting. Ella didn't know much about pheromones, but since immortals had heightened senses, perhaps they were more sensitive to their effects than humans?

Running her fingers through her hair, Ella debated whether she should bring it up. Someone must have researched it or at least considered it.

Eh, what the heck. The worst that could happen was Vanessa smiling at her indulgently and explaining why it was total nonsense. Ella was not a scientist and therefore was allowed laypersons' stupid questions.

Not a big deal.

"What if the affinity immortals feel for Dormants is caused by pheromones? Immortal senses are sharper in every other way, so why not that?" When Vanessa didn't immediately dismiss it, Ella continued. "And the same can be true for the destined mates thing."

"There might be a connection. Testing in humans produced no definite results, but we haven't tested immortals. Except, it could explain why immortals feel affinity toward Dormants, but not the other way around."

Well, that was it for her theory. It had been worth a shot, though.

"That might explain why Julian is so sure that I'm his true-love mate, while I'm not. But on the other hand, he fell for my picture. We can't blame pheromones for that."

Damn, it was all so confusing. Like a puzzle made up of mismatched pieces.

Vanessa leaned back and sighed. "We are complicated creatures, Ella. It's impossible to reduce everything to hormones and pheromones, although some scientists love to do that. Many factors are at play. Julian might have been infatuated with your pretty face in the picture, but until he met you in person he couldn't have been sure that you're the one. It takes time, and with immortals it also takes sex."

That was an odd thing for a therapist to say. "Sex helps determine true-love, since when?"

"Immortals, when they are exclusive with each other, form an addiction. When bitten enough times by the same male, the female becomes addicted to him and repulsed by other males. Eventually, her scent changes in a way that affects the male in the same way. Even if they were originally not each other's true-love mates, they become that."

No one had told her that.

Did her mother know?

"That's one hell of a pill to swallow, and not as romantic as Julian made it sound. Addiction is not love."

Vanessa smiled exactly like Ella had imagined she would, with the indulgent expression reserved for the lay and the stupid.

"No, addiction is not love. But in our case love comes first. Immortals, like their godly ancestors, are lustful and promiscuous by nature. If they don't feel a special connection to their mate, they are not going to be faithful. As long as the female gets bitten by more than one immortal, the mixture of venoms will prevent her from getting addicted to just one, and her scent is not going to change, meaning that none of the males will become addicted to her either."

Ella groaned. "I think I feel a headache coming on. This is all so complicated. How come no one has told me about the addiction?"

"It's not well known and certainly not something that we discuss over coffee. Most of us don't have mates or even a prospect of one, so it's not an issue. Why does it bother you, though? Isn't fidelity something you would want from your mate?"

"Of course. But not because he is forced into it. I want it to be his choice, in the same way that I want it to be mine. Faithfulness is much more meaningful when it's observed despite outside temptations, and not because of their absence, especially when that absence is chemically induced. Talk about Stepford Wives."

Sighing, Vanessa leaned forward. "Give it some thought, and I'm sure you'll see the beauty of it. For most the addiction takes months to set in. If it's not the real thing, you'll have plenty of time to walk away and seek another partner."

"But I don't want another partner."

"We will talk about it in our next session." She smiled. "Perhaps we will actually get to discuss your experience. As I said before, I was very impressed by what you said in the recording. I think it was a breakthrough for you. But since I have another session scheduled right after yours, we will have to address this in our next one. How about tomorrow?"

"Same time?"

"Works for me."

Ella hesitated. "I know that you're busy, and there are girls here who need your help much more than I do. I hate taking up so much of your time."

And she wasn't even using that as an excuse.

"I'm not the only therapist here. We have plenty of volunteers who the other girls can go to. You, on the other hand, can talk only to me."

"That's true."

JULIAN

"Here is your swipe card." Julian handed it to Yamanu.

"Did anything get stolen?" the Guardian said as he regarded the new security measures at the construction site. "That's one hell of a fence."

Turner had recommended a site management service that provided tall fences that were wired to an alarm company. It was pricey, but with the proceeds from the ring, Julian no longer needed to count the pennies.

"Come inside, and I'll show you. Squatters used one of the bedrooms upstairs, and we need to get rid of everything in there."

Since Yamanu hadn't been there on Friday or Monday, he hadn't seen the fence getting installed or heard the story.

"That's strange." The Guardian followed Julian upstairs. "The building stood empty for months, and no one trashed the place."

"Yeah, well. They did now."

Grimacing, Yamanu pinched his nose even before Julian opened the door. "I can't believe they've stunk up the place so bad in one weekend. Did they piss on the floor?"

"Possibly. They were a couple of nasty druggies."

As they hauled the bed out of the room, Julian told the Guardian a shortened version of what had happened, omitting most of the drama.

"I'm so proud of you, kid. If I weren't carrying furniture, I would give you a good slap on the back. Correct me if I'm wrong, but I don't remember you attending any of the self-defense classes. How did you know what to do? Did you train elsewhere?"

Julian shook his head. "I let instinct take over. The beast knew what to do." He grimaced at the memory.

The thing was, he couldn't recall any actual thoughts, just the fury that had consumed him when those druggies threatened Ella. It had incinerated every civilized part of him and called up the inner caveman he hadn't even known was living inside him.

Grinning from ear to ear, Yamanu tossed the bed on top of the pile of construction debris outside. "Come here, my boy." He pulled Julian into a bro embrace, knocking the hell out of him as he slapped his back. "The beast is your friend. Embrace him."

When they were back in the room and away from human ears, Yamanu leaned against the wall and crossed his arms over his chest. "What did you do with the bodies?"

"I didn't kill them, only knocked them out. Ella wouldn't let me finish the job. I called Turner and he handled the cleanup. Those two are going to spend a lot of time in jail."

Looking disappointed, the Guardian nodded. "How much of the stuff did they have here?"

"Not enough to put them away for such a long time. I have a feeling Turner arranged for more to be delivered." Julian lifted the desk. "Grab the other end. We don't want the humans to start wondering."

"Sure thing."

As they took it out of the room and started down the stairs, Julian's phone rang in his back pocket.

"Damn, that's Ella."

Yamanu chuckled. "No kidding. With that ringtone, I didn't think it was your mother. Go ahead and answer it. I'll take the desk downstairs by myself. The guys think I'm a freak anyway."

The snippet from *My Girl* had seemed like a cool idea when he'd assigned it to Ella's contact, but maybe it wasn't. It was too obvious.

"Hi, sweetheart. How did it go with Vanessa?"

"Great. That's what I wanted to talk to you about."

Ella had said great about talking with a shrink? Something wasn't right.

Taking the steps two at a time, he went into one of the rooms upstairs and closed the door behind him. "Okay. I'm alone now. Shoot." He leaned against the wall.

"So, we started talking, and one thing led to another, and then Vanessa said something about pheromones influencing who we are attracted to."

As a therapist, Vanessa wasn't as well acquainted with human physiology as a medical doctor.

"Studies show that humans emit very little, and that their pheromones have no measurable influence on arousal."

"Yeah, Vanessa said that not much is known about pheromones. Did anyone test immortals for it?"

"Maybe, but if it was done no one has told me."

He heard her huff. "I can't believe that I'm the first one to think of it. What if immortals emit more pheromones than humans or more powerful ones? What if your enhanced senses pick up on some Dormant-specific pheromones, and that is what you interpret as affinity? I know from Vanessa that affinity can also be felt without sexual attraction attached to it, but I went on the internet and read that pheromones are not only for sex. Animals use them to communicate many other things. That could also explain the alarm immortal males feel when they meet a new one of their kind. You guys probably emit warning pheromones, and after you get used to them you don't sense them anymore. That's why immortal males don't feel alarm around male friends and relatives."

Ella sounded so excited, and what she'd said made a lot of sense, but he didn't think Amanda could have overlooked something as obvious as this. She'd probably investigated it and had realized it didn't work this way.

He felt bad about bursting her bubble. "I'm sure Amanda checked this out. Searching for Dormants is her thing."

"What about your mother? She said that before heading the rescue operations, she researched immortal genetics."

"She didn't find anything useful."

"Yeah, but did she investigate pheromones?"

"I don't know. I'll have to ask her."

"Please do. And one more thing. When were you going to tell me about the freaking addiction?"

Damn, it hadn't even crossed his mind. "We are not doing anything. So, I didn't think it was important to mention."

"But we are going to at some point. Don't you think I should have been given a warning?"

He raked his fingers through his hair. "When the time comes, sure. Frankly, I didn't think about it at all. My mind wasn't there yet."

"Does my mother know? Is it too late for her?"

Why was she so upset about it? The addiction wasn't a bad thing. It was just a side effect of the devotion between true-love mates.

"I don't know whether she does or not, that's between her and Magnus. And if she does, I'm sure she is not as upset about it as you seem to be."

Ella huffed again. "You want to tell me that it doesn't bother you to be ruled by some weird chemical reaction?

Wouldn't you rather be faithful out of love and devotion to your partner than something you have no control over?"

"What if love and devotion are also chemical reactions? Have you thought of that? What if free will is an illusion and everything we do is determined by our genes and hormones and the inherited structure of our brains?"

As a long moment of silence stretched over the cellular connection, Julian wondered whether Ella was mulling over what he'd said or just taking time to rein in her anger.

"Do you really believe that?" she asked.

Did he?

"Not entirely, although I should. There is enough evidence to demonstrate that. A brain injury can change a personality, Alzheimer's robs people of their personality, and some drugs alter perception. So, if I were a purely logical creature like Turner, I would probably say that yes, that's all there is to us, and that nothing metaphysical or mysterious like a soul exists. But then I'm reminded of all the things that have no scientific explanation, like precognition and remote viewing."

Ella chuckled. "Why go that far? What about quantum physics? Does that make any sense? Or string theory? If that's real, I don't know why people having souls can't be."

At least she didn't sound angry anymore. "Does getting addicted to me really bother you that much? Because I have no problem being addicted to you for all eternity."

"That's so sweet and so creepy at the same time. I need to give it some thought. When are you getting home?"

"Six or six-thirty."

"Can I see you?"

"Of course. I need you. I'm already addicted to you without any chemicals involved."

"Oh, Julian, that's so sweet of you to say. Even though you're such a creepy geek sometimes, I love you so much."

He laughed. "Love you back."

ELLA

*I*n her mother's car, Ella dropped her head against the headrest and closed her eyes. "I hate disappointing Julian, but all I want to do when I get home is shower and sleep." Hopefully, without dreaming because she had no energy for Logan either.

Vivian patted her knee. "I'm sure he'll understand."

"Yeah, he will, but he will still be disappointed. I should call him right now so he can make other plans. It's not healthy for his psyche to spend time only with me. Julian needs guy buddies."

Vanessa would have been proud of her. She was spewing psychobabble like a pro. Not all of it was bullshit, though. As Ella could attest, mood certainly affected the body.

Yesterday, even though her presentation had been emotionally draining, she'd felt upbeat and motivated by the positive response. Today, on the other hand, she had listened passively to two horror stories, and to top it off, Tessa had a meltdown.

Ella had a feeling she would have to find a new filming assistant because Tessa wasn't coming back.

Maybe Julian could suggest a replacement?

Selecting his contact, she smiled at his picture. She should make it her screen saver, but then she'd be staring at it all day long, kind of like he had done with hers.

She wondered if he still did that.

"Ella, are you on your way back?"

"I am. I'm hitching a ride with my mom. Tessa had to leave early."

"Why? What happened?"

Ella sighed. "I shouldn't have asked her to do this. After I talked with you, we filmed two stories, and by the second one Tessa just fell apart. We had to call Jackson to come get her."

"Poor girl. She must be very sensitive."

Evidently, Julian didn't know about Tessa's past, and since Tessa preferred it that way, Ella honored her wishes. "Yeah, it's difficult to stomach. In fact, I'm afraid that when we work on the editing, you are going to have a meltdown as well."

"You don't give me enough credit."

"On the contrary, my love. I'm giving you all the credit. You're a sensitive and loving soul. It will be difficult for you."

"I can handle it. How are you holding up?"

"I'm drained. Emotionally and physically. All I want to do is take a quick shower and crawl in bed."

"Do you want me to come and tuck you in?"

"It sounds lovely, but I'm really beat. Can I take a rain check for tomorrow?"

"Sure."

"You're the best, Julian. I love you."

"Love you too, sweetheart. Sleep well."

"I hope so." Ella ended the call.

Next to her, Vivian was grinning like she'd won the lottery. "You didn't tell me that you were in the I-love-you stage. When did that happen?"

In the past, Ella would have run to her mother with every piece of exciting news, but those days were long over. And it wasn't the type of conversation she wanted to have over their mental link either.

"It's very recent. Saturday night."

Her mom arched a brow. "That's it? Saturday? That's all you're going to tell me?"

Ella dropped the phone into her purse. "There isn't much to tell. We talked, and Julian told me that he loved me, and then I told him that I loved him too. Not a big deal."

"Well, I think it is. Congratulations."

"Thank you. By the way, do you know about the addiction?"

"What addiction?"

Crap. Magnus hadn't told her. Should she?

Yeah, she should. Magnus might not be aware of it, but as a daughter, Ella couldn't and shouldn't keep such important information from her mother.

"Vanessa told me that over time the venom is addictive if a woman is exposed to the venom of only one male. The way it works is that you will want Magnus exclusively, and any other guy that you might have normally found attractive will repulse you. The only way not to get addicted is to have more than one immortal partner bite you."

Vivian frowned. "That's the first I've heard of it. Magnus hasn't said anything about it. I wonder if he knows."

Her mother didn't sound upset, but Ella felt like she should give Magnus the benefit of the doubt. The guy had been awesome to her mom and to Parker and her. He deserved some slack.

"Vanessa said that it's not something they talk about because it doesn't concern most of them, only those who find Dormant or immortal mates. And since that's so rare, Magnus might not be even aware of it."

Vivian shrugged. "It doesn't matter. Magnus is the one for me, and I don't want to feel anything for anyone else. And I certainly don't want any other immortal to bite me. It is what it is. It's not like he's doing it on purpose to get me addicted to him. It's just how it works for them."

"Well, the good news is that he's addicted to you, too, or will be. Vanessa said it takes time for the addiction to set in."

"At least it's fair."

"Yeah. And it gives one hell of a motivation to make up your mind early on if you want a guy or not. Dragging things out with someone you don't love is dangerous for immortals."

Ella wondered if that was why Carol had ended things with Robert. She hadn't mentioned anything about the addiction, so maybe she hadn't been aware of it either.

As tight as the immortal community was, it seemed like vital information wasn't getting communicated properly to its members. The village needed an adult sex education class immortal style.

"Did you and Julian get closer?" Vivian asked.

"Emotionally, yes. Physically, no."

"Are you concerned about the addiction?"

"That's not the reason, Mom. I have Mr. D to deal with, and my issues to overcome. When that is resolved, I can start thinking about intimacy with Julian."

"Perfectly understandable. I don't want you to feel pressured into anything. Take as long as you need. But if you love Julian, and he loves you back, the addiction thing shouldn't stand in your way. It's a small price to pay for love, and even a smaller one for immortality."

Her mother's attitude toward this was probably the right one. It was the way it was, and if Ella wanted Julian or any other immortal mate, she had to deal with it. It wasn't as if Julian intended to get her addicted to him on purpose, and wishing things worked differently for immortals was pointless.

ELLA

"*H*ello, my precious Ella." Logan pulled her into his arms gently and kissed the top of her head.

That was so out of character for him that for a moment Ella thought she was really dreaming, her own dream, and not dream-sharing with the Doomer.

"I have good news for you. Your interview is set for next Wednesday. You should be getting the email tomorrow, or rather Kelly Rubinstein is getting an email. That girl has some impressive grades, and her extracurriculars are even more so." He chuckled. "My friend was ecstatic about expediting your interview. I didn't need to put any pressure on him at all."

It was on the tip of her tongue or, rather, at the end of her synapse to ask Logan if he'd used compulsion on the guy, but then she wasn't supposed to know that he could do that.

"Which extracurricular impressed him the most?"

"The charity you're supposedly running. The people helping you are real pros. I checked out Kelly Rubinstein, and she has a Facebook page with history and friends, including your pictures with a bunch of teenagers. How did they pull off a thorough job like this?"

Ella had no idea that Roni had gone to so much trouble for her. She needed to make him something special as a thank you.

"They are Special Ops. They can do anything. You know, access to government databases and things like that."

She had no idea what she was talking about, but that was fine. An eighteen-year-old wasn't supposed to know how those things worked. Playing dumb was her best defense.

"I wish I had access to your friends," Logan said. "I could use a good hacker."

Was he fishing for information, trying to find out who was helping her? She hoped it wasn't because he suspected his enemies were involved and still believed it was the government.

She shook her head and smiled up at him. "As I said, they are my mom's friends. I don't even know them."

He let go of her and then took her hand. "Let's take a walk. Look around you."

"Where are we?"

"Amsterdam. You liked the canals in Hamburg, so I thought you would like another city that had them."

"I do." She stretched up on her toes and kissed his cheek. "You're being very thoughtful. Thank you for everything you're doing for me. I'm so excited about this interview." Just not for the reason he thought she was.

Frowning, he stopped and turned toward her. "You don't sound excited. You sound tired. What happened?"

"I had a rough day, that's all. A friend of mine had a mini meltdown, and dealing with that was draining. I had to call her boyfriend to come pick her up because she couldn't even drive herself home."

"What triggered that?"

She had a feeling that he wasn't really interested, which made sense. He didn't know Tessa, and even if he did, he probably wouldn't care either. Logan was being really nice to

75

her, but that was because he had an ulterior motive and not because he was a nice guy.

"She heard a very disturbing story that reminded her of bad things that had happened to her when she was younger. I feel guilty for dragging her into this. I knew she had issues."

Logan forced a smile. "I should let you get some real sleep then. I'm sure that in the morning everything will look brighter."

She nodded. "You are probably right. I feel tired even in the dream."

He kissed the top of her head. "Sleep well, my Ella. Good night."

When he was gone, Ella didn't continue sleeping. Opening her eyes, she looked out the window and watched the dark silhouettes of branches swaying in the wind. It had been a mistake to open the shutters after she'd turned the light off, but she wanted to let in fresh air. From her bed, the branches looked menacing, like gnarly arms and fingers tipped with claws.

With a voice command to the home system, she lowered the shutters and turned the light on in the bathroom. Huddling under the blanket, she thought about what Logan had told her.

Next Wednesday was only a week from now. Was it enough time to set up the trap?

This was actually happening. Up until tonight, it had felt like a game, but now reality was knocking on her window with dark, claw-tipped fingers.

For some reason, Ella didn't feel as excited as she thought she would be. Was it anxiety? Or maybe she was a little conflicted about entrapping Logan?

The thing she needed to remember was that he was planning the same thing for her, and if he was not, he wouldn't be there and nothing would happen. So, her guilt was utterly misplaced.

He'd been nice to her lately, which had softened her up toward him, but it had been only a convincing act. If he really cared for her, he wouldn't have evaporated when she was sad. It seemed that Logan didn't like dealing with her when she was in a bad mood.

Good to know for next time she needed to get rid of him fast. All she had to do was make a sad face, shed a few tears, and *poof*, he would be gone.

KIAN

"*I* have to go." Kian grabbed his laptop and headed out.

The text from Ella had arrived a little after two in the morning, but he'd only seen it when he'd checked his phone three hours later.

Syssi stopped him at the door. "Wait. I'll pour your coffee into a thermal mug. The guys can wait a minute longer."

After telling her the exciting news, he'd made a few phone calls and arranged a meeting.

"Thanks." Kian took the mug and kissed her cheek. "I'll make it up to you tonight."

Syssi smiled and waggled her brows. "A foot massage would do."

"It's a deal."

It had been a long time since he'd gone to work that early in the morning or scheduled a meeting before nine. He didn't like leaving the house without making love to his wife first, but as he'd promised, he would make it up to her later.

Smiling, he thought about the pleasure sounds she made when he kneaded her little toes. For some reason, that was her favorite part.

Thermos clasped in hand and a laptop tucked under his arm, Kian took the stairs up to his office two at a time.

One week wasn't long, and there was much to do. Surprisingly, Lokan had come through for Ella and expedited her interview for next Wednesday. Kian wondered whether the Doomer had collected favors owed or just compelled someone to push her up in the list. Not that it mattered one way or another, but he was curious. What business could the Brotherhood possibly have with the university that someone on its staff would owe Lokan a big favor like that?

As far as he knew, Navuh's sons didn't get to study abroad, but then his information about the Doomers' royal family was scant and unreliable.

"Good morning, boss." Onegus walked in with his own mug and took a seat at the conference table.

"Good morning, indeed. The rat has set the trap that he's going to get caught in."

Onegus rubbed his hands. "Who else is joining us at this ungodly hour?"

"Turner and Bridget, of course. And also Magnus and Julian because of their personal involvement. I'll leave it up to you to choose which Guardians you want to take to Washington."

Onegus arched a brow. "I'm going? I thought Turner was. This is his kind of operation."

"I am," Turner said as he and Bridget walked in. "You should stay here." He pulled out a chair for Bridget. "I want security around the village reinforced and put on high alert." He pulled out a chair for himself and sat down.

When Magnus and Julian entered next, Kian motioned for them to take their seats.

"Lokan might have shared more than Ella's dreams," Turner said. "If he has access to her mind and can read her thoughts from afar, he knows that she is with us, and he could have used bits and pieces of information she's subconsciously collected to deduce our location. He also might know that we are coming for him. This could all be an elaborate setup to lure Guardians away from the village so it would be open to attack. It's a remote possibility, but one we cannot ignore."

Turner was paranoid, but his advice was solid nonetheless. The village should be put on high alert.

"Do you think we should order a lockdown?" Kian asked.

In case of emergency, the entrance to the underground tunnel could be blocked by what looked like a rock formation, and no one could come or go until it was open again.

"That's an extreme measure," Turner said. "And probably over the top. If it were up to me, you know I would have done it. But it is your call."

Kian turned to Onegus. "What do you think?"

"Locking down the village should be reserved for real emergencies, and by that I mean an actual attack. I don't think it should be done as a precaution in case of a very remote probability of one."

Bridget nodded. "No offense, Victor, but I'm with Onegus on that."

Turner shrugged. "If later we have reason to suspect that one is coming, we can up the alert level and issue a lockdown command."

"What's the plan?" Magnus asked. "I assume you have one."

"I do." Turner opened his briefcase and handed everyone printouts.

"When Kian called me this morning, I got in touch with my contacts in Washington. We have an entire hotel reserved to ourselves, so Ella and Vivian will be surrounded by Guardians. We will also have five taxis at our disposal. Each time the ladies have to travel, they will be using a different car."

"How are we getting them there?" Julian asked. "Are we taking the jet?"

"We are taking both. The Guardians and I are going to leave tomorrow and lay the groundwork. The ladies will go on Monday. I'll make decoy travel arrangements for them by train. And I'm also thinking of putting two female agents on it in case Lokan thinks to check on that. Now that he has Ella's fake name, it will be easy for him to find where she bought tickets. An internet connected world is one with no privacy."

He looked at Magnus and then at Julian. "You two can either leave with us tomorrow and join the preparations in Washington, or you can stay here and escort the ladies on the plane ride on Monday. But if you want to take part in capturing Lokan, you'll have to come earlier and participate in the prep."

Magnus and Julian exchanged glances.

"Tough choice." Magnus smoothed his hand over his goatee. "Naturally, I don't want to leave Vivian alone for nearly a week. But I want to be on the ground when shit is going down."

Turner nodded. "I'm counting you in for tomorrow's departure."

Magnus nodded.

"How about you, Julian?"

"I'm with Magnus. Who is going to escort Vivian and Ella?"

"Arwel and Bhathian. The two used to work together and they make a good team."

"That's what I thought when we originally paired them." Kian snorted. "But back then Bhathian didn't have Eva and was always grumpy as hell, and Arwel, well, we all know what bothers him. But I agree that they are the perfect escorts. Arwel because of his telepathy, and Bhathian because of his brawn."

"Is that enough, though?" Julian asked. "What if Lokan ambushes them in the terminal? If he can access Ella's brain, he would know she's coming on a private jet and where she is landing."

Turner's lips curved up in a rare smile. "We won't tell Ella the exact travel plans. All she will know is that she and Vivian are flying to some remote private airport in the area. It's better not to tell Vivian anything either, so she doesn't accidentally blurt something out."

"She won't," Magnus said. "But if that's how you want it, I have no problem with that."

"Good. Now let's move to organizing the Guardians. I'm going to take as many as can fit in the two jets." Turner handed Bridget another printout. "These missions will have to be postponed and the schedule reworked."

"I'm on it."

JULIAN

"Are Vivian and Ella going to the sanctuary today?" Julian asked as he and Magnus left Kian's office.

"Vivian doesn't have a class scheduled, and Ella was supposed to film, but she is without an assistant. I don't know if she can do it all by herself."

"Did Tessa quit for good?"

Magnus shrugged. "I don't know, but it makes sense that she would after the panic attack she experienced. Apparently, the girl is too sensitive for that kind of work. Ella is made from stronger stuff."

Even though Julian didn't agree with Magnus's assessment, he liked how proud of Ella the guy had sounded.

"Do you mind if I tag along? I want to talk to Ella."

The Guardian smiled and clapped him on the back. "You are always welcome in our home, Julian. You are part of the family, and that is regardless of what the future holds for you and Ella, although I'm sure you are going to get your happily ever after, as Vivian likes to say."

"Fates willing."

Magnus nodded. "I think they are."

When they neared the house, Vivian opened the door

before they even made it to the front porch. She must've been waiting by the window, no doubt anxious to hear how the meeting went.

"Hi, Julian. Did you have breakfast?"

He rubbed his empty stomach. "After Kian called, I was too nervous to think about food."

The truth was that he still hadn't gone grocery shopping, and neither had Ray. His only option had been heating up a frozen pizza, which was gross for breakfast and took too long.

"Good, so you can join us. Ella and I made mountains of pancakes."

Julian sniffed. "I can tell. Lots of cinnamon."

Inside, Ella was setting the table, anxiety rolling off her in an atypical outpouring of emotion.

He walked up to her and pulled her into his arms. "It's going to be okay. You have nothing to be afraid of."

She pushed on his chest. "You think? Don't talk to me like I'm a baby."

"Ella," her mother warned. "Watch your temper. Julian is just trying to comfort you."

"It's okay," Julian said. "You can punch me if you want." He patted his chest. "Come on, right here. I can take it."

Fisting her hands, she gave him a couple of playful punches. "Thanks. It helped."

"Is that all you got?" He slapped his own chest. "Punch me harder."

"I don't want to. Sit down and eat your pancakes."

Parker came in with a bottle of syrup. "You want some?"

"No, thanks." Julian sat down and spread a napkin over his thighs. "I like mine with butter and honey."

"Your loss, dude. This is good maple."

After Magnus poured everyone coffee, Vivian lifted her mug and waited for him to sit down. "So, what's the plan?"

"The Guardians leave for Washington tomorrow, and that

includes Julian and me. You and Ella will fly out Monday and meet us there."

"On the clan's private jet?" Ella asked.

"Yes."

"Kian said something about flying us to some remote airport and us taking a rented car from there. Is that still the plan?"

"I'm not sure what Turner is planning. He's the mastermind." He hated lying to Ella, but there was no way around it. Turner was right about that.

Vivian shook her head. "Why do you guys need to go with the other Guardians?"

Magnus put his fork down and wiped his mouth with a napkin. "We need to familiarize ourselves with the terrain and with the flow of foot traffic, find good spots for Guardians to hide around campus, and a thousand other details that go into planning and executing a successful operation. Simply put, if Julian and I are not part of the prep, we can't participate."

"How many Guardians are going?" Ella asked.

Julian glanced at Magnus. "About thirty, right?"

"More or less. Turner is taking as many as he can fit into the two aircraft."

Ella whistled. "That's a lot. Who is going to run the rescue missions if so many are going to Washington?"

"Bridget is going to reschedule or cancel them," Magnus said.

She shook her head. "I feel bad about it. There are only two of us, and we really don't need so much security. Those poor girls are suffering, and now their rescue is going to get postponed or canceled."

Julian reached for her hand. "It's not only about keeping Vivian and you safe. In the long run, catching Mr. D is more important than the missions that will get canceled. The information we can get out of him will save many more lives from ruin."

"How do you figure that?"

"If we know where the island is, we might be able to save the women who are held there against their will."

Magnus shook his head. "Sorry to disappoint you, Julian, but we won't be able to do that even if we know where it is. The Brotherhood has thousands of warriors. We can't attack their home base, and we certainly can't bomb it because of all the innocents who live there."

Ella threw her hands in the air. "So, what's the point of catching Mr. D if we can't do anything with the information we can extract from him?"

Magnus smirked. "I didn't say we can't do anything, just that we can't attack the island and free the women. There are other things we can do."

"Like what?" Vivian asked.

Magnus shrugged. "I'm sure Kian and Turner have a plan."

ELLA

*W*ith Magnus and her mother out on a walk with Scarlet, and Parker in his room, Ella and Julian were left alone in the living room with no chaperones, which for some reason filled Ella's head with naughty thoughts.

It was silly. She could be alone with Julian whenever she wanted. Magnus and her mother didn't even know that they were supposed to chaperone them.

A glance at Julian revealed that he either sensed her interest or had the same naughty thoughts. His eyes were glowing, and he seemed uncomfortable.

"Would you like to have coffee out on the front porch?"

That was as public as she could make it, but since their house was in the new part of the village, the only possible passerby was Merlin. Still, someone might decide to visit Merlin. But that was unlikely this early in the morning. She doubted the doctor was even up. From what she'd learned about him, Merlin was a night owl and liked to sleep in late.

"Good idea. I'll pour us what's left in the carafe."

Joining her on the loveseat swing outside, he handed her a full mug. "I fixed it the way you like it."

"Thank you." She took a sip. "I guess that with you and Yamanu gone, the work on the halfway house is going to stop."

"Yamanu is not coming. He is staying in the village to protect it if needed."

The wheels in her brain spinning fast, it didn't take her long to realize why the village needed extra protection. "Kian fears that Mr. D saw what's inside my head and figured out where the village is?"

"Turner, not Kian. He says it's a remote possibility, but he is a very careful guy."

Ella shook her head. "I wouldn't be able to find this village, so even if Mr. D could see what I did, there is no way he could find it. But that's irrelevant because he can't get into my head."

"You don't know that. When you met him, he'd not only peeked into your memories and found out about the telepathy you and your mother share, but he also made you forget whatever he talked with you about. As I said before, he is a very powerful immortal, and you should never underestimate him."

Ella smirked. "That may be true, but I found a way of getting rid of him really fast if I need to."

"How?"

"Last night when he entered my dream, I was sad over what happened with Tessa in the sanctuary. He didn't like dealing with my bad mood and poofed out as soon as he could. I figured anytime I don't want him to hang around my head, I can bring up sad memories. Until this is over, I plan to be sad often."

"Don't overdo it. What if Turner is wrong and he wants you for you and not the telepathy? He might change his mind if you keep acting depressed."

Ella chuckled. "Suddenly you don't mind me being nice to Mr. D? Should I up my game and pretend to seduce him?"

Julian's eyes blazed blue. "Just keep stringing him along. After centuries of having any woman he wants, the Doomer probably appreciates the chase more than the catch."

That soured her mood. "Do you think he thralls women into going to bed with him?"

"He doesn't need to. Or did you forget the giant brothel the Doomers have at their disposal on the island?"

"Right. I did. But he is stationed in the States, so he doesn't have access to it."

"There is no shortage of the paid variety here. Those who are voluntarily in it for the money, and those who are coerced by threats."

She wondered whether Logan frequented the kind of brothels the clan routinely raided to rescue girls who'd been sold into sexual slavery. He wasn't a good man, she had no such illusions, but he was also vain, and he appreciated luxury. Logan probably paid for the best escort girls money could buy, not some poor girls who'd been drugged and beaten into cooperation.

Unless he was perverted and enjoyed inflicting suffering.

She wouldn't put it past him. In fact, he would have made a much better choice as the lead for the *Fifty Shades* movie than the actor they'd chosen for that role. Still, if she were a casting director, she would have selected Logan to play Lucifer, and not some playboy billionaire with a kinky twist.

The king of the underworld suited him better.

"What are you smirking about?" Julian hooked his finger under her chin and turned her so she had to look at him.

"Nothing important. I was pretending to be a casting director in my head."

He lifted a brow. "Do you do that often?"

"Yeah, I do." She sighed. "I was having fun casting Mr. D as Lucifer, but I need to focus on casting someone new for the role of my filming assistant. I'm afraid Tessa is out. And now with you gone for the week, I also need someone to help me with editing. I want to put those videos up and start the fundraiser. I can't be the director of a charity that doesn't exist yet."

"Try Sylvia. She's not too busy, and she should be a quick learner after the many years she's spent studying."

"Isn't she dangerous to electronics, though?"

"Not unless she wills them to malfunction. At least that's my understanding. Roni wouldn't have let her into his lair if she was going to damage his equipment."

"Do you have her number?"

"I have Roni's." He put his mug down on the floor and pulled out his phone. "I'll share the contact with you."

"Thanks."

Ella waited for him to put the phone back in his pocket before lifting her bottom and planting it in his lap. "If I'm not going to see you for almost a week, I need the kiss of all kisses to remember you by."

"Do you now?" He wrapped his large palm around the back of her neck, massaging the side with his thumb.

With his other arm wrapped around her waist, he had her trapped, but Ella didn't feel even a smidgen of panic. Only desire.

"Kiss me, Julian." She wound her arms around his neck.

His fingers gently rubbing the back of her head, he tilted his head and brushed his lips over hers. Soft and yet firm, cold and yet hot.

As the world spun around her, Ella moaned. When was the last time they'd kissed? Had it been Monday? Yeah, after they were done filling in the applications. But it felt as if he hadn't kissed her in ages.

He was going slow, drawing the kiss out and making her impatient for more, his tongue flicking over her lips, delving inside her mouth, and then retreating to lick her lips again.

As she arched into him, pressing her hardening nipples against his chest, his hand brushed lightly over the side of her breast, sending tiny bolts of lightning into her feminine core and igniting her desire.

"Touch me, Julian," she breathed into his mouth.

Without warning, he left her mouth and dipped his head, taking her nipple between his lips together with the bra and shirt covering it.

"Julian," she groaned.

Reaching for the hem of her shirt, she started lifting it up. But as suddenly as he'd taken her nipple, Julian let go of it, lifted her off his lap, and set her down beside him.

"Lean into me," he whispered. "Your shirt is wet."

A moment later Scarlet bounded onto the porch, her tail wagging and her tongue lolling.

Damn. Vivian and Magnus were back from their walk.

Chuckling, Ella murmured into Julian's shirt, "Saved by the dog."

VIVIAN

*T*he walk had done little to alleviate Vivian's anxiety. Despite Kian and Magnus's reassurances, she had a bad feeling about them using Ella as bait to trap the Doomer prince, but she saw no way of backing out of it or convincing Ella to reconsider.

Not that at this stage of the game it was an option for either of them. Perhaps if Ella had been less enthusiastic and confident about her ability to lure Lokan, Vivian could've argued against it.

Probably not even then.

After all that the clan had done for her family, and how important catching Navuh's son was for them, refusing was not an option.

Talk about peer pressure.

If they backed down, living in the village would become intolerable. Everyone would pretend to understand, but on the inside, they would resent her and Ella, thinking of them as cowardly and ungrateful.

That was not how Vivian envisioned her and Ella's future in the village. Even Parker and Magnus would be affected.

As the door opened and Ella came in with Julian, Vivian

plastered a pleasant smile on her face and took the empty mugs from his hands. "Would you like more coffee?"

"I need to change." Ella was holding her shirt away from her body. "I spilled coffee on myself." She darted into the hallway.

Looking after her retreating back, Julian sighed. "I would have loved to stay and have another cup with you, but I need to get moving. Yamanu is waiting for me at the halfway house. I need to make arrangements for the project to keep going while I'm gone."

"Can't you have someone else supervise the job?" Magnus asked.

"Not on such short notice, and Yamanu can't take my place because he needs to stay in the village during the heightened alert. When we started the project, I thought to save money by managing the job site and subcontracting the work. Now I regret not hiring a general contractor to handle everything."

"What about the pros Kian uses in the real estate development?"

Julian shook his head. "They don't do renovations." He turned to Vivian. "I guess the next time I'll see you will be in Washington."

Swallowing, she nodded.

"Good luck."

Listening to the guys talk about remodeling had been a momentary distraction, but Julian's reminder spiked her anxiety back up.

Vivian waited for the door to close behind him before walking up to Magnus and wrapping her arms around him. "I don't know what I'm going to do without you. You've become such a vital part of my days and my nights that I'm going to feel lost and lonely while you're gone."

He held her to him tightly, rocking her in place. "Are you having separation anxiety, lass?"

That wasn't the type of language Magnus used. Had he been consulting with Vanessa without telling her?

"Who have you been talking with?"

"Andrew. He says Phoenix cries every morning when he leaves for work, and it breaks his heart even though she stops the moment the door closes behind him."

"So, what are you saying, that I'm acting like a little girl?"

He shook his head. "No, love. It's just that this is the first time we are going to be apart since we met, and that's why it feels so uncomfortable. But it's not going to be the last. I'm a Guardian, and although most of the time I will be assigned to local missions, from time to time I will have to leave for several days. You'd better get used to that."

Resting her forehead on his chest, Vivian nodded. "I know. I'll have to keep myself super busy, that's all. Perhaps Vanessa can use my help with more things than just the sewing class. I just hope she'll be okay with me bringing Parker over. He's fine by himself for a few hours, but I don't want to leave him alone for entire days."

As she rambled on and on, Magnus rubbed slow circles on her back, waiting patiently for her to calm down. Even though they hadn't been together all that long, he knew her so well because he paid attention.

She lifted her head and kissed his lips. "I love you. You're the best."

Wearing a fresh shirt, Ella walked in and cast an amused glance at them. "Are we still going to the sanctuary today, Mom? Or do you want to spend every moment smooching with Magnus until he leaves?"

Kissing the top of Vivian's head, he gently disentangled himself from her arms. "I wish we could, but I have a briefing I need to attend."

"When?" Vivian asked.

"After lunch."

"Good, so we can eat together." She turned to Ella. "I

called Vanessa and canceled for today. We need to go shopping."

"What for?"

"Clothes, shoes. You have nothing decent to wear for the interview. You can't go wearing your Frankenstein boots or sneakers."

Over her head, she felt Magnus nodding as if to encourage Ella to say yes.

Sweet guy.

"Well, I need to add a few items to my wardrobe, and if it helps to take your mind off worrying, I'm all for it. But not today. After Julian comes back from the halfway house, I want to spend some time with him. Besides, we can go virtual shopping and order everything online."

"Things won't arrive on time."

"We can pay for expedited shipping."

Poor girl. She was still wary about leaving the safety of the village. "Are you afraid of going anywhere other than the sanctuary?"

Ella shrugged. "It hasn't even crossed my mind, but now that you mention it, I was reminded of what a hassle it was to put on my full disguise. I can't stand the contact lenses, and trying on clothes with sunglasses on will be too weird."

"Online shopping it is, then." Vivian headed to the kitchen and opened the fridge. "I'm just afraid of ordering shoes and then finding out that they don't fit. We don't have time to send them back and order another size." She pulled out lettuce and a wedge of parmesan cheese for a Caesar salad.

Ella followed her to the kitchen and leaned against the counter. "I need to go talk to Eva. I haven't thought about wearing the disguise while touring Georgetown, and the contacts are a pain in the derrière. I need to ask her if there are regular looking glasses that can fool facial recognition software."

Vivian frowned. "I hadn't thought of it either. Perhaps we both should go see her. We need better disguises."

Pulling out her phone, Ella glanced up. "I'll ask her if she can see us after lunch. Okay with you?"

"Perfect. We can do that while Magnus is at his meeting."

"Right. And I need to go visit Tessa too. Do you want to come with me?"

Vivian smiled. "I have a great idea. How about we make something special for lunch and bring it to her? I'm sure she is in no mood for cooking."

Ella waved a dismissive hand. "I don't know if she cooks at all. Jackson could be bringing stuff from the café. Besides, it isn't as if either of us is a great cook. I'm not going to take Tessa your meatloaf, if that's what you have in mind."

Vivian cast her a reproachful look. "I know more than one recipe, and besides, it's the thought that counts."

"I meant no offense, Mom. I love your meatloaf, but many people don't like that kind of food. If I bring Tessa something, I want to make sure she enjoys it. Like a box of Godiva chocolates."

"Do you have any left?"

Ella was a sucker for those. If she had any, they were most likely gone by now.

"I do. After I cleaned his kitchen, Merlin gave me a huge pack full of small boxes. I had Julian keep them so I wouldn't eat all of them at one sitting, but I have two boxes here. I can wrap one up and give it to Tessa."

"Perfect."

ELLA

"I have just what you need," Eva said. "Believe it or not, Roni printed them for me on a 3D-printer."

Vivian shook her head. "Technology is progressing at an amazing speed. I read that scientists at the Tel-Aviv university were able to 3-D print a small scale human heart using human cells. Pretty soon organ donations will no longer be needed. No more waiting in line for hearts and kidneys and the like. Each hospital will have a 3-D printer and replacement parts will be custom made for any patient that needs them."

Eva grinned. "I just love it. Yesterday's science fiction is today's reality. Like Jules Verne's stories. The inventions he wrote about were fantasy back then, but they became reality." She pushed to her feet. "Let me get my magic makeover case."

In his bassinet, Ethan was making cute little sucking noises, and Ella got up to get a better look. He was sound asleep, probably dreaming about nursing.

Such an adorable baby, and those pink cheeks were just asking to be kissed. Hopefully, he would wake up before they left so she could hold him for a little bit. Having the baby pressed against her chest felt like an infusion of good. It really was a bundle of joy.

Ella wondered if that feeling was produced by the same chemical reaction Julian had talked about, or if it was unique to babies. Hugging adults, or even Parker, had never flooded her with as many feel-good endorphins.

"Do babies have this effect only on women or on men too?"

"What do you mean?" Vivian asked.

"Whenever I've held Ethan, and I've only gotten to do it twice, I felt like I was high. It felt euphoric. So, I'm wondering if only females feel that because their bodies prepare them for motherhood, or do males feel that too?"

A sadness settled over Vivian's features. "Your father's eyes would roll back from pleasure every time he held you and later Parker." She chuckled. "But only until you started crying or made a stinky in your diaper. Then he would quickly give you back to me."

When Eva came back hefting a huge trunk, Ella rushed to help her. "This looks heavy."

Eva huffed. "Don't be silly. I'm at least twice as strong as you are." She put it down on the floor, crouched next to it, and sprung the coded locks. "Open sesame." The lid popped up.

Inside, several compartments of various sizes were separated by dividers. Eva pulled a makeup case out and opened it.

"I have three new pairs of those specialty glasses, but with clear lenses this time so they look like reading glasses. They are called adversarial, probably because they can fool your adversaries. They aren't the prettiest, and if you want, I can ask Roni if he can print something better looking." She handed one pair to Ella and the other to Vivian.

The frames were made from simple black plastic, but they

weren't as hideous as Ella had feared something made with a 3-D printer would be.

"Can't we order nicer ones from a store?" Vivian asked.

"They are not commercially available yet. The instructions are not publicly available either, but you know Roni. When he wants to get his hands on something, he finds a way."

Ella took the glasses off and examined them closer. "Did he hack the instructions?"

"According to him, he did not. The inventors are sharing them with people in their close circle, and William knew a guy who knew another guy. That sort of thing." Lifting a handheld mirror from her case, Eva handed it to Ella. "Here, put them back on and take a look."

"They are not bad." Ella ran her fingers through her hair, spiking it. "Hipster style meets grunge punk. I like it." She handed the mirror to her mother who didn't look happy.

"Ugh, it's going to look awful with my black wig, but whatever. I'm not entering a beauty pageant."

"What else can you do for us?" Ella asked. "We need things that are not difficult to put on and keep on."

Eva looked her up and down. "You're fine. If you want, you can go to William's lab and have him run you through his program while you're wearing the glasses. If you pass the test, then there is no reason to go any further. And the same is true for your mom." She turned to Vivian. "But keep the wig on. Your hair is very distinctive, especially when combined with your tiny frame."

"I will."

"I have one here that might look better on you than the one Amanda gave you." She pulled out a shoulder-length wig. "It's not all black, so it looks more natural. Try it on."

The wig was dark chestnut, and it looked like it was real hair. Either that or it was made from better materials and didn't look as fake as the one Amanda gave Vivian. Except,

Ella thought that it was kind of gross to wear someone else's hair.

"I love it. Thank you," Vivian said. "I don't look like a vampire in it. I'm normally pale, but when I'm stressed, I look like a ghost."

"Then I suggest you put on a lot of makeup." Eva smiled evilly. "You don't want to scare your prey off."

Vivian swallowed. "I need to buy more foundation."

Way to go, Eva. It was good that the woman wasn't a doctor because her bedside manner left a lot to be desired. She would've scared her patients to death.

Then again, her direct approach had worked for Tessa. After killing her tormentor, Eva had nursed the traumatized girl back to health, which meant that she wasn't as callous as she appeared. Or maybe Tessa responded better to tough love?

"How is Tessa doing?" Ella asked. "Did you talk with her since yesterday?"

"Jackson took her horseback riding. That boy is a genius. It would've never occurred to me that such an activity could have a therapeutic effect. But apparently, it's working for Tessa. When she called me earlier, she sounded fine."

"Well, his mother is a therapist. He must've asked Vanessa for advice."

Eva cocked an eyebrow. "Did you see any horses in the sanctuary? If that were Vanessa's idea, she would have a stable on the grounds."

"Horses are expensive and need a lot of care," Vivian said.

Eva waved a dismissive hand. "She could have made do with some cats or goats to pet."

Cats and goats were not in the same category as horses, but Ella wasn't going to point it out. No one liked a wiseass, and Eva was a bit scary. Pissing her off was not a good idea.

"Why not dogs?" Vivian asked. "Small ones, that is. I can see how some girls might be afraid of big dogs."

Ella took the glasses off and put them in her purse. "Dogs pee and poo where they are not supposed to. Scarlet still has accidents."

Vivian grimaced. "Tell me about it. I ordered half a dozen of those disinfecting spray bottles."

"Scarlet is so funny." Ella chuckled. "She always looks so guilty after doing something she knows is a no-no. As soon as she makes that face, we go looking for her mess right away."

As a sound of protest came from Ethan's bassinet, Eva walked over and picked him up. "Are you hungry, my sweet little boy?" She kissed his cheek.

The baby cooed and reached with his tiny fist, closing it around a strand of her hair.

"Don't pull on Mama's hair, precious." Eva smoothed a finger over his tiny ones but didn't attempt to pry them open.

Ella wondered if the baby would let go on his own. Perhaps when Eva started feeding him?

"We should go." Vivian pushed to her feet. "Thank you so much for all your help."

"My pleasure. And if I don't see you before you leave, good luck. I wish I could be there, but since my Bhathian is escorting you, I know that you are in good hands."

2 2

JULIAN

*W*hen Julian made it back to the village, it was after ten at night and he still needed to pack, but he had to see Ella before leaving. The flight was scheduled for early in the morning the next day, and he didn't think she would be awake to say goodbye.

Should he ask her to spend the night with him?

The yearning to hold her in his arms until the last moment was so intense that it made breathing difficult. A problem, since he was running.

Fifty feet or so away from her house, Julian slowed down to a walk and evened out his breath. There was no need for Ella to know how obsessed with her he was, and that he had run all the way from the pavilion.

Except, as soon as his foot touched the first of the three steps leading up to her front porch, Ella opened the door and stepped out. "Did you run all the way here?"

"What gave me away?" He climbed the stairs and took her into his arms.

"I timed it. You called me when you left the construction site. And I calculated the drive and the walk. You are seven minutes early."

It seemed that he was not the only one obsessed.

His heart felt lighter at the realization. "How are we going to survive these five days?"

She wrapped her arms around his neck. "We will have to talk on the phone a lot and video chat."

All kinds of visions crossed his mind, some naughtier than others.

"What's that smirk about?" Ella asked.

He kissed the tip of her nose. "You're not the only one with a vivid imagination. I entertained a few ideas for those phone calls."

Catching his meaning, she blushed. "We can't. Not yet."

He made a face. "It doesn't count when there is no touching involved."

"I'm sure that some touching was going on in your vivid fantasies."

"Guilty."

Ella sighed. "Just a little bit longer, Julian. By next Wednesday, I will be free. Hopefully. If everything works out as planned." She pushed out of his arms and took his hand. "It will be one hell of a disappointment if Mr. D doesn't show up, and all this careful preparation is for nothing. I will feel like such an idiot."

As they started walking down the pathway, Julian wrapped his arm around Ella's waist. "Do you know the phrase about the leopard and how he cannot change its spots? The same is true of the Doomer. It would be unchar-acteristic for him to help you out of the goodness of his heart. He wants you. He admitted it."

"True." She shrugged. "Everything is set in motion, so there is no point in speculating. Whatever happens, happens. Just promise me to be extra super-duper careful. I won't survive it if anything happens to you." Her voice wobbled a little.

"Hey." He stopped and hooked a finger under her chin. "Look at me."

She had tears in her eyes.

"Nothing is going to happen to me. Thirty experienced Guardians can take on a platoon of Doomers. The most formidable warriors on the planet are going to guard you and your mom. I'm just tagging along because I'll expire from worry if I'm not there with you."

Wiping the tears with the back of her hand, she smiled. "And I thought that I was being melodramatic. Sorry for the mini-meltdown."

"Speaking of meltdowns, how is Tessa doing?"

Holding hands, they resumed their walk.

"Better. Jackson took her horseback riding. Except, I don't know what did the trick, him taking the day off to be with her or the horses."

"A little bit of both, I guess." He squeezed her hand. "I'm not going to bore you with a geeky explanation about why horseback riding releases endorphins."

"Why not? I love it when you tell me interesting facts. I can then use them in conversations and sound smart."

"You are smart." He leaned and kissed the top of her head. "But I'll save it for after we come back. Right now I want to hear about you and your day. Did you talk with Sylvia about assisting you in the sanctuary?"

"I did. She's going to help me film and also help edit the videos."

"Editing was supposed to be my job." On the one hand, Julian had been looking forward to spending long hours with Ella, but on the other hand, he hadn't been looking forward to the emotional pain of hearing horrible stories.

"It still is. I just want to edit the first three videos and put them up before I leave for Washington. I want to have this fundraiser up and running. Sylvia is going to help with those. When we come back, you'll help me with the ones I'm going to shoot tomorrow and the day after."

"Did you get more volunteers?"

"No, but I'm going to. Tomorrow I'm shooting the other two from the original four, and I hope more will sign up. We don't need all of them to do it, but the more the better."

"Good luck."

"Thank you." Ella looked down, found a small loose rock, and kicked it. "This project keeps me going. Whenever I feel scared or overwhelmed, or when bad thoughts intrude, all I need to do is think about the fundraiser to get excited and positive again."

It was a little disappointing that thinking of him was not enough to chase the gloom away, but he was happy that she had something to keep her upbeat.

Having a goal, especially a worthy one like that, was a powerful motivator.

Julian wished he had something like that to get him excited. Something he felt super passionate about. He could jump on the fundraiser wagon and help Ella or focus on remodeling the halfway house. Both were worthy endeavors, but they didn't get his juices flowing. He needed a challenge, something he was exceptionally good at, or believed he could be. Regrettably, he hadn't stumbled upon that one thing yet.

He was excited about catching the Doomer, though. Which brought back Ella's suggestion of him joining the Guardian force. Perhaps as a medic?

Nah, that wasn't it either.

Who did he want to be when he grew up?

Ella waved a hand in front of his face. "A penny for your thoughts."

"They are not worth even that. I was trying to figure out what would excite me as much as the fundraiser excites you."

"I don't think you can go looking for it. Fate has a way of putting the right person in the right place for the right job.

The choice we have is either to step up to the plate or not. If you asked me a month ago if I was interested in fundraising, I would have said no way. I was convinced that I wanted to be a nurse. But one thing led to another and here I am, all consumed by this project that is way too big for me, but that I want to tackle anyway."

"You no longer want to be a nurse?"

"I'm not sure what I want."

"A doctor. You should study to become a doctor."

She shook her head. "I don't think so."

He chuckled. "That makes two of us. Neither of us know who we want to be when we grow up."

"Oh, I know who I want to be." Ella looked up at him and smiled. "I want to be Ella Takala, Director of Save the Girls."

23

ELLA

*A*s they got back to her house, Julian swept Ella into his arms and sat with her on the loveseat swing.

"I need a kiss that will hold me through the next five days." He palmed the back of her head and took her lips.

Ella threw her arms around his neck and pulled him down to her, savoring the ferocity of his kiss. His mouth was hard on hers, taking, demanding, and beneath her his erection prodded her through his jeans.

God, she wanted him. She was ready, and even if it wasn't going to be perfect because of the baggage she was bringing along, she didn't want to wait any longer.

Except, that was a lot of empty bravado when she knew nothing could happen between them tonight.

With an effort, she pulled away and put a hand on his chest. "Next Wednesday, Julian, we are going to celebrate Mr. D's capture. The Guardians can bring him back here and we can stay in Washington for a few days. We will go to see all the monuments, eat in fancy restaurants, and spend our nights together."

Julian shook his head. "Don't."

"Don't what?"

"Make victory plans."

"Are you afraid to jinx it?"

"It's not about that. Don't rush things because you feel bad for me." He smirked. "When you're so ready that steam is coming out of your ears, then we will revisit your proposition."

Smiling, Ella clapped her hands over her earlobes. "I think it's happening already. I can feel the steam billowing out."

"Not yet, but it will. I guarantee it."

"I believe you, and I love you."

"I love you too, sweetheart." He lifted her off his lap and helped her stand. "I don't want to go, but I should."

Stretching up on her toes, she kissed his cheek, then the other one, and last she kissed his lips. "Good night, Julian. Call me when you get settled in Washington."

"I will."

She opened the door and went in, but before closing it, she stood there for a long moment and watched him walk away.

The next five days were going to be difficult but doable, with plenty of video calls and long talks into the night.

Yawning, Ella closed the door and tiptoed through the dark house to her room. Five minutes later she was in bed and hugging her pillow.

Showering could wait for the morning.

A soft kiss on her lips woke her up, and then a hard male body pressed against her, strong arms wrapping around her and pulling her closer. Smiling, she wrapped her arms around Julian's neck, her fingers stroking his hair.

Except, something didn't feel right. His hair was shorter, and coarser, and his body was leaner than she'd remembered. This didn't feel like Julian at all.

Gasping, she opened her eyes and leaned away.

"Did I scare you?" Logan asked. "You were smiling a moment ago. Did you expect someone else?"

Crap, she was in her room, in her own bed, and Logan was there with her, which meant that he was seeing into her mind. That was bad, really bad.

"I didn't expect to find you in my bed. Usually you take me somewhere nice."

"My apologies." He snapped his fingers, transporting them to a different room.

"Where are we?"

"My bedroom."

She looked over his shoulder, but it was too dark to see. "Can you turn on a light?"

"I can do better than that."

As the ceiling disappeared, revealing a starry night, Ella gasped with delight. It was magical. If only she knew more about the constellations, she could figure out where they were, but regrettably her knowledge was limited to their names. She couldn't discern the patterns in the sky.

Turning on her back, she crossed her arms over her chest. "This is beautiful, thank you. But you really shouldn't have taken such liberties. I told you that I'm not that kind of girl."

He leaned over her, caressing her cheek with his finger as he regarded her with his intense dark eyes. "I've done exactly what you've told me. I've taken you on walks in beautiful places, and I've behaved like the perfect gentleman. Then you explained to me how modern girls don't play games and hook up with anyone they want. I thought you were hinting at something."

"I also told you that I'm not ready to hook up with anyone."

"Don't you find me attractive?"

"I find you disturbingly so."

He arched a dark eyebrow. "What does that mean?"

"You're a dangerous man, Logan. You admitted as much. I should be afraid of you, not attracted to you."

Smirking like the devil he was, Logan rubbed his finger

over her lips, the small touch sending goosebumps all over her arms. "Let me tell you a secret, little Ella. Women are attracted to dangerous men. Have you ever heard the phrase like a moth to a flame?"

"I have. And that's exactly how I feel." A slight exaggeration, but there was enough truth in it to sound believable.

His other hand smoothed over the curve of her hip. "It's a dream, Ella. You're in no danger from me or anyone else in here. You can have some harmless fun in dreamland."

She took his hand and moved it off her hip. "I'm not ready for fun. Not after what I've been through, which was not fun at all. In fact, I started seeing a therapist."

"And how is that working for you?"

"It's good. I only had one session so far, but I think I made some progress."

A grimace spreading over his handsome face, Logan turned on his back and crossed his arms under his head. "Americans and their shrinks. Do you really think some bobbing head knows better how to heal your mind than you do yourself?"

She couldn't agree more. "I'm giving it a try. If it helps, fine, and if it doesn't, I'll quit."

"You are a smart girl, Ella. You don't need the shrink or anyone else to tell you how to feel."

Damn. How did he know all the right things to say? Was he reading her mind after all?

"What if I feel sad?"

"It's okay to feel sad and angry and frustrated. This futile pursuit of feel-good and happy is a very Western sentiment. Suffering is part of the human experience."

She turned on her side and looked at him. "Are you suffering, Logan?"

"Every goddamned day of my life."

That was surprising. "You don't look like you do."

"Because I don't dwell on it. I plot and I scheme and I act.

110

Instead of lying on a couch in a shrink's office and complaining about my troubles, I fix them."

"What if you can't fix something?"

"Then I put some work into searching for the right tool until I find it."

Reluctantly, she liked his attitude. A lot.

"I'm tired and I need to sleep, Logan. For real. Can we continue this conversation tomorrow?"

"On one condition. I want a kiss goodnight."

Oh, boy. This wasn't good.

"Not in bed. How about you take me to some romantic location and we kiss there?"

He didn't look happy about her request, but he did as she asked anyway. Snapping his fingers, he had them standing at the top of the Eiffel Tower.

"Is that romantic enough for you?"

"Oh, yeah. Thank you."

Wrapping his arm around her shoulders, he chuckled. "In reality, it's not as romantic as I made it for you."

"What's the difference?"

"I removed the metal grid and replaced it with glass panels." He glanced down at her. "You didn't notice the change in attire either. How do you like the gown?"

With the magnificent view all around her, Ella hadn't paid attention to anything else. Now that he called her attention to it, though, what she had on didn't feel like the nightshirt she'd gone to bed in.

He snapped his fingers again. "Here is a mirror."

The gown was indeed beautiful, and she appreciated Logan's good taste, but with him standing next to her, it was difficult to concentrate on her own reflection.

Regal was the word that came to mind. Right after dangerous and sexy as sin. Logan looked like the prince he was. Correction, the grandson of a god.

Lucifer had nothing on him.

24

AMANDA

"*M*aster Parker." Amanda ruffled the kid's hair. "I came to check on your progress. Have you been practicing your powers?"

Vivian chuckled. "He's been tormenting Ella, and he even tried it on Scarlet."

"Did it work?"

"Nope." Parker shook his head. "She's cute, but she's stupid."

Amanda affected a scowl. "I hope you are referring to the dog and not your sister."

He grimaced. "Ella is not cute."

Exchanging glances, Vivian and Amanda burst out laughing.

"What?" Parker threw his hands in the air. "She might look cute, but she's not. Sometimes she's really nasty to me."

"She's not." Vivian motioned for Amanda to take a seat on the couch. "Can I offer you some coffee?"

"No, thank you. I've had too much already. But I'll take water. Do you have something cold and carbonated?"

"I'll get you a Perrier."

"Perfect. Thank you."

Amanda waited for Vivian to come back before turning to Parker. "Come sit with your auntie and tell me about your compulsion experiments." She put the Perrier bottle on the coffee table, crossed her legs, and rested her hands one on top of the other on her knee. Her teacher's pose.

"I figured out why sometimes it works and sometimes it doesn't." He sat on the other side of the couch.

The kid was still uncomfortable around her, but that would pass. She liked him, and hopefully in time he would feel the same about her.

"Do tell." Patting the spot next to her, Amanda motioned for him to get closer.

"There are several things I need to do at once, and it's not easy. First, I need to concentrate and visualize what I want the person to do, then I need to really want them to do it, and finally I have to use the voice."

Up until the comment about the voice, it sounded a lot like thralling.

"Can you demonstrate?"

He frowned. "You're an immortal. It's not going to work on you."

"I know. I just want to hear that special voice you use." She pulled out her phone and pressed record.

If this had to do with sound waves, William could analyze it. Although on second thought, it would be better if Parker came down to the lab and they recorded him using proper equipment.

Still frowning, Parker shook his head. "I can't think of anything I want from you. It can't be something I'm not really interested in."

Remembering his transition party demands, Amanda reached into her purse and pulled out her wallet. "If I detect something special in your voice, I'll give you a twenty." She pulled the note out of the wallet and waved it in front of Parker. "Do you want this?"

He nodded. "Then ask me for it."

Parker nodded, took in a deep breath, closed his eyes for a moment, opened them and leveled his gaze at Amanda. "Give me the twenty dollars, please."

"Here you go." She handed him the note.

Snatching it, he quickly put it in his pocket. "Did you hear anything in my voice?"

She hadn't, but it was important not to discourage him. The more confident Parker felt, the better he would do.

"I'm not sure." She glanced at Vivian. "Can he practice on you? I want to see him in action."

"Give me a moment." Vivian got up and rushed into the kitchen.

A moment later she came back with a small packet of roasted almonds. "These are like catnip for Parker."

The kid's eyes widened. "I didn't know we had any left."

"I hid them from you because you weren't eating anything else. Try to get me to give them to you." She dangled the small package from her fingers.

Amanda could almost feel the vibration of Parker summoning his powers, but then again, she wanted to feel something, so she could have been sensing what wasn't there.

Lifting his hand high in the air, he commanded, "Throw the almonds to me."

Vivian's hand shook as she tried to resist the command, but it was no use. The pack went flying straight into Parker's raised hand.

"What did you feel, Vivian?"

"It's the weirdest thing. It's like he took command of my arm and it did what he told it to do. My own body betrayed me." She looked up at Amanda. "What if it's a placebo effect?"

"Let's see how Ella reacts. Is she home?"

"She is in her room with Sylvia. They are working on editing the first two videos she shot at the sanctuary."

"Congratulations. I didn't know she'd already started.

How is it going for her?"

Vivian sighed. "She lost Tessa. The girl couldn't stomach it. Sylvia volunteered to take her place."

"That bad, eh?"

"I don't know. Ella didn't let me see any of them. I'm afraid that I'll have to wait for her to upload them to YouTube first. She thinks I can't handle it."

Amanda lifted the Perrier and unscrewed the top. "Perhaps she's right. It's one thing to listen to a stranger's horror story, and another thing entirely to hear your own daughter recounting her nightmare."

Glancing at Parker, Vivian shook her head, indicating that they shouldn't talk in front of him. It was her prerogative as his mother, of course, but Amanda didn't believe that a teenager Parker's age couldn't handle some nasty.

"I'll call her," Vivian said.

For a moment, Amanda expected her to pull out a phone, but when Vivian just gazed at the direction of Ella's room, she was reminded that mother and daughter had a more direct way of communicating.

She heard the door open, and then Ella's light footsteps as she rushed into the living room. "Hi, Amanda. Mom said that you need me for something."

Amanda nodded. "I want Parker to show me how he compels you to do something that you don't want to do."

"Great." Ella rolled her eyes. "Just do it quickly and don't embarrass me. I want to be done with those three videos tonight."

Vivian didn't look happy. "I thought you were only working on the two you filmed on Tuesday."

"I also have mine from Monday."

"Please don't put it up. What if Gorchenco can recognize you? You were his wife, for God's sake. He can probably detect every inflection in your tone, and he knows your body language."

Ella waved a dismissive hand. "Once we are done with editing, I'll let you watch it and you'll tell me if I'm recognizable. After all, I was married to the Russian for only a few days, but I've been your daughter for eighteen years."

That seemed to mollify Vivian. "Promise?"

"Yeah. Now. Let's get on with the compulsion."

While they'd been talking, Parker had time to prepare, and he was ready with his demand. "Make me a sandwich exactly like the one you made me yesterday."

"Crap." Ella tried to shake it off, and then headed to the kitchen. "I don't understand how it works," she said as she pulled the ingredients out of the fridge. "I know he's about to do it, I brace to resist, and then I have to do it anyway. It's like he's taking control of my body. But when he did it unknowingly, it felt different."

"How so?" Amanda asked.

"Since I didn't resist, I didn't feel as if my body was obeying a command. I thought that I decided to humor him, that it was my decision."

Fascinating. Apparently, compulsion was undetectable unless the compelled knew it was coming. Amanda wondered what happened when the command went against the compelled one's moral code. Did they try to fight it, or did they convince themselves that they actually wanted to do what they were compelled to do?

It seemed that compulsion worked a lot like hypnosis, just with more muscle behind it. Resisting it was more difficult.

It could explain how otherwise sane people could be turned into a murderous mob by a charismatic leader. The question was whether those types of leaders used mass hypnosis or were gifted with the unique ability to compel.

It would be interesting to introduce Ella and Vivian to a powerful hypnotist and see if hypnosis affected them similarly to compulsion, and then ask them to compare the two.

25

JULIAN

"*I*s this also a clan-owned hotel?" Julian asked as their van pulled up to the building.

"Not this time." Turner slung the strap of his duffel bag over his shoulder and opened the sliding door. "I have many friends in Washington. Or rather acquaintances who owe me favors. This place is reserved for special operations. There are several of them scattered throughout the city. Different sizes and different levels of concealment."

Julian followed him inside. "Are we going straight to the campus? I wouldn't mind stopping somewhere for a bite to eat."

Turner smirked. "We are going to enjoy the cuisine of the student cafeteria."

"I don't miss that."

"We don't have time." Turner slapped his back. "The campus is sprawling and we need to get familiar with it while not attracting attention."

The clerk at the hotel's front desk was clearly not trained in the hospitality business. With a nod of acknowledgment, he handed Turner a bunch of plastic entry keys with sticky notes marking the room numbers attached to them.

Was he an agent? And if he was, which department did he work for?

"Thank you," Turner said as he took five and handed the remaining ones back. "The rest of my crew is arriving shortly."

The clerk nodded again.

"Are we sharing a room?"

Turner lifted a brow. "Do you want to room with someone else?"

"I was hoping to have one to myself. If everything goes well, Ella and I might stay over and do some sightseeing. We can come back on a commercial flight."

"No problem. We have rooms to spare." Turner turned around and went back to the front desk. "We will need one more room."

The clerk grimaced as he handed him the key. "I'll have the cleaning crew prepare it for you."

"Much appreciated."

The guy nodded.

Turner handed Julian a card. "We are on the ground floor. I'm number three and you are number five."

As he followed the guy down the corridor, Julian rubbed his jaw. "If Lokan has Ella followed to her hotel, he might notice that the majority of the guests are men. It could tip him off."

"I've thought of that. We will have female company."

Hopefully, he didn't mean the paid kind. Maybe the other guys would be happy about it, but Julian didn't think his mother would appreciate it if her mate arranged for it.

He stopped next to Turner as the guy opened the door to his room. "What kind of female company? Are we talking agents or call girls?"

"Neither." Turner got inside and motioned for Julian to join him. "Remember the women we rescued from the Doomers a while back?"

"What about them?" Julian closed the door and looked at the room.

Crappy, that was what Ella would've called it. Then again, it was probably what Vivian could have afforded on her own, so it fit the profile. Except, that was not how he wanted to spend a romantic weekend with Ella. Once the mission was done, he would get them a nice room in a luxury hotel.

"You were away at school, so I don't know how much of the story you've heard."

Julian sat on the bed. "Only that the Guardians rescued the girls and then torched the place. Also, something about taking them to a retreat in Hawaii."

"After the rescue, Amanda thralled them to forget that they had been held captive by the Doomers. She made them believe that they had spent the missing time training for a new job. Kian hired all of them to work in the clan's new hotel in Hawaii, and many of them stayed on."

"Cool. I'm glad that they were taken care of. But what does their story have to do with this?"

"I was getting there. We got them tickets to a hospitality convention in Washington D.C. and booked their stay right here in this hotel."

"Smart. Was it your idea or Kian's?"

"Actually, it was your mother's."

26

ELLA

"I have to go," Sylvia said after the rough edit on the first video was done. "I still have homework to do."

It seemed that Sylvia didn't like to work hard, or maybe she had a soft heart and the stories had disturbed her, but she was embarrassed to admit that. The result was the same, though. Ella was left to do the rest on her own.

"Thanks for your help. It would have taken me forever to figure out the editing software if you weren't here to show me how to use it."

Sylvia smiled. "I'm glad I was able to help at least a little. I'll come back tomorrow if I can."

That didn't sound promising. "Thanks. I really appreciate you doing this for me."

"No problem. Good night."

After she left, Ella sighed and went back to work. The truth was that without Sylvia it would have taken her the entire evening just to learn how to do the most basic things, and she would've gotten none of the editing done. Now, she might be able to finish the first two videos tonight.

When her phone rang long hours later, Ella snatched it off the charger and plopped on the bed. "Hi, Julian."

"You sound tired."

"I'm exhausted. I've been working on the recordings since morning and I only have one and a half done."

"Is Sylvia still there?"

Ella snorted. "She went home hours ago, saying she had homework to do. I think she either got bored or upset over the story we were working on."

There was a slight pause before he asked, "How are you holding up? It must be difficult for you."

Ella closed her eyes and sighed. "Maybe the first round was. But after that it became technical. I don't really listen anymore. I guess I'm like a surgeon, performing the operation on the organ without thinking about the patient. It's easier that way."

"Whatever works, sweetheart. I wish I could be there with you and help you out."

The truth was that Ella preferred not having Julian work on the editing with her. Spending time together could have been fun, but the subject matter was too difficult for him to stomach. It would have killed him to have to listen to those stories and be unable to do anything about it.

Ella hadn't realized that until she'd started the editing process, but the most potent emotion she'd experienced hadn't been pity for the girl. It was an intense hatred for the scum who'd hurt her and a powerful need to avenge her.

It would've been so much more difficult for a guy like Julian who had the soul of a Guardian.

"How are things in our nation's capital?" She changed the subject.

"All I've seen is the hotel and the Georgetown campus. We've spent most of the day scoping the place and getting acquainted with the grounds, which are sprawling. It's a beautiful place, though. Maybe we can tour it together after this is over."

Smiling, Ella lowered her voice. "Did you get a solo room?"

"I did, but it's not the kind of place I want to spend time with you."

"Why, is it dingy?"

"Kind of. It's old and moldy."

"My mom and I are going to stay there too, right?"

"Yeah. But that's different. This hotel is part of the setup. It's close enough to the campus without being too pricey, so it fits the profile of students coming in for a tour. In fact, Turner arranged for us to pose as potential football recruits. We even had a fake meeting with the coach who is a friend of Turner's from his military days."

Ella could only imagine what the guy had thought when he'd seen Turner. "How did he explain his youthful looks?"

Julian chuckled. "With his usual lack of expression, Turner told the guy that he'd gone for a hair transplant and a laser resurfacing on his skin because he'd married a much younger woman and didn't want to look like her father. He even showed him my mother's picture."

"Bridget is beautiful."

"The coach thought so too. It's good that Turner is not the jealous type because there were a few hubba hubba's and whistles thrown in."

"You like Turner, don't you?"

"He's okay. And he is a perfect match for my mother. Not to mention a real asset for the clan. Even before Turner's transition, Kian relied on him to organize complicated missions. But back to us. I think I like your idea of staying over the weekend. Not here, of course. Somewhere nicer. If you're still game, I should make reservations before there are no decent rooms left."

That was different from just staying a little longer in the

same place. A romantic weekend in a nice hotel was a much bigger deal. She would be obsessing about it and imagining what was going to happen, which could be a problem when Logan entered her dreams. Until he was captured, she needed to keep coasting on neutral with Julian.

"I don't want to jinx it. Let's wait until this is over."

"It was your idea."

He was right. It had been momentary bravado. Or perhaps it had been just a good moment. She had those occasionally, feeling like her old upbeat self, but they didn't last long. That was the downside of the project she'd undertaken. It was a daily reminder of what she'd been through.

"I know, but making reservations in a different hotel takes it to another level. Besides, my head is full of organizing the fundraiser. I can't concentrate on anything else." Hopefully, that was enough said for Julian to understand. "I have one video ready, and I need to figure out how to put it on YouTube, and then how to upload it to the fundraising site. It's all new to me, and I'm freaking out a little. I think I bit off more than I can chew."

She was talking a mile a minute to hide her discomfort, but that didn't mean that she was making it up. Up until now, she'd talked a big game without having the knowledge to back it up. Not that she couldn't figure it out, eventually she would, but it was stressful.

"I was lucky that Sylvia was familiar with the editing software and showed me how to use it. If not for her, I would still be struggling with it. But I don't have anyone to help me with the other things. Do you know anyone who puts up videos on YouTube? Because I've never done it before."

"You could ask Roni or William. Not that they post anything there, but I'm sure it will be easier for them to figure it out than it will be for you."

"That's an awesome idea, but how do I get to them? Do I just ask someone where the lab is and go there?"

"First of all, yes, you can do that. But you can also call Roni. By the way, you should ask him what to do to get more views. I don't know much about it, but there are keywords and phrases you can include that will make it come up in more searches and suggestions."

"Good idea. I'll do that. I didn't even think about search engine optimization because I don't know anything about it. Do you think Roni or William do? They are not into marketing or promoting stuff."

"Don't worry about it. Those two can figure anything out."

"Yeah, but do they have time? I'm sure they have better things to do."

Julian chuckled. "You're tired, Ella. Go to sleep and tomorrow everything will look less daunting."

"Yeah, you're right. I should."

27

ELLA

*B*efore getting in bed, Ella browsed the internet, looking up information about Georgetown. If Logan entered her dream tonight, and she had a strong feeling he would, her head would be filled with tidbits about the university, the grounds, the dorms, the cafeterias, and all the other things a prospective student would be interested in.

It was what Logan would expect from someone who was excited about actually going to a prestigious place like that.

As Ella drifted off, images of the various academic halls were playing like a slide show in her head, and when the dream began, she was strolling along a path on Healy Lawn, with Logan at her side.

"Do you like it here?" he asked.

"It's beautiful. I can't wait to actually see it with my own eyes instead of on a computer screen."

"You are seeing it."

She turned to him and smiled. "Are you creating the scenery, or am I?"

"It's coming from my memory. I've been to the campus recently, and I walked down this path."

"Oh, yeah? What were you doing there?"

He wrapped his arm around her waist. "Talking with my friend about a certain young lady I wanted him to admit to the undergrad program."

He was tipping his hand, revealing that he was in Washington. The question was whether it had been a slip, or had he done it on purpose, hoping she would suggest a meeting?

"I can't thank you enough for arranging this for me. I've never dreamed of getting into such a prestigious university. President Clinton went there, Justice Scalia, the CIA Director, several congressmen and Wall Street moguls. I will probably feel like the country mouse visiting the city. Royalty from around the world send their kids to Georgetown for heaven's sake."

He laughed. "Don't worry about it. Ordinary people go there too. Not that you're ordinary, far from it. You're more extraordinary than all those snobs whose parents are famous politicians, which makes them American royalty, or those who are royal by birth. And if you are concerned about not having money to flaunt, I'll take care of this for you as well."

Crap. She needed to think fast because that could be a test. If any of this were real, she would not accept money from him, but if she said so, she might blow the whole thing up.

What to do?

"I can't take money from you, Logan. A favor is all I can accept."

"It's not going to be my money. My friend will arrange a full scholarship for you, and whatever you planned on spending on tuition and living expenses, you'll be able to spend on things to impress your new snobby friends with."

Was this another trick? Was Logan a compulsive liar?

Because if he was planning to snatch her and her mother, there was no reason for him to arrange a scholarship for her. Why make it up? She was coming for the interview anyway.

"That's awesome, but I feel guilty about accepting this.

I'm sure there are more deserving students than me for a full-ride scholarship."

He hugged her closer to him. "You are more deserving than most. You're smart, resourceful, and you are willing to work hard. Besides, you need it. I'm sure that with no father to support the family, finances are tight. Last I checked, dental hygienists don't make much."

Why didn't it surprise her that he'd investigated her?

Did he think that she was desperate for money and he could use it to his advantage?

But then if she never got to actually study at Georgetown, she would have no need for it.

She sighed. "Thank you. I really need a scholarship because I can't afford a place like that. I can take out student loans and work part-time while I'm studying, but I'm afraid that as a nurse I will not make enough to repay the loans in a reasonable time. The financial burden would be suffocating."

Logan seemed so pleased with himself, so genuinely happy to be able to help her, that Ella was starting to seriously doubt his motives.

Perhaps Julian and Kian and the others were wrong about Logan, and he wasn't rotten to the core. What if he was helping her just to gain her approval and get her to date him?

Have sex with him?

Seemed like a lot of trouble to seduce a girl, when it was obvious that Logan could have anyone he wanted. Not only was he incredibly handsome and rich, but he could also compel or thrall compliance.

Still, it might be an ego thing. Even a Doomer might want to seduce a girl the old fashioned way, by courting her and making himself indispensable to her, and her falling for him because she thought he was wonderful.

Especially someone like Logan who wasn't an ordinary Doomer. He was the son of their leader, which made him Doomer royalty.

Curiosity burning hot in her gut, she had to find out even though asking point-blank was risky. "Are you going to be in Washington when I'm there?"

A sly smirk lifting one corner of his lips, he looked into her eyes. "I might. Do you want to see me?"

She shrugged. "You still scare me a little, but after all that you have done for me, I should at least invite you to dinner. My mother would have to come along, of course, but given your traditional upbringing, you shouldn't be a stranger to the concept of a chaperone."

Pausing their stroll, Logan turned to her and put his hand on her shoulder. "You must realize that if I want to abscond with you, your mother is not going to be an obstacle for me."

"Do you still want to kidnap me? Or would you rather I came willingly?"

She was playing with fire, but the game demanded that she act as if it was real. Anything else would seem suspicious to Logan. He was smart, and he didn't trust anyone. A man not easily fooled.

"Would you come willingly to me?"

Stretching on her toes, she kissed his lips lightly. "That depends on you. I expect to be treated like a lady and courted properly. If you ask me on a date and don't try anything shady, then I'll gladly agree to another one, and then the next, and the one after that."

The sly smirk was back. "I was under the impression that you are a modern, liberated woman, and that you feel free to hook up with whomever you choose."

"I am all that, but I also have standards. A guy has to work hard to get me to open up to him, and he has to prove that he's worthy of me." She grimaced. "I thought like that before the degrading experience I went through, and even more so after."

His expression somber, he hooked his finger under her chin and tilted her head up. "I'll treat you like you are my princess and I'm your knight." He kissed her softly, his arms wrapping around her tenderly.

A lover's kiss.

The guy was either the best actor on the planet, or she'd misjudged him completely.

VIVIAN

"*R*eady to go home?" Vivian glanced around the makeshift studio Ella had organized in the classroom.

She was impressed. Ella was making this happen without much help and with no prior training. Maybe it was the advantage of youth because Vivian couldn't imagine undertaking such a huge project. Heck, organizing the sewing class had seemed like a big deal to her.

Ella still believed that she could conquer the world, and Vivian had a feeling she could. Her daughter was incredible.

"Yeah. I'm done. Let me just stow the camera away." She put it back into its case. "The lights can stay where they are. It took me over an hour to get them positioned just right, and Vanessa said that I can leave everything like it is for the next shoot."

"How did it go?"

"I only did one today. With the hours it takes to edit them, I'm in no rush to tape more. Besides, I didn't have an assistant. Sylvia couldn't come."

"Did you talk with Tessa?"

Ella slung the camera bag over her shoulder. "I did. She

said she'll be good to go by Monday, but I told her we were leaving for Washington, and she'd have a longer break. I don't think she should come back though. No reason to make herself miserable."

They walked out of the classroom and headed out to the parking lot.

"You'll need someone to drive you. I'm not here every day."

"I don't plan on being here every day either. And besides, after we are back from Washington, I'm asking Kian for a car. I'll take it as payment for entrapment services rendered."

"Every clan member gets a car. It's not a payment since it doesn't really belong to them. The cars are owned by the clan."

Ella put the bag in the trunk. "I know. But it's cool to think that I'm getting paid." She grimaced. "Although perhaps it is better that I'm not. I dream-shared with Mr. D again, and he was so super nice that I'm really starting to doubt that he has nefarious intentions. He said he's going to arrange a full-ride scholarship for me. Why would he do that if he knew I would never use it? And there wasn't even a reason for him to lie about it. It's not as if I'll cancel my trip to Washington because I'll suddenly realize that I can't afford Georgetown."

Vivian added her own bags to the pile and then walked over to the driver's side. "Maybe he wants to make sure that you arrive as planned. Just as we are preparing and laying a careful net for him, I'm sure he's doing the same for us. The scholarship was just extra honey to make the bait more appetizing."

"I hope you're right. I would hate to get everyone's hopes up for nothing. Not to mention the resources. If this is all for nothing, I'll have to compensate the clan for their expenses and not the other way around."

Vivian waved a dismissive hand. "It's just nervous jitters.

Besides, the trap is Kian and Turner's idea, not yours, so they bear responsibility for it. What you're doing for the clan is priceless. Meaning that I would have never agreed for you to risk yourself for monetary compensation."

As she turned the engine on, Ella pulled out the new glasses Eva had given them and put them on. "I don't know if there is a saying like this, but you can't live on good deeds, lofty ideals, or even satisfaction. I need money."

That was true. Ella was working her butt off and not getting a penny for her efforts. "Did you upload the video you finished editing to YouTube?'

"Not yet. I talked to Julian last night, and he suggested I ask Roni for help with that. I'm just thinking of a nice way to do it. I can't offer him anything in return, and I hate asking for a favor I can't repay."

"You're not asking anything for yourself. The entire clan is involved in this humanitarian effort. I'm sure he will be glad to help. But if you like, we can invite him and Sylvia to dinner. It's going to be easier to ask for a favor in an informal setting."

Pulling out her phone, Ella glanced at the time. "We can stop at the supermarket and get stuff. But let me check with Sylvia first. They might have plans for tonight. What time should I tell her?"

"Let's make it seven so we'll have plenty of time to cook."

Ella's fingers flew over the screen as she typed up the message.

When Sylvia didn't respond, Ella shrugged. "Do you want to stop on the way for takeout? Parker wouldn't mind a hamburger, and neither would I."

"Sounds good to me. But let's get groceries just in case."

The return message came while they were waiting in line in the drive-through.

"She says they would love to and apologizes for not

answering before. She was in class and her phone was turned off."

Vivian was glad. Friday dinner without Magnus and Julian would have been a sad affair. In fact, maybe they should invite more guests to make it even merrier?

"What do you think, should we invite Ruth and Nick too?"

Ella scrunched her nose. "Ruth is a really good cook. We are not in her league."

"We don't have to be. Let's make something simple that is impossible to mess up. How about fettuccini with mushrooms and a couple of your specialty salads?"

"Parker will want meat, and so will Roni. I don't know about Nick, but he probably is a meat eater too."

"What about fish? I can make salmon. That always comes out good."

"That could work. I like it, and so does Parker, probably because it's soft and doesn't irritate his gums. I hope the others will like it too."

"Salmon it is, then." Vivian smiled at Ella. "Having dinner with friends is more about the company than the food. It doesn't have to come out perfect."

"No, but it should be tasty and plentiful. Otherwise they won't come again."

ELLA

"*I*'m stuffed." Roni pushed his plate away and reached for the pitcher of water. "Everything was excellent."

Ella wondered if this was a good time to ask for his help.

"Thank you for inviting us," Sylvia said. "I feel so bad about not helping Ella today, but I had an important class I couldn't miss."

Smiling, Ella waved a dismissive hand. Sylvia had just provided her with the opening she needed. "Don't worry about it. I shot only one video, but there is no rush. I have four already, two of them edited and ready for upload to YouTube, but I don't know how to do that. I'm sure it's not a big deal, but with everything new there is a learning curve. And once that's done, I need to actually set up the fundraiser, again not something I've done before."

Nick put his fork down. "I can help you out with YouTube. It's so easy that I can do it right now. Just bring me your laptop."

That was unexpected. Ella hadn't thought of Nick, but she should have. Eva had told her that the guy was a whiz with electronics and surveillance equipment.

"Thank you. But would you mind showing me how to do it? I'd rather not have to run for help anytime I need to upload a new video."

"Sure thing."

As Ella pushed to her feet, her mother cleared her throat. "Can this wait until everyone is done eating? And we also have dessert."

Glancing at Ruth who was still picking at her salmon, Ella sat back down. "I'm sorry. You're right. It's just that I'm so excited and eager for the fundraiser to start."

Across the table, Parker looked at her as if she'd offended him.

"What's your problem?"

"You could've asked me. I know how to do it. But no one ever thinks I can do stuff because I'm just a kid."

He wasn't wrong. She should've thought about him, but to admit it would be like throwing more fuel into his fire.

"Do you know anything about search engine optimization?"

He shook his head.

"Well, that's what I need the most help with. It's not enough to upload the videos. If I want anyone to see them, they need to be discoverable."

"I can help with that," Roni said. "I can have these videos suggested to tons of people. What I need from you is a list of things your target audience is interested in, so I can have your videos suggested to them."

"Who is the target audience?" Ruth asked.

Ella thought that everyone should watch it, but perhaps certain segments of the population would react more strongly to the message. "Teenage girls and their mothers, I guess. Which I should have thought of before. Damn."

"Why? Is that a problem?" Vivian asked.

"If I want them shown to teenagers, I need to make sure that the videos don't contain anything inappropriate for a younger audience, but that's almost impossible given the subject. And what's more, girls under eighteen should be aware of the risk. Traffickers don't shy away from taking minors."

"Not in the States, I would think," Sylvia said. "If a minor goes missing, the police get involved. It's easier and less risky for the traffickers to go after legal adults."

Roni put his glass down. "You can make two kinds of videos. One aimed at the over-eighteen crowd that will show the videos you are shooting at the sanctuary, and another one for minors that's more of a general warning and has no details. I would even make two separate channels so there is no confusion between the two."

It was a good idea, but it meant doubling the work. In fact, Ella wasn't sure she could edit the recordings so much. She would need to shoot new ones with teenagers in mind.

"Yay, more work for me."

"You can hire someone to doodle cartoons for you," Parker said. "Like they do in infomercials. You'll need to write a script, though."

That shouldn't be too hard. She could write highly modified versions of the stories the girls told. Except, it was more work and she was already overwhelmed.

"I need to find someone to do that. I don't have time to write scripts in addition to everything else I'm doing. And where am I going to find a doodler?"

"Many clan members are creative," Sylvia said. "You can post a note on the virtual bulletin board."

"I don't have money to pay them."

Next to her, Ella saw Vivian's shoulders start to shake. "What's the matter, Mom? Are you crying?"

Vivian let out a snort and then started laughing. Strange woman. Was missing Magnus making her crazy?

"What's so funny?" Parker asked.

Waving a hand, Vivian caught her breath. "It's funny what

the brain can come up with. When Parker suggested making doodle presentations, I thought that it was a cool idea and that there could be a whole series of simple cartoons showing different dangerous scenarios a girl can find herself in. But then I thought that someone would need to write scripts for the narrator to read."

She reached for her glass, took a long sip, and then put it down. "Naturally, the first person that came to my mind was Eva because she wrote a book and has some experience with creating stories. But since she somehow managed to turn her romance novel into a detective story full of gore and blood, she would probably do the same with the cartoons, writing terrifying stories that were way worse than the ones the girls recorded."

Nick joined in the laughter. "I can imagine that. My boss trying to write a romance is a joke. But she can write killer detective and spy novels." He laughed even harder. "Killer stories about killers."

If he only knew the half of it.

Nick and Sharon didn't know about Eva's vigilante days, and she'd told Tessa only recently. Surprisingly, she'd told Ella too.

But that was because of Ella's weird effect on people. Come to think of it, if she really had a unique ability to have people open up to her and tell her things they didn't tell anyone else, it might be a special talent she had in addition to the telepathy she shared with her mother.

And if it was indeed a talent, and not a case of having the kind of personality that invited confessions, it would grow stronger after her transition just as Parker's compulsion ability had.

In a way, what she did was sort of unintended compulsion. It was as if people felt compelled to tell her their secrets. The difference was that she didn't do anything to force the confessions, and later people didn't regret opening up to her.

Or perhaps they did?

Ella wondered if Eva had had second thoughts about sharing her dark past with her and Tessa.

The answer could shed light on whether Ella had done anything to actively compel the confession. Maybe she'd just been at the right place at the right time and armed with the right attitude.

JULIAN

*A*s he came out of the bathroom, Julian checked his phone for a new message from Ella. It was getting late and he was tired after a full day of preparations.

She'd said she would call or text as soon as she was done with Nick and Roni, but it seemed the three of them were still working on uploading the YouTube videos.

It shouldn't take that long, unless Roni started working on the search engine optimization. Why would he do it on a Friday night while his mate was waiting, though?

The guy didn't need Ella to do his hacking magic or whatever it was he planned to do. He could do it from his house or on Monday from the lab.

Except, Ella might have wanted to see how it was done.

Julian smiled. The girl was like a sponge for information, her brain going a hundred miles per hour all hours of the day. And she wasn't just absorbing it, she was turning it into a fountain of creative ideas.

His mate was awesome.

He couldn't have asked for a more perfect match. The more he got to know her, the more the age difference that had bothered him in the beginning was becoming irrelevant.

Ella was bright and confident in her own way, and she didn't treat him like the older guy she should defer to.

Heck, she didn't give him an inch, and he loved that she wasn't a pushover. A lot of it was bravado, and on the inside she hid insecurities, but those were the result of her captivity, and in time they would fade away.

He would make sure of that.

His mate shouldn't feel tainted, or undeserving, and he was going to reassure her day in and day out that she was pure and kind and selfless, and that she deserved every bit of happiness that life with him would bring.

When his phone finally pinged, Julian let out a relieved breath, read Ella's short message, and called her.

"It's about time, I was about to hit the sack. It's after three o'clock in the morning here."

"I'm sorry about that. But it didn't feel right to leave Roni and Nick to do the work while I went chatting with my boyfriend."

"What took so long? Is it complicated?"

"No, not really, but they also helped me with establishing the fundraiser. We are up and running. Or rather crawling, but we are up."

"Congratulations."

"I'm crossing my fingers. Do you have a clan member who's a witch? Because I could totally use some good luck charms or incantations."

He chuckled. "The closest we have is Merlin. But he's all about potions. I don't think he does charms."

"A potion is not going to do it, but enough about me. How was your day?"

"Grueling. Turner is having us check out every corner of the campus and memorize it. After today, I can find any place here blindfolded. Tomorrow, he's going to assign positions. He must really be concerned with Mr. D. I think he takes him more seriously than he took Gorchenco."

"He should, and he shouldn't."

"What do you mean?"

"As you've pointed out, Mr. D is a god's grandson. He is smart and has powerful abilities. So that's a good reason to take every precaution Turner can think of. But on the other hand, he might have no nefarious intentions other than to win me over."

Julian shook his head. "He's playing you. Did he invade your dreams again?"

"He did. He said he's arranging a full-ride scholarship for me. Why would he do that if he knows I'm not going to go? But that's just a side note. He's acting as if he's really happy to help me get a great education. He is either an amazing actor, or I am clueless because I'm inclined to believe him."

"The guy is old. He's had centuries to hone his acting skills. Doomers are not into charity and doing good deeds, they regard humans as only a little better than sheep, and getting an education is not high on their priority list even for themselves."

Ella sighed. "You can't generalize. Look at Dalhu and Robert. Not all Doomers are evil."

Julian was getting annoyed. It was good that this was coming to a head because Lokan was messing with Ella and little by little pulling her over to his side.

"Your own impression from him was that the guy was bad."

"True, but then when you're the son of a despot, you can't act like a nice guy even if you are one on the inside. Every dream we share, he sheds more of his thorns."

Pushing up to his feet, Julian started pacing the small room. "Don't tell me you're falling for his lies, Ella."

What he actually wanted to ask was if she was falling for the Doomer. But that would have been stupid. Ella would've denied it, probably because she hadn't even realized that it was happening. Lokan was messing with her head big time.

141

"I'm not sure. But all this guessing is futile. We will know in a few days. I can't wait to see the campus and go touring the city with you. How is the weather? Is it cold?"

"It's very pleasant here. After all of this is over you might consider going here for real. You don't need any charity from the Doomer. The clan will pay for your tuition and your living expenses."

There was a moment of silence, and then she sighed. "It sounds lovely, but I don't want to leave the village. I decided to go to a local college."

It should've been good news, and he should've been happy about her decision, but Julian didn't want Ella giving up on her dreams or even compromising them on his account.

"Is it because of me?"

"Yes, but not exclusively, so don't let it go to your head. I just found a new home and an extended family. Leaving it to go to college and hang around a bunch of humans I have nothing in common with doesn't appeal to me at all. I'd rather stay in the village and commute to a local college every day. That way I can have it all."

"It's a compromise."

"Why would you say that? It's not like there is a shortage of great universities in Los Angeles, and with my fake transcripts and list of achievements I can get into any of them. I don't see it as a compromise at all. On the contrary, I think I'm being very smart about it. Besides, I don't like being away from you. It's been only two days and it feels like you've been gone for weeks."

The vice that had squeezed his heart when Ella had waxed poetic about Lokan not only loosened but fell off completely.

Ella loved him.

"Same here. It's tough being away from you."

"You see? And you want me to go away to college?"

"I would've gone with you."

That stunned her for about three seconds. "Really? And what would you have done? Studied for another degree?"

"Maybe. Or I would have found a job wherever you went to school. There's no way I can live without you. I love you."

"Oh, Julian. I can't live without you either. I love you so much. You're the best guy on the planet."

ELLA

*E*lla was about done packing her suitcase when her phone rang. Expecting Julian, she snatched it off the nightstand, but it wasn't Julian's handsome face on the screen.

"Hi, Tessa."

"Are you very busy? I wanted to stop at your house and give you a good luck charm."

"Oh, thanks. I was telling Julian how I needed one to make the fundraiser successful."

"How is it going so far?"

"The first day it was nothing but crickets, the second we got a trickle of donations, mostly from clan members, and today it's too early to tell."

"It's going to pick up. Those things take time."

"That's what Roni is telling me. I'm crossing my fingers."

"The good luck charm is for the trip, not for the fundraiser. But I'll get you another one for that."

"Thanks. That's so thoughtful of you. I'm almost done packing, but my mother and I need to be at Kian's office in about an hour. So, hurry up."

"I'm walking toward the door as we speak."

"I'll turn on the coffeemaker."

In the kitchen, Ella found her mother scrubbing the counter. Again.

"You're going to rub it down to nothing and we will have to order a new counter."

Vivian gave her an evil look when she pulled the coffeemaker out. "Don't make a mess. I want to leave the house clean."

As if it was going to stay that way. Parker and Scarlet were supposed to stay with Merlin, but Ella doubted he would be spending the entire time there, and for sure he wouldn't want to sleep there. Her brother was going to want some quiet time to himself, and he was going to make a mess in the kitchen.

"I promise to clean up. Tessa is coming over. What do you want me to serve her? Water?"

Vivian waved a hand at the fridge. "We have soft drinks."

"We should leave them for Parker. Merlin is a fun guy, but he forgets to go grocery shopping. I'm glad we cooked enough to feed both of them while we are gone."

Provided everything went according to plan, Vivian would come back home Wednesday night. Ella planned on spending the weekend with Julian, but nothing had been decided yet.

"Wonder invited Parker to come to stay with her and Anandur."

"I didn't know that. Should we take the food to her place?"

That could be a good solution. Their house was not a disaster zone like Merlin's. On the other hand, she wasn't sure they would be okay with hosting Scarlet.

Vivian shook her head. "Parker prefers staying at home by himself and hanging out with Merlin when he gets lonely."

"What's the matter? Is he over his crush on Wonder?"

Her mother snorted. "He's not, but that's exactly why he doesn't want to spend so much time in her house. It's stressful for him."

That was true. Ella had forgotten how nerve-wracking crushes could be. She'd had one when she was Parker's age, and it was on the UPS guy of all people. She remembered how excited she would get whenever they were expecting a delivery, but she also remembered how sweaty her palms would get whenever he smiled at her, cute twin dimples forming in his cheeks.

With perfect timing, Tessa rang the bell at the same time the coffeemaker finished brewing.

Opening the door, Ella glanced at the small package Tessa was holding. "What's in there? Can I open it now?"

"Sure." Tessa handed her the package.

"Come on in. Coffee is ready."

"It smells clean in here," Tessa said as she followed Ella to the kitchen. "Hi, Vivian. I wanted to come and wish you luck before you left for Washington."

Her mother smiled. "Thank you. That's very thoughtful."

Ella poured the coffee into three mugs and put them on the counter. "Didn't you notice that the marble top is missing a quarter of an inch?"

Tessa examined the counter and then looked up with a puzzled expression on her face. "Did you do something to it?"

"My mother went into a cleaning frenzy over the weekend, which is what she always does when she's stressed. This counter got scrubbed at least five times."

"Don't mess it up." Vivian wagged her finger at them. "Besides, I did more than clean. We went grocery shopping, and then we cooked so Parker would have food while we were gone, and then we cleaned."

"I stand corrected." Ella leaned toward her mother and

kissed her cheek. "I'm just teasing. You are right about cleaning being calming."

"For me it's arts and crafts," Tessa said. "Making this thing gave me hours of calm." She motioned to the package. "Open it."

Ella tore through the wrapping paper and pulled out a dream catcher. "It's so pretty. Do you think it will protect me from the dream walker?"

Tessa shrugged. "It's worth a try."

"It's gorgeous. Thank you. Although right now I'm more concerned about him not showing up in my dreams. Do you think the dream catcher can help me lure him back? He didn't come Saturday or Sunday night, and I'm starting to worry."

Tessa arched a brow. "Why, do you think that something happened to him?"

"No, I'm worried that he is busy doing whatever he does for Navuh and that he won't come to Washington. I don't know what I'm scared of more. Mr. D trying to snatch me or not showing up at all."

As the doorbell rang again, Ella and Vivian exchanged glances.

"Did you invite anyone else?" Vivian asked.

"I didn't. Let me see who it is."

Maybe it was Merlin with a good luck potion, or perhaps just a relaxing tonic. Both she and Vivian needed it.

"Ray, what a pleasant surprise." Ella forced a smile.

If he thought to start something while Julian was away, she would promptly show him how wrong he was.

"I came to wish you luck, and I brought you invitations to a concert I'm giving next week." He handed her an envelope. "I included tickets for your brother and Magnus as well. I hope you all can come."

That was innocent enough.

"Thank you. I would love to come, and I'm sure my

mother and Magnus would love to as well. But Parker, not so much." She opened the door wider. "Please, come in. Would you like some coffee?"

"Thank you. I would love some."

Half an hour later, Vivian started getting antsy. "We need to go. I don't want to be late for the debriefing."

Ray got the hint and rose to his feet. "Thank you for the coffee, and again, good luck. I'll keep my fingers crossed when I'm not playing."

Tessa hugged Vivian briefly and then crushed Ella to her chest. "Be careful."

"I will."

KIAN

ands tucked into his back pockets, Kian stood next to his office window and gazed at the village square below. It wasn't as if he had nothing to do, but with the nervous energy coursing through him since morning, he had been too distracted to concentrate on work, and the foot-tall stack of files on his desk remained untouched.

In less than fifteen minutes, Vivian and Ella were scheduled to arrive for the debriefing, which gave him just enough time to grab a quick smoke. He wasn't supposed to do that during his workdays. The deal Kian had made with himself was that he was only going to indulge while relaxing outside in his garden, but here and there he snuck one in.

Especially when he felt tense and frustrated like he was now.

Grabbing a pack of cigarillos and a lighter from his desk drawer, he headed out into the corridor and opened the door to the emergency escape stairs leading to the roof.

His not so secret hideout.

Bridget, whose office was a couple doors down from his, knew he was sneaking out there, but she was cool about it, keeping it to herself and refraining from making comments.

When Kian needed a few moments alone, the last thing he wanted was for people to know they could find him on the roof.

He lit up as soon as the roof door closed behind him.

Staying in the office while Turner led a mission that Kian would have loved to be a part of was frustrating as hell.

Since when had he become a glorified pencil pusher?

He used to lead missions like that.

Catching Lokan was going to be the biggest coup the clan had ever scored against the Doomers, and he was going to miss out on that because Turner had declared him a security liability.

Fucking Turner.

Kian was still the American clan's leader, and until bloody Turner had shown up and taken over operations, Kian had been in charge of defending the clan and heading missions.

So what if Turner was better at it? It didn't make Kian a fucking liability or obsolete.

Taking a long puff, he blew out the smoke and looked up at the sky. He was damn good at it too. The rescue he'd headed in what was now the sanctuary had been a complicated operation, and he'd pulled it off without losing a single Guardian. And that had been despite several glitches.

The operation before that, however, was a different story.

Amanda's so-called rescue had been a joke. Not his fault, though. How could he have known that his sister had not only fallen for the Doomer but had him wrapped around her little finger?

Fates, what an embarrassment that had been.

Perception had a way of warping reality into what was expected. Mistakenly interpreting Amanda's scream as resulting from torture and not a climax, Kian had rushed headlong into danger. He would've never made such a mistake if it was any other female. But he'd found it inconceivable that Amanda could be having sex with a Doomer.

Back then he'd thought of them as worse than worms and couldn't forgive her.

A lot had changed since then, and Dalhu as well as Robert had managed to overcome Kian's centuries of deep-seated hatred that put every member of the Brotherhood in the same dirty basket.

Grudgingly, he had to concede that not all Doomers were pure evil, and as in any society, some were better than others.

Perhaps Turner was right, and Kian was too hotheaded and emotional to lead this particular mission. He'd been lucky with Dalhu because the guy had operated solo and had had no malevolent intentions toward Amanda.

It could easily have been a trap, one Kian had run head-long into without thinking.

True, capturing Navuh's son didn't carry the same emotional intensity as rushing to save his sister, who he'd thought was being tortured, but it was tantalizing enough to cause him to make a move just as stupid.

Turner, cold fish that he was, had no such problems. With him it was always mind first, heart second. Besides, the two organs differed disproportionately not only in influence but also in size. Turner's brain was huge, and his heart was tiny.

With Kian, it worked the other way around. Not that his brain was small, just that his heart was so much bigger.

Stubbing the cigarillo out, he threw it into the metal trash can and headed back to his office.

When he got there, he found William waiting for him by the door. "I'm not late, am I?" he asked as he opened the door.

The guy pushed his glasses up his nose. "No, I'm early."

He'd been wondering for years why William needed glasses and had learned the reason only recently. There was nothing wrong with William's vision, but his eyes were sensitive to the computer glare and the glasses had a special filter for that. Still, William never took them off. He might have just forgotten to do so when he left the lab, which

151

didn't happen often, or maybe he thought of them as an accessory.

"Did you bring the trackers?"

"I have them here." William followed him inside and pulled out a small box from one pocket and a second one from the other side. "The miniaturizing is amazing. Each of these boxes contains ten trackers."

He joined Kian at the conference table and opened one.

"There is a tracker in there?" Kian lifted an earring that was just a small stud. "Where is it?" He turned the thing around.

"This is it. You're not going to find anything. There is a tiny transmitter embedded in the gold." William lifted a hairpin. "I like this one the most. No one would suspect a plain thing like this to be anything out of the ordinary. Ella and Vivian can put several in their hair."

"Which reminds me that their passports were delivered earlier. Kian got up and walked over to his desk. "One for Mrs. Victoria MacBain and the other for Ms. Kelly Rubinstein." He took the envelope out of the drawer and brought it over to the conference table.

"They should start practicing the fake names right away," William said. "By the way, you didn't say anything about getting them earpieces."

"Unless you can get something as tiny and inconspicuous as these trackers, they can't use them. If Lokan is setting a trap for them, he would be watching them closely. But that's not a problem. Ella and Vivian will never be out of sight or earshot. Thirty Guardians should have no problem keeping a close eye and ear on our two ladies."

JULIAN

*J*ulian loaded a tortilla with steak strips and bell peppers. "This is really good." He rolled it up.

"Not bad," Liam said after biting into his taco. "I'm not crazy about Mexican, but as fast food goes there is nothing better. You can tell that the ingredients are fresh. They don't pull it out of the freezer and stick it in the microwave."

The Guardians had split up for dinner, checking out eateries surrounding the campus. There were many of them, which meant going solo, or in his case being paired with Liam. Which rankled, but Julian wasn't technically a Guardian.

Still, Turner could have entrusted him with such a simple assignment as keeping his eyes open for Lokan.

Hacking into every available surveillance camera on campus and the area around it, William and Roni were scanning for the Doomer, but not every place was equipped with them, and Turner believed in boots and eyes on the ground.

"When are the ladies arriving?" the Guardian asked.

"I'm waiting to hear from her. She said she's going to call me once they're up in the air."

When he'd called earlier, Ella said that Tessa and Ray were there, which had pissed him off big time. What had Ray been doing at Ella's house? Had the sly bastard waited for Julian to be gone before making his move?

If he had, the guy was either an obtuse idiot or a sucker for pain.

Ella hadn't shown any interest in him, and after his stupid comments, she'd barely acknowledged his presence. Once this was over and they got back, Julian was either going to get a new house or ask Ray to move. His bachelor days of living with roommates were over. He had a mate now, and she was the only one he was going to share a house with. Except, of course, for the children they would one day have, Fates willing.

Since Ella had told him about her decision to stay in the village and commute to college, he'd been thinking about it a lot, but he hadn't said anything to her yet. Not only was it premature, but it also might fill her head with stuff that shouldn't be there while she was dealing with Lokan.

As his phone rang, Julian quickly wiped his sticky hands with a napkin and accepted the call.

"Hi, sweetheart. Are you in the air?"

"Yes."

"I can't wait to see you."

"About that." She sighed. "My mother and I were instructed by Kian not to interact with any of you. We are to act as if we don't know any of the hotel guests."

Julian's heart sank. He'd been counting the minutes until he got to see Ella again, and now she was going to be within reach, but contact was disallowed.

"It's probably Turner's doing. The guy is paranoid."

"I think he is right. If Mr. D finds a way to follow us, it will look suspicious if we mingle with the other guests at the hotel. We are not supposed to know anyone."

Curiously, Lokan hadn't visited Ella for the past two nights. Had he been busy setting the trap?

If he had, the guy was incredibly sneaky because none of the Guardians had reported noticing anything suspicious. Not only that, none of the cameras around campus, and there were many, had caught him hanging around.

Perhaps he was using a disguise? Or maybe in addition to his other talents he could also do what Sylvia did and manipulate electronics?

Except, if Julian believed in the Occam's razor principle that the most straightforward and simple solution was most likely the correct one, then Ella's hunch was right, and Lokan wasn't coming.

Or, maybe he'd been busy and was going to arrive tomorrow, or on the day of the interview, and wing it. With his power of compulsion, Lokan didn't need much of a setup.

"Julian? Are you there?"

"Yeah. Sorry for zoning out on you. I've been thinking about what you've said regarding Mr. D not coming. There is no trace of him."

He glanced around the restaurant, checking that the clientele was still comprised of humans, and switched to a whisper just in case. "William and Roni have been running the camera feed from all around town through William's facial recognition software, and they got nothing so far. He didn't check into any of the hotels and hasn't been to any restaurants with cameras. He either isn't here, or he's staying in a private house and ordering meals delivered to him."

"That's possible. I have a feeling that he is stationed in Washington, so it makes sense he has a permanent place here. You should tell Roni to check older feeds and see if he shows up in any of the restaurants. Friday, he told me that he'd been to the campus recently. There must be footage of him."

"I'll tell Turner."

"You know, there could be another possibility. He could be using the same kind of glasses Eva gave my mother and me. If William is running the feed through his software, it's not going to pick him up."

"Why would he do that? Unless he suspects something, there is no reason for him to avoid detection."

"Not necessarily. He might be doing it as a precaution. He is still an immortal who needs to hide the fact that he doesn't age. Besides, he might have other enemies. He is a warlord, after all."

"True, but we don't have the personnel to check that much feed by eye, so that's a moot point. We just need to assume that he is here and keep our eyes open."

Ella sighed. "It's going to be torture to know that you are in the same building and not be able to go to you, but it is for the best. I need to keep my head in the game, so to speak."

"We can still talk on the phone."

"Thank God for that. I was afraid Turner would prohibit it as well. But I guess he trusts the clan's phones are secure against hacking."

"They are. We use our own satellite and the signal is encrypted."

She chuckled. "I don't even know what that means, but it sounds impressive. Listening to Nick and Roni when they were helping me with the charity setup, I felt like an uneducated schlump. I didn't know half the terms they used."

Smiling, Julian switched the phone to his other ear. "Don't tell me that you've decided to study computer engineering instead of nursing."

"No way. But I'm no longer sure that I want to study nursing either."

"Have you given some thought to what you want to study instead?

"I'm still thinking it over. Physician's assistant sounds cool, but I need to get an undergrad degree first, the same as nursing." She laughed. "We could open a hug clinic together. You'll be the physician, and I'll be the assistant."

"Sounds awesome, but we will hire professional huggers. I'm not letting you hug any guys older than twelve or younger than seventy."

"Deal."

34

ELLA

*A*s the jet started its descent, Ella pulled out her makeup case and went to work on her face. Next to her, Vivian put on the chestnut wig Eva had given her and pulled out her own case.

"Should we put in the trackers now?" Ella asked Bhathian.

The Guardian nodded. "From now on, always have at least a few on you. The Doomers could strike at any point."

Ella swallowed.

It was show time, and she was ready, but that didn't mean she wasn't scared. Getting captured by Logan and his henchmen was a remote possibility, but it was still there. As someone who'd just recently gotten free, that was a terrifying prospect, and she got nauseous every time she thought about it.

Which meant that she did everything to avoid those thoughts and switched to something else. Contemplating her future in college and what she wanted to study usually did the trick or thinking about the fundraiser and all the things she still had to do.

Like finding a doodler and a scriptwriter. Her post on the clan's bulletin board had yielded no results so far.

"They are so tiny," her mother said. "And surprisingly pretty."

The case containing the ten trackers was no bigger than a bracelet's jewelry box, and as she opened it, Ella once more marveled at the miniaturization. The question was whether Logan was aware that such tiny trackers existed. If he was, he would search for them, and as small as the devices were, they weren't invisible.

After putting on the earrings and the pendant, and sticking four pins into her hair, Ella was still left with three little studs she could attach to her clothes. But to do that, she needed to go to the bathroom.

With Arwel and Bhathian in the small cabin, it wasn't as if she could attach a stud to her panties.

When the jet touched down, Ella unbuckled and pushed to her feet.

"Is it okay to take the seatbelt off?" Vivian asked.

Arwel nodded.

"I'm going to attach the remaining studs to my clothes. I suggest that you do the same, Mom."

Vivian waved a dismissive hand. "I have the earrings on and two pins in my hair. I think that's enough for now. I'll put the rest on when we go to the interview."

"We might never get to the interview, Mom. As Bhathian pointed out, the enemy may strike at any time. Besides, it could very well be that there is no interview, and that Mr. D was lying the entire time."

On their private channel, she sent, *I'm going to put one in my panties. You should do the same.*

Isn't that going too far?

Maybe, but I'd rather be safe than sorry. One captivity in a lifetime is enough.

You're right. I'll wait until you're done.

Ella nodded and ducked into the bathroom. Unlike the dim light in the cabin, the one in the tiny compartment was bright, and as she looked into the mirror, Ella realized that she'd put on too much makeup.

Then again, it had been a while since she'd gone all out with it, so maybe that was just right.

The nearly black purple lipstick was a cool addition to her disguise. It was so strong that she'd been able to draw a new lip line with it, changing the shape of her mouth.

Between the makeup, the glasses, and the hair, she looked nothing like the old Ella. If she ever got to that interview, however, that grungy look was going to get her rejected for sure. It was a good thing that she had no intention of going to Georgetown.

With the rest of the studs attached to her clothes, Ella pushed the door open and stepped out. "Your turn, Mom."

"You went a little too heavy with the makeup."

"I know. I'll fix it when we get to the hotel. On the way, it's better to have more than less."

Vivian grimaced. "We will have to do something about your looks for the interview. This makeup and this hair don't go with the nice outfit we got for that."

"I'm not really going to Georgetown, Mom, so it doesn't matter if I make a good impression on the interviewer or not. Once this is over, Kelly Rubinstein will cease to exist."

"I don't see why. With the Doomer out of the picture, you don't need to abandon this identity, and if you get accepted, you should go. With the clan paying for your education, you can go for the best there is, and it doesn't get much better than Georgetown."

"I decided that I want to stay home and go to a local college. There is no shortage of them in Los Angeles. And with my fabulous grades and the clan's financing, I can pick the best." She winked.

Her mother smiled. "Is it because of Julian?"

"Yes, but not only. I found a home in the village, and the

extended family I always wanted to have. I don't want to leave that and go room with strangers in some dingy dorms."

35

JULIAN

irst-floor hotel rooms that faced the street were usually the least desirable, but Julian was very happy to have one. Standing by the window, he waited for the taxi to arrive. The driver was one of the Guardians whose name he'd forgotten. Another Guardian driven taxi had picked up Arwel and Bhathian, and it was trailing Ella and Vivian's in case they encountered trouble on the way.

When the cab finally stopped in the front, Julian let out a relieved breath. He'd had no reason to anticipate anything happening to them en route, but then he didn't know what to expect and when.

There was still no sign of Lokan or any other Doomers, and it worried him. Julian vacillated between thinking that Ella's hunch was right and that Lokan wasn't going to show up, to imagining crazy scenarios with a bunch of Doomers arriving at the time of the interview and taking the entire admissions office hostage.

It could happen.

Except, they had enough Guardians stationed around the building to deal with that. Lokan and his cronies wouldn't get anywhere near that office. Especially since he wouldn't suspect anyone lying in wait for him.

Julian smiled when Ella got out of the taxi. Despite the glasses she had on, he could see the heavy purple makeup around her eyes, and her lush lips were painted with lipstick so dark that it looked black. But she was adorable even in her full Goth costume.

He missed his little pixie girl with her spiky pink hair and monster boots.

Rubbing his aching heart, he tried to imagine how he was going to survive having her so near and not going to her. Perhaps he should ask one of the Guardians for a reinforced pair of handcuffs. He should cuff himself to the bed because he was bound to sleepwalk to her room.

As she and Vivian entered the hotel, he contemplated going out to the lobby so he could at least look at her and smell her.

A text from her surprised him.

Hi, we are here at the hotel, safe and sound. I thought we had the entire place to ourselves, but I see women in the lobby. Who are they?

Julian chuckled, regretting not having the ability to read Ella's mind. Who did she imagine the women were?

He texted her back. *I will tell you only after you try to guess.*

I heard them talking about a hospitality convention they were attending. Are they working for Turner's friend?

Not as exciting as he hoped. Usually, Ella's imagination was more inventive, and he expected her to suggest that they were secret agents, or call girls, or secret agents impersonating call girls.

He texted back. *I was expecting some wild speculations from you. But your guess was half right. They work in one of the clan's hotels in Hawaii. Turner thought it would look strange if there were only guys staying here with the two of you, so he arranged for them to attend the convention.*

Smart guy. He thinks of everything.

It would seem that way. Text me again when you're settled in your room. I have instructions for you and your mom for tomorrow.

She sent him the thumbs up emoji.

His phone rang a moment later with the tune he'd assigned to Turner.

"Ella and Vivian are here. Come to my room."

"On my way."

Since the door was slightly ajar, Julian knocked and walked right in.

"Close the door behind you," Turner said. "And put some music on."

Julian walked over to the nightstand and found a classical station on the radio. "Is that good?"

"A little louder." Turner walked over to the door connecting his room to the next and knocked.

When Vivian opened it and peeked in, Julian cast him a murderous glare.

The sly bastard had arranged connecting rooms for himself and the ladies, while feeding Julian crap about not having contact with them until after the mission.

"Give us a moment," she whispered. "We need to freshen up, and then we'll be right there."

Turner waved a hand. "Take your time." He looked at Julian. "I should have waited a little longer before knocking. I forgot that ladies need more bathroom breaks than guys do."

"You planned this all along while feeding me bullshit about not seeing Ella."

Turner shrugged. "You chose to have a separate room."

"Let's switch."

"You can move back with me if you wish. That's the best I can offer."

"Why?"

"Because this is not a honeymoon, and this room is the

headquarters. If you stay here, Magnus would want to stay here too, and you can imagine the rest."

As always, Turner was right, but he should've mentioned the adjacent rooms instead of pulling Julian's leg about not seeing Ella until Lokan was captured.

When mother and daughter entered a few moments later, Ella's face was clean of makeup, her natural beauty even more breathtaking than Julian had remembered.

Ignoring Turner and Vivian, he pulled her in for a quick embrace. "I missed you."

She clung to him. "I missed you too. This is such a surprise. I thought we wouldn't be allowed to see each other until this is done."

"Me too." He cast another angry glare at Turner. "Apparently, this was Turner's idea of a joke. Not a good one."

"Is Magnus coming?" Vivian asked.

"He is bringing takeout. I figured you'd be hungry after your trip."

Ella waved a dismissive hand. "Who can eat? My stomach is tied in knots."

"Same here," Vivian said.

"Take a seat, ladies." Turner motioned to one of the queen beds. "We have things to go over."

"Shouldn't we wait for Magnus?" Vivian asked.

"It doesn't concern him directly."

Ella took Julian's hand and pulled him to sit with her on the bed.

"Tomorrow you are going on a campus tour," Turner started. "Four Guardians are going to make the tour with you, pretending to be prospective students, but you shouldn't acknowledge them."

Julian squeezed Ella's hand. "I wanted to do the tour with you, but Turner didn't allow it."

"Why not?" Ella looked up at Turner.

"Because you two would not have been able to keep from

casting loving glances at each other, and you're supposed to pretend that everyone on the tour is a complete stranger. Also, don't forget to use your fake names. Kelly and Victoria. I suggest that from now on, you use them exclusively."

Ella nodded. "Not a problem for me, since I call my mother Mom most of the time."

"I'll have to practice," Vivian said.

"Did the dream walker visit you lately?" Turner asked.

"The last time was Friday night, and nothing since. Maybe I'm too nervous to dream-share?"

Turner tilted his head. "Was that your experience? Have you been nervous or anxious on the night he didn't come?"

Ella sighed. "I don't know. I'm just throwing ideas around. It bothers me that he didn't come so close to the interview. I expected him to visit me nightly to make sure that I'm coming."

Turner didn't look worried. "There could be many reasons for his absence, the main one that he can't sleep at the same time you do. If he's on the island and busy, he can't take naps in the middle of the day to visit you."

36

ELLA

*A*s Ella stood on the lawn with the rest of the students and their parents, waiting for the tour guide to arrive, she stole quick glances at their faces, trying to find the Guardians. She'd recognized Kri as soon as they'd gotten there, but not the others. Evidently, she hadn't met any of the three, which made it easy not to acknowledge them.

Stop looking, her mother sent.

It's normal to check out people in your group. I can even start talking to Kri, pretending that I want to make friends.

Turner said not to, so don't.

Fine.

As the tour guide arrived and introduced herself, Ella hardly paid any attention to the girl, scanning the vicinity for Logan instead.

"Please, follow me," the guide said, and the group started walking.

It was probably her overactive imagination, but Ella could feel Logan's eyes on her. He was watching her from some-where. Ella had read that people could feel it when they are being watched, even if it was through a camera lens. The roofs were too steep for him to hide there, but he could be at one of the windows, or he could be flying a drone.

Those usually made a buzzing noise, but if it was high up she wouldn't hear it.

Damn, she felt as if ants were crawling up her arms. If he got near her, he could thrall her, get into her mind, and see the plan. The entire operation was hinged on the Guardians catching him before he could do that.

Not to mention his ability to compel her and any other human. God only knew what he could do with that. On the one hand she was scared shitless, but on the other hand, she had a morbid curiosity to see him in action.

The waiting and guessing were the worst part.

You're doing it again, her mother sent.

I can't help it. I feel as if he is watching me. We shouldn't have come for the tour.

That would have been suspicious. All prospective students and their parents go on one. That's part of the experience.

How would you know? You've never gone to college.

I've read about it.

About an hour later, when the tour was over, Ella was exhausted, not from walking but from the constant state of vigilance and stress.

Her phone pinged with an incoming message from Turner. *Follow Kri. She and the other Guardians are going to a restaurant named Matchbox for lunch. Try to choose a table close to them.*

Ella sent the message to her mother.

Turner had decided against earpieces because they were hard to hide, so all communication was done through the phones. But at least she and her mother had the trackers all over them.

Oddly, those reassured her more than the presence of Guardians did. If anything happened and Logan managed to somehow snatch them, they could be rescued in no time.

"Hi." A girl walked up to Ella. "I'm Kristen." She offered her hand. "I heard you mention that you're interested in the nursing program. So am I."

"I'm Kelly." Ella shook the girl's hand. "And this is my mother, Victoria."

The girl gasped. "You are her mother? I thought you were another student. You look so young. People probably mistake you for sisters all the time."

"Thank you." Vivian offered Kristen her hand. "We are heading to a place called Matchbox for lunch. Would you like to join us?"

"I would love to. I was there yesterday, and the food is really good."

"Great, so you can lead the way. I was about to ask someone for directions."

"Follow me."

As Kristen chatted with Vivian, Ella resumed her scanning. The girl was a good cover, and she wondered whether Turner had sent her.

Or could she be a spy for Logan?

She glanced at the girl out of the corner of her eye. Kristen seemed genuine enough, but that didn't mean anything. Logan could compel any human to do his bidding.

"Where are you staying?" Kristen asked, raising Ella's suspicions.

"At the Hilton," her mother deadpanned.

Good for you, Mother.

Vivian smirked.

"Which one?" Kristen kept pushing.

"The one on 22nd Street. The Hilton Garden Inn."

Ella was impressed. *Where did you get that from?*

It was in the instructions Kian gave us. I actually read and memorized them.

That's why I didn't. I knew you would.

Vivian smiled indulgently. *Glad to be of service.*

Unaware of the conversation going over her head, Kristen kept talking, telling them about the hotel she was staying in and why her parents couldn't join her for the tour.

Ella sent to her mother. *Do you think she's working for Mr. D?*

Anything is possible.

VIVIAN

*A*s they got back into their hotel room, Vivian kicked her shoes off and plopped on the bed. "I need to start exercising. I'm so out of shape it's ridiculous."

They'd been walking all day, and after a while even her most comfortable shoes had started to chafe.

Thank God for the taxi and the Guardian who'd driven them back to the hotel. Or rather thank Turner for arranging it.

According to their driver, Guardians had been following the two of them around, hoping to flush the Doomer out, but he was still a no show.

Kristen and her questions had seemed suspicious at first, but they'd learned pretty soon that she was asking everyone where they were staying and what they thought about their accommodations because she was collecting information for her blog. It could've been a great cover story, but Vivian believed that it was true.

She and Ella were just jumpy and seeing shadows where there were none.

Lying on the other bed, Ella turned on her side and propped herself on her forearm. "You won't have to do anything special once you transition. I don't see Bridget or Amanda exercising."

"Amanda runs on the treadmill. I don't know about Bridget."

"You're avoiding the subject, and by that I mean your transition, not your exercise routine."

"I'm not. Once this is over, I'm going for it. I promised Magnus."

"Finally." Ella got up and pulled out a coke from the mini fridge.

"I miss Magnus." Vivian sighed. "Maybe I can ask Turner to invite him to his room so we could be together for at least a little while."

"Do it. I'm sure he wouldn't mind. And I want to see Julian too."

Vivian wasn't sure at all. "Should we open the connecting door to Turner's room?"

"I don't think they are there. I can't hear anything, and these walls are not soundproof."

Vivian got up and pulled out a water bottle from the fridge. "I sleep better knowing that Turner is next door. It's funny how I don't feel safe with all the Guardians surrounding us, but I do with him, even though he's not a warrior."

"He was. But I know what you mean. It's like he has the answers for everything and always knows what to do. The Guardians follow his orders."

Pulling her phone out of her purse, Ella checked her messages. "Nothing from Julian. I'm going to text him." She typed a quick message.

"I should text Magnus too. He's supposed to be wherever I am, so he should be here in the hotel."

"He was probably following us all day long." Ella snorted. "If I couldn't detect him or any of the other Guardians watching over us, it was silly of me to think that I could spot Mr. D."

When Ella's phone pinged with a return message, she read it out loud. "Turner and I are on our way back. What do you want for dinner? We can bring takeout."

Vivian waved a hand. "I don't care. Whatever they bring is fine. I just want to see Magnus."

"I'll ask Julian to ask Turner if it's okay."

For a moment, Vivian thought to tell Ella not to bother him, but then reconsidered. Seeing Magnus was worth the little embarrassment. Everyone knew that mates were inseparable. Poor Bhathian hadn't stopped scowling since they'd boarded the plane.

Only Turner seemed indifferent, but that was because the guy didn't show emotions. Vivian was sure he missed Bridget as well and was talking on the phone with her whenever he could.

"He says Magnus can join us for dinner."

"Wonderful. Thank you. And thank Turner too."

"I already did." Ella sat on the bed and crossed her legs. "Georgetown is so beautiful. I wish the campus were in Los Angeles."

"You can still decide to go here."

Ella shook her head. "I made up my mind. I want to stay home, with you and Magnus and Parker, and, of course, Julian. I'm also not sure about nursing anymore. The village doesn't need more nurses. I don't know how I feel about working in the outside world. I kind of like living in this secret universe, surrounded by my people. I would like to find something I can do that would be beneficial for the clan."

Vivian had a feeling she knew where this was going. "You want to head that charity, don't you?"

Ella smiled. "Passionately. I'm much more excited about that than I ever was about nursing."

"What does one need to study to manage a charity?"

Ella tossed the empty coke can in the wastebasket. "Some kind of management, I guess. I would assume a Master in Business Administration degree is good for that, but maybe there is something more specific."

Vivian scooted back against the pillows and patted the spot next to her. "We can find answers on the internet. Bring your laptop."

This could have waited for later, but they were both anxious about the interview tomorrow, and this was an excellent topic to take their minds off it.

As Ella joined her on the bed, Vivian wrapped her arm around her shoulders. "Just like old times. Remember how you and Parker would come to snuggle in bed with me and have me read you a story?"

Leaning, Ella kissed her cheek. "Yeah, I loved doing that even though the stories Parker wanted you to read were lame." She opened the laptop. "Let's ask Oracle Google what should I be when I grow up."

"It's amazing how you can find everything online these days."

"Here is one." Ella clicked on a link. "Online bachelor's degree in nonprofit management." She read the description out loud. "I don't even have to go anywhere. I can study at home." She turned to Vivian. "Isn't that awesome? I can do homeschooling like Parker, but for college."

"Let me see."

It looked legitimate and it was accredited, but Vivian had always imagined Ella getting to do what she couldn't, and that included going away to college and experiencing youth to the fullest.

But it seemed that her daughter had found love at a young age, and same as her mother was willing to skip all that to be with her guy. Unlike Vivian, though, Ella was making a conscious choice and wasn't forced into it by circumstances.

Or maybe she was?

Vivian had no doubt that part of the decision to stay in the village had to do with Ella's captivity and her fear of the outside world. Or more specifically the Russian mobster who was probably still searching for her. And then there was the evil Doomer who was planning to kidnap her.

"I have to check how the fundraiser is going," Ella said. "Maybe I'm flapping my wings in the wrong direction, and this entire project is a flop."

"I'm crossing my fingers."

As Ella looked at the figures, her eyes widened. "Oh, wow. It's doing much better than I thought it would. We've collected seven thousand three hundred and seventeen dollars."

"Is that a lot?"

"I think it is. We only uploaded the video on Friday night, and Roni said he was going to work on the algorithm on Saturday. I think this is pretty amazing."

38

ELLA

*W*hen Logan entered her dream, Ella felt a weight lift off her chest. And when he wrapped his arm around her, she sighed and leaned her head against his solid chest. "I've missed you the last couple of nights. Where were you?"

"I've been busy."

"Doing what?"

He smirked. "Warlord stuff. I didn't have time for naps."

So, Turner had been right and Logan was on the island, or he had been.

"Which is what? Are there any wars going on that I'm not aware of?"

"There are always conflicts somewhere on the globe. Many don't make the news in the States, or anywhere else in the western world."

"Why is that?"

He shrugged. "Politics, I guess. Some conflicts are more newsworthy than others even though they might be insignificant in comparison."

She'd learned as much from Gorchenco. It was interesting how the bad guys had a better grasp on global affairs than the good guys, or maybe just the misinformed masses. Naturally, it wasn't because the warlords and mobsters cared more, but because they profited from conflicts large and small and, therefore, made it their business to know.

Unlike other warlords, though, Logan didn't live in the war zone. His island was probably the safest stronghold on the globe because no one knew of its existence.

"Are you back home, wherever that is? I assume that night and day are flipped over there."

He chuckled. "They are flipped over where you are. Are you home? Or are you at Georgetown already?"

Boy, was he a good actor and an expert deflector. She couldn't detect a note of falsehood in his tone. He must have known she was there already, even if all he'd done was to hack into university computers and check the tour's roster.

"My mother and I arrived Monday night. We did the tour today and tomorrow is the interview."

He squeezed her shoulder. "Are you excited?"

Ella hoped she was as good an actor as Logan and could fake as flawlessly. Then again, she was excited, just not for the reason he thought.

"I'm nervous. What do you think I should wear? My mom bought me a pantsuit, but I think it's too formal. I usually wear jeans, but jeans are too casual. Maybe I should wear a skirt? But I don't know which one. A short one to show off my legs, or a long one that will make me look modest and romantic. Help!"

That's how teenage girls talked when they were excited, right?

Not too long ago she'd been one too, but she could barely remember herself from the days before Romeo. Had she talked like that?

Logan laughed. "Just be yourself and wear whatever makes you feel confident. If you put on something that you don't normally wear it will make you even more nervous."

"That's good advice."

It really was. That's what she would've told Maddie or any other friend going for an interview. Except, Logan wasn't her friend, or was he?

"You're welcome. Anything else I can help you with?"

"How should I talk? Should I use a lot of fancy words to show off my vocabulary, or should I talk like I normally do?"

He stopped walking and turned her toward him. "You know that it doesn't matter, right? My friend is going to recommend your acceptance even if you come in wearing a bikini." He chuckled. "He might get a stroke seeing you in one, so I don't recommend it. Since I don't know anyone else on the board of admissions, we need to make sure my friend lives to conduct another interview."

Logan had a sense of humor? That was new. He was like a chameleon, changing his colors according to who he needed to charm, and it was working.

"I can't thank you enough for making this happen for me."

"I know how you can thank me." He waggled his brows. "I want a kiss. I want much more than that, but I'll settle for a good and long thank-you one. Or two, or three."

Ella wanted to ask about his plans to take her out on a date, and whether he wouldn't prefer a real kiss to a virtual one, but she was too much of a chicken to do that.

Except, chicken or not, she needed to find out what his plans were. Or at least get an inkling.

Wrapping her arms around his neck, she smiled. "What about the real-life date you've promised me? Wouldn't you like your thank-you kiss to be real?"

He arched a brow. "In front of your mother? I don't think so. I may be an evil warlord, but I do have some basic manners."

This wasn't the answer she needed.

"Is that why you decided not to meet me after all? Was it

because I told you that my mother would have to come along?"

Instead of answering her question, he asked one of his own. "When are you going back home?"

Ella did some quick thinking. If he'd been held up and couldn't make it, she could salvage the situation by waiting for him.

"We are staying for the weekend. I want to absorb the atmosphere, and my mother wants to visit the monuments."

"That's good. I have a few loose ends I need to tie up before I can leave here, but I think I can be done by Friday. We can meet on Saturday." A sly smirk lifted the corner of his lips. "Are you going to make it worth my while?"

"You just said that you're not going to kiss me in front of my mother."

"I can come to your hotel at night and throw pebbles at your window."

Ella laughed. "Where are you getting these crazy ideas from? Old movies?"

For the first time since she'd known him, Logan seemed uncomfortable. "Where I come from, I'm like royalty, and I don't have much contact with ordinary people. What I know is from watching movies and reading books."

Knowing that what he was telling her was the truth, Ella felt touched and a little sad for him. As Navuh's son, Logan's life was probably all about the Brotherhood and taking care of its various interests. Even if it allowed him to live in the lap of luxury, it didn't allow for experiencing most of what she considered worth living for.

Family and friends.

No wonder he liked sharing her dreams and getting exposed to the ordinary in a very extraordinary way.

Or, he was playing her.

Yeah, that was more likely. Julian had told her not to underestimate the Doomer. Logan had had hundreds of years to perfect his manipulating technique. He was appealing to her softer side.

He wasn't the only one with tricks up his sleeve though. By now she'd gotten to know Logan a little. The Doomer had an enormous ego and a soft spot for pretty girls.

Smirking, Ella rubbed his neck with her thumbs. "I'm sure that doesn't apply to kisses. You've probably kissed many girls." She'd almost blurted thousands, catching herself at the last moment. She wasn't supposed to know that he was much older than he looked.

"I'm an exceptional lover, and all of my vast experience is hands on."

Yep. An overinflated ego and then some.

He dipped his head until their lips were almost touching. "Enough stalling. Am I going to get my thank-you kiss or not?"

Looking into Logan's dark eyes and the red flakes of light sparkling in them, Ella realized that this was most likely the last time they were going to kiss. Heck, it was the last time she was going to kiss any guy other than Julian.

She'd better make it count.

39

TURNER

*T*urner parted the drapes and looked out the window, scanning the street for any suspicious activity. It was superfluous, he'd assigned Guardians to do that in shifts throughout the night, but it was a habit and a healthy one at that.

He had a knack for spotting things that others didn't and for seeing patterns in seemingly random occurrences.

Not this time, though. He was either pitted against a superior opponent who was even more paranoid than he was, or their underlying assumptions were all wrong and they were wasting their time because the Doomer wasn't coming.

A light knock on the connecting door preceded the thing opening a crack, and then Ella's head peeked inside. "Is it too early for the briefing? I heard the door open and close several times, so I knew you and Julian were awake."

They were supposed to meet at seven, but given Ella's troubled eyes, she was anxious to start. Or maybe she wanted to see Julian, who'd moved in with him to be closer to her.

"Come on in. Julian and Magnus are bringing breakfast. They should be back soon."

She walked in and sat on Julian's bed. "Mr. D came into my dream last night."

Turner perked up. "That's great news. What did he tell you?"

"That he's been busy, and that he might get here on Saturday. And that was only after I dangled a date in front of his nose."

"Did you believe him?"

The girl shrugged. "I don't know. If he were a regular human, I would have been sure that he was telling the truth. But Julian and you warned me that I shouldn't do that."

"And you are very smart for heeding that warning."

"Thank you. Just in case he wasn't lying, though, I told him that my mom and I planned on staying in Washington over the weekend. He might have been detained by his father, or by some emergency, and it would be a shame to miss this opportunity by giving up too early."

"Excellent. Did he ask you where you were staying?"

Ella shook her head. "Nope. Does it mean that he knows?"

"We should assume that he does. He could've sent people to follow you back here. That's why we went to all the trouble of staging things, including bringing in the ladies from Hawaii. They have no clue why they are really here, so they can't divulge any information if asked."

"But you don't know that for sure."

"No, I don't, and we have loads of monitoring equipment in addition to the Guardians. If anyone followed you, we would've known."

Roni and William hadn't come up with anything either, but Lokan might have achieved that by wearing specialty glasses. Still, none of the Guardians had spotted him either, and they'd been searching relentlessly.

On the face of things, everything pointed to Ella's conclusion being right. The Doomer wasn't coming. Not yet, anyway. But every instinct in Turner's body screamed that Lokan was there and that he was setting up his trap.

Pushing up to her feet, Ella walked over to the window and peered outside. "Where did Magnus and Julian go for food?"

"The corner deli."

"I think I can see them coming, but with my human eyes I can't be sure."

Turner walked up to her and stood behind her. "It's them. Is your mother coming?"

"Yes, I am." Vivian walked in through the connecting door. "Good morning. Was the meeting pushed forward earlier and no one told me?"

Ella shook her head. "I wanted to tell Turner about the dream visit and I didn't want to wait. Julian and Magnus are bringing breakfast."

Vivian regarded Ella's sweatpants and T-shirt. "After we are done, you need to get ready. Did you decide what you want to wear for the interview?"

"Not yet. I'm too nervous to think about outfits."

As the door opened, and the men walked in, the mood in the room changed markedly.

"Yay, coffee." Ella rushed up to Julian and wrapped her arms around his neck, ignoring the cardboard tray he was holding. "Good morning," she whispered and kissed his cheek.

Vivian was a little more circumspect about her excitement to see her mate, but not by much.

Regrettably, it wasn't the time or place for a love fest.

"Let's go over everything one more time while we eat." Turner motioned to the two beds, and pulled out the only chair in the room for himself.

Grabbing a coffee off one of the trays, he focused on the ladies. "I know that all of you are concerned with Lokan's compulsion ability, but let's not forget that his men can thrall too. Fortunately, you can prevent them from getting into your head. All it takes is keeping your mind closed off."

"How am I supposed to do that?" Vivian asked.

"A suspicious and contrary attitude. Thralling is easy when the victim is unaware. When a person suspects the thraller, it is much more difficult and requires a stronger thralling ability." He turned to Julian. "I can't thrall well yet, so you'll have to do that. Try to get into Vivian's head."

She lifted a hand. "Wait a minute. Maybe Magnus should do that?"

"You trust Magnus, so you are not going to fight it as hard."

"I trust Julian too, but I'm more comfortable with Magnus."

"That's who we got, so that's what we have to work with. I want you to think of something you wouldn't want Julian to find out. Like a birthday present that you bought for him and want to keep it a surprise."

"Got it." She smiled at Julian. "Go for it."

The guy frowned. "I can't get in. She's blocking me."

Vivian's eyes widened. "I am? I don't know how I'm doing it."

"I told you that it's easy. Once you are aware of it, you can deny entry. Doesn't always work, but just as with hypnosis, if the subjects are reasonably intelligent and resist the hypnotist, it can't be forced on them."

"I wish it worked the same with compulsion," Ella said. "But I know for a fact that it doesn't. As hard as I try, I can't resist Parker's commands."

"We should have brought him along," Julian said. "He could command Ella not to succumb to Lokan's compulsion."

Turner shook his head. "I don't think it would work if Lokan uses his full power up close."

"It's worth a try," Vivian said. "Let's call Parker and ask

him to command both of us to resist the Doomer's compulsion."

"Does it work over the phone?" Julian asked.

Vivian pulled the phone out. "We didn't try it, but if it can be done in a shared dream, I'm sure it can be done over a cellular signal."

"Mom, what's up?" Parker answered.

"I want you to command Ella and me to resist Mr. D's compulsion."

There was a long moment of silence before he answered. "I can give it a try. I'm imagining how much I hate him, and how I don't want him to get anywhere near you or Ella. I hope it will help."

"Just do your best, sweetheart."

40

ELLA

*A*s Ella came out of the bathroom, her mother looked her up and down and then nodded her approval. "You look lovely."

"Thank you." Ella stifled the impulse to roll her eyes.

No matter how many times she'd told her mother that the interview was irrelevant, Vivian insisted on treating it as if it was for real. Perhaps it was easier for her to focus on that than on what this was really about.

Humoring her, Ella had put on a long flowing skirt that wasn't new, and a matching blouse that was. The shoes were also a new purchase, comfortable and old-fashioned, with a low chunky heel and a strap across the top.

Only after she was fully dressed, standing in front of the mirror and examining her reflection, had Ella realized that she'd followed Logan's advice. She felt comfortable and confident in her own style of clothing. Pant and skirt suits were a reminder of her captivity, of dressing up to please the whims of her owner and not her own taste and preferences.

She'd smoothed her pink hair back instead of spiking it, had gone easy with the makeup, and had donned the pretend reading glasses Eva had given her. They weren't stylish and made her look bookish, but she actually liked them.

The most important part of her attire, though, were the trackers. A matching set of earrings and pendant, four hairpins, and three tiny dots that were attached to the inside of her clothing.

It was a little early, but Ella was too nervous to wait. "Ready to go, Mom?"

"Yes." Vivian picked up her purse. "Let's text our taxi driver."

When the Guardian picked them up from in front of the hotel, they did their best to act as if he was just a driver, and when they arrived at campus, Vivian pretended to pay him.

He returned her credit card and smiled. "Good luck."

Knowing that Magnus and Julian had been following them in another cab, Ella tried not to look over her shoulder.

Instead, she looked at her mother. *Do you think it will be okay if I pull out a mirror and pretend to check my hair?*

Vivian shook her head. *Save it for when we actually need it. I'm sure the guys are behind us.*

As they walked to the admissions office, Ella barely breathed, expecting an ambush at every corner. It was so damn nerve-wracking that she let out a sigh of relief when they got there.

"Please take a seat," the receptionist said. "These gentlemen are ahead of you, and then it's your turn."

"Thank you."

Ella eyed the two, but they seemed precisely who they were supposed to be. One was a guy about her age, although he looked much younger, and the other was obviously his father and looked to be in his mid-fifties.

No immortals posing as humans here, she sent to her mom as she took a seat.

When Vivian started chatting with the father, Ella smiled

at the son and then pulled out her phone, pretending to read. She was in no mood for small talk, and besides, her throat was dry. She'd forgotten to get a water bottle and wondered if it was okay to go get one.

A quick text to Julian solved her dilemma.

There was a vending machine out in the corridor, and a couple of Guardians were hanging around in its vicinity. Kri was across from it in the ladies bathroom, stationed there in case Ella or Vivian needed to use the facilities.

She tapped her mother's shoulder. "I'm going to get a bottle of water Do you want anything from the vending machine?"

"Water would be lovely, thank you."

Ella pushed to her feet and looked at the father and son. "Would you like me to get you anything?"

"I'll come with you." The son started to get up.

His father stopped him. "You can't leave. That door may open at any moment and it will be your turn."

Deflated, the guy sat back down. "I guess I'm stuck. Can you please get me a coke?" He handed her two bucks.

"Sure. Diet or regular?"

"Regular. Thank you."

The trip to the vending machine and back was uneventful, but at least she got to see the two Guardians monitoring the corridor.

On the way back, she saw a girl and her father leave the waiting room, and when she entered it, the son wasn't there.

Ella handed the father the coke and the change. "Sorry I was too late."

"He'll have it when he gets out. Thank you for buying it for him."

"You're welcome."

She wondered if the father had stayed behind because it had been his choice or because parents weren't allowed inside.

Not that she cared one way or another, but Vivian seemed so excited about the interview that she would probably be disappointed if she was left out. Besides, it wasn't a good idea for them to separate.

Walking up to the secretary, Ella waited for her to get off the phone and asked, "Can my mother come in with me, or does she have to stay outside?"

The woman smiled indulgently. "It's up to you. Professor Perry is not going to kick your mom out." She leaned closer. "On the contrary, he'll be mad if she doesn't come in. Students are off limits. But mothers are not." She winked.

Ella glanced at Vivian. She was indeed beautiful, and the boy's father was practically drooling over her. Was that the reason he'd stayed behind?

It never ceased to amaze her how stupid some men got over pretty women.

"My mom is taken."

"Pfft." The woman waved a dismissive hand. "As if that has ever stopped him."

Time dragged on, and with it the stress buildup. Despite the Guardians Ella had seen with her own eyes, and the many others hiding in various places, she watched the door, expecting Logan to saunter in at any moment.

In the movie she'd created in her head, he would walk in, order everyone to keep quiet, compelling their silence so no one could sound the alarm, smile at her evilly, and crook his finger, beckoning her to him.

She would try to resist, but it would be no use. He would compel her and her mother to follow him, maybe stealing a kiss before ushering them out of the waiting room.

Outside, there would be a horde of Doomers, holding the Guardians in chains, but just as all hope was lost, Magnus and Julian would come and save the day.

How?

Her imagination had no answer for that.

So yeah, she was an optimist at heart. In her imagination, even the worst case scenario had a happy ending.

41

JULIAN

*T*he men's room was the last place Julian would've chosen as headquarters for their stakeout, but Turner had convinced him that it was perfect.

A Guardian named Edan was shrouding the place in such a heavy cloak of dread that human males chose to bypass it and continue to the next bathroom down the hall. And if an immortal happened to wander in, there would be one less Doomer for them to worry about.

Not that there were any.

The small surveillance cameras they'd installed around campus revealed nothing suspicious, and a whole lot of nothing was happening in the interviewer's waiting room, except for some guy flirting with Vivian.

Magnus was probably going out of his mind. The feed from the room was broadcasting on the private channel all the Guardians had access to through their phones. Julian had no doubt that Magnus was watching it as avidly as he was.

Turner, on the other hand, was watching the feed from the interviewer's room.

Not that anything interesting was going on there either.

The tiny portable transmitter was mounted on the wall across from the interviewer, so all that was visible was the professor's pudgy face and the young guy's back. There was no sound, or maybe Turner was just keeping the volume off.

For the first fifteen minutes or so the two had talked, and then the professor had turned around to the monitor mounted on the wall behind him and had started playing a documentary about the university's history. It was running for over twenty minutes already and didn't seem to be nearing the end.

"Do you think he shows that to every student?" Julian whispered.

They were supposed to keep silent in case of immortals overhearing them, but since none were around except their own people, it didn't matter.

Turner shrugged. "It's an easy way to make the interview seem longer than it is and justify more hours," Turner whispered back.

Minimizing the window, Turner brought the rest of the feeds up on his tablet and scanned them quickly. There was even one transmitting from Ella and Vivian's room in the hotel.

Where a whole lot of nothing was going on as well.

"He's not coming," Julian whispered.

Turner shook his head. "My brain agrees with you, but my intuition doesn't. Which is a first for me. I never rely on feelings."

Intuition was not a feeling. It was a collection of clues too small for the conscious mind to notice, but not for the subconscious that collected everything.

The problem was that Julian's intuition was saying the exact opposite, and, since getting to Washington, he and Turner had been exposed to the same input. The only difference was Turner's experience, which allowed his subconscious to make more connections and see more patterns than Julian's.

Trusting Turner's gut more than he did his own, Julian tensed. Something was about to happen. The question was when, where, and how.

ELLA

a whole freaking hour had passed since the guy had gone into the interviewer's office. Ella had finished her water and needed to pee, but she was afraid to leave in case the guy finally got out.

On the other hand, it was a bad idea to keep holding it in throughout the interview, especially if it was going to last so long.

She tapped her mother's shoulder. "I'm going to the bathroom."

Vivian gave her a pained look. "I need to go, too." She rolled her eyes at the guy's father.

"So, come with me. We can tell the receptionist that we are going and will be right back."

"Good idea."

After a quick stop at the secretary's desk, they rushed out and headed to the bathroom, passing two Guardians posing as students on the way.

"I don't really need to go," Vivian said. "But that guy was getting overly friendly. Can we hide out in the bathroom until he leaves?"

"Sure." Ella smiled and switched to a silent mode of

communication. *We can ask Turner to let us know when it's safe to come back.*

It could've been beneficial to keep the channel to her mother open, but Ella was afraid that by doing so she was going to open her mind to attack. Her best bet was to keep her shields up and reinforce them as much as she could.

In the bathroom, they found Kri, dressed in a custodian's coveralls and polishing the counters.

"Good afternoon, ladies," she greeted them.

Ella stifled a giggle. "Good afternoon to you, too."

With her height and broad shoulders, Kri wasn't a very believable custodian, and besides, she'd joined them on the tour of the campus as a student. Then again, some students took on jobs like that to help with their living expenses.

Once Ella was done, she double checked that the transmitters were still attached to her clothing before getting out. A moment later her mother joined her at the sink. "We should go back. I just hope that Larry and his son are gone already."

No such luck.

When they got back, the father was still sitting in the waiting room. Not for long, though. A couple minutes later the son got out.

"What took so long?" Larry asked.

The guy glanced at a receptionist before answering. "A long documentary about the university's history and every important person who ever attended it or donated big bucks to it." He rolled his eyes. "There were a lot of both." He turned to Ella. "Good luck. Professor Perry is a nice guy. The hardest part of the interview was watching that movie."

"Thanks."

"You can go in," the receptionist said. "Professor Perry is ready for you."

The guy must have a bathroom in there. Otherwise he would have needed a pee break, Ella sent to her mother.

Vivian smiled. "Let's not keep the professor waiting."

The interviewer's office was made to impress, with fancy bookcases lining both its sides, and heavy furniture that looked as old as the university.

"Welcome." Professor Perry got up and headed straight for Vivian. "Ms. Kelly Rubinstein and her lovely mother, Mrs. Victoria MacBain." He shook Vivian's hand first and then Ella's.

"Second marriage?" he asked as he pulled out a visitor chair for her mother and then for Ella.

"I've remarried after Kelly's father passed away."

"My condolences," he said as he took his seat behind the desk.

Finally looking at Ella, the professor gave her a quick once over. "My friend spoke very highly of you, but he failed to mention how pretty you are."

Ella affected a polite expression. "Thank you for the compliment, but I'm very glad that he didn't. I would like to be judged based on merit and not looks."

"You are a wise young woman." He lifted his notepad and took a look. "Very impressive grades. And you also organized a charity?"

"Yes, I did."

"Tell me about it."

Ella had that part prepared. It was a variation on the one she was actually working on, but instead of helping girls who'd been lured away from their families and violated, her invented charity was about helping victims of child abuse. A much less controversial subject.

Once she was done, he asked some more questions about the charity, and after she answered those, he asked why she'd chosen Georgetown.

"That's an easy answer. Georgetown is one of the most prestigious universities in the country, and the campus is beautiful. Also, its nursing program is extremely well regarded."

Her answer seemed to please him. "I think you are a very good fit for us. And it has nothing to do with my friend putting in a word for you. You're an excellent candidate, Kelly." He turned around and clicked the monitor on. "But if you are still not sure that this is the place for you, this documentary is going to convince you."

As the movie started playing, Professor Perry rolled his chair sideways and out of the way, taking the notepad and pen with him.

Now the movie made sense. Instead of summarizing the interview after the student was gone, he was doing it while the movie was playing and saving himself working after hours.

What else seemed clear was that Logan hadn't planned a trap and everything he'd told her was aboveboard.

She owed him a big apology. Except, she could never tell him what she'd suspected and why.

About ten minutes into the movie, the professor got up, walked over to one of the bookcases, and pulled out a book.

Evidently, he was done summarizing the interview and was going to spend the rest of the time reading.

43

MAGNUS

*A*rwel clapped Magnus's back. "Relax. It's only harmless flirting."

Sitting on a bench in front of the admissions office, they were supposed to be watching the entry, with Arwel monitoring moods and intentions for any disturbances.

But since nothing was happening, Magnus busied himself with watching the feed from the waiting room.

"The asshole is drooling all over Vivian. He's been slowly inching closer to her, and now he's practically sitting in her lap. I want to get in there and teach him some manners."

"Patience, my friend. His son is going to come out soon, and they are going to leave. The worst that could happen is Vivian having to stop by the ladies room to clean his drool off her shoes."

As worst case scenarios went, that was, of course, a joke. Magnus had bigger worries on his mind. But it seemed that this operation was a bust, and that the Doomer really wasn't going to show up.

Not today anyway.

The question was whether he'd told Ella the truth and would arrive on Saturday.

Magnus wasn't sure which outcome he was hoping for. On the one hand, catching Lokan was important to the clan, but on the other hand, he would have preferred to keep Vivian and Ella as far away from danger as possible.

Next to him, Arwel was doing his thing, with his eyes closed and his head tilted back, tuning into the vibes coursing through the campus.

"Are you getting anything?"

Arwel shook his head. "I'm getting plenty, just not anything that is interesting to us."

"Let me guess. The asshole in the waiting room is thinking dirty thoughts about my mate, and his kid is anxious."

"The kid was anxious, and now he is bored, and you're right about the horny bastard." Arwel scratched his head. "There is something else too, but it's faint and it's subtle. Like a low-level excitement." He waved a dismissive hand. "It's probably nothing. Someone looking forward to a hookup."

Magnus snorted. "This place is packed with young humans. All of them are thinking about hookups twenty-four seven."

Turning back to his phone screen, he focused on the door to the interviewer's room. Instead of looking at the human male making advances toward his mate, he should be watching that door, which was the only way into the inner office. They had checked the room the night before last, verifying that there was no back exit.

About ten minutes later, it opened and the young human stepped out, smiled at Ella and said something to her.

"Hallelujah, the kid is out, and he's taking his father with him."

Arwel nodded. "I can feel his relief, and also the older man's disappointment."

"Ella and Vivian are going in. Do you feel them?"

"I can feel Vivian, and she is excited, but Ella's shields are

199

up, and she emits next to nothing. I can't get a reading on her emotions."

"That's good, isn't it? She is less vulnerable."

"It's very good, and I need to ask her how she does it. Maybe she can teach me how to protect my mind. I would love some peace and quiet in there."

Magnus felt an unreasonable wave of pride wash over him. Even though she wasn't his flesh and blood, he couldn't help thinking of Ella as his daughter. When an old and experienced Guardian like Arwel believed he could learn something from such a young girl, Magnus couldn't help but feel pride in her achievements.

"I doubt she can help me, though," Arwel added. "Ella learned how to block her mother when she was very young, and she probably does it without thinking. Besides, she needs to block only one person. I'm not that lucky."

"There shouldn't be a difference between blocking one and many. You should talk to her. If she can help you, great, and if she can't, at least you tried, right?"

Arwel nodded. "When we get back, I'll stop by your place."

"I'm not sure you'll find her there. Once this is over, I have a feeling she's going to move in with Julian."

Arwel arched a brow. "It's getting serious between them, eh?"

"Very. They are obviously destined for one another."

44

ELLA

*E*lla watched the professor from the corner of her eye, expecting him to take the book and go back to his chair. Instead, he put it on another shelf and remained standing with his hands clasped behind his back and his face turned toward the movie.

Maybe he got tired of sitting?

But then she heard a noise that didn't come from the loudspeakers playing the movie's soundtrack. Something creaked, then whined, like a very old door being pushed on squeaky hinges.

Did you hear that? Ella sent to her mother.

What are you talking about?

Never mind.

The small hairs on the back of her neck prickling, she turned her head in the direction of the noise and saw the professor just standing there. He either hadn't heard it or was ignoring it.

It was probably nothing. The admissions office was located in an old building, and it made all kinds of weird noises, which everyone who worked there was most likely used to.

She was just jumpy, that's all.

Turning back to the movie, Ella tried to ignore the creaking, but then Vivian's back stiffened, indicating that she was probably hearing the weird noises too.

They both turned their heads at the same time.

"Not a sound, ladies." Logan stepped out from behind the bookcase that had been somehow pushed forward. "And don't move a muscle either," he said as calmly as if he was saying hello.

The professor dipped his head in greeting and said nothing.

The power behind Logan's compulsion made Parker's seem like child's play. What Logan had done in her dream hadn't been even a minuscule fraction of what he was doing now.

Ella was paralyzed, stuck in the same pose and mute. She couldn't even look at her mother because her head had been turned toward the noise when Logan issued the command. Hell, she couldn't even move her eyes.

The one thing he couldn't control, though, was her mind.

As Logan instructed the professor to go through the opening, Ella sent to her mother, *Shields up, Mom. And don't worry. The Guardians are going to be here any second*. She then slammed her own shields into place.

When the professor had gone through the secret opening, Logan walked over to them, leaned, and kissed Ella's forehead. "I'm sorry about this, Ella, but I need you and your mother for a special mission. Once that is done, I will let you both go. I promise."

Where were the freaking Guardians?

"Please get up, ladies, and follow the professor. Take your purses with you."

Ella fought the compulsion with all she had. If she could only stall for a couple of minutes, the Guardians would burst through the door and end this.

She was too damn weak, and the only thing that seemed to be working was her tear ducts that started leaking. She couldn't even raise her hand to wipe them away.

Like a couple of zombies, she and her mother did as they were told, got up and headed toward the protruding bookcase.

Walking through the opening, they entered a tunnel that would've been completely dark if not for the professor holding up his phone with the flashlight activated. Logan entered behind them and closed the way.

"Keep walking," he told the three of them.

Was the professor under Logan's control too?

Had Logan somehow tampered with the camera inside the room? But how?

And what was that mission he'd talked about?

Damn, she couldn't open her mouth to ask, and she could barely see because the tears were blurring her eyesight and she couldn't wipe them off.

They must've walked about a third of a mile when they met up with one of Logan's men.

"Stop," he issued the command from behind them.

As the man, or rather immortal, handed Logan a duffle bag, Ella's panic intensified. What was in there? Gags? Blindfolds? Handcuffs?

Turning toward the professor, who was standing just as motionless as Ella and Vivian, Logan pointed at another tunnel forking away from the one they were walking in. "You are free to leave, Perry. Once you get out, you will remember nothing of what happened from the moment you saw me earlier today. Am I clear?"

The professor nodded.

"You can start walking, Perry. Ladies, you stay right where you are."

As the professor walked away, Logan turned to them, his forehead creasing as he took in Ella's tear-stricken face.

"There is no reason to cry, Ella." He wiped her tears with his thumbs. "No one is going to touch you or your mother without your permission, and that includes me. This is not about sex, like it was with Gorchenco. I need your minds, not your bodies."

As if she was going to believe the liar. But that was neither here nor there. Soon, the Guardians would come and rescue them.

Why hadn't they already?

As Logan unzipped the bag, the last thing she'd expected him to pull out were two string bikinis.

"Please hand me your purses." He took them and gave them to his guy. "When I say now, I want you to take off all of your clothes, toss them in front of you, and put these on." He looked at his man. "Turn your back to the ladies."

When the guy did as he was told, Logan pulled two sets of exercise clothes and two pairs of flip-flops out of the bag and put them on the floor at Ella and Vivian's feet.

"I'm going to turn around. When you have the bikinis on, stop, and wait for further instructions." He turned his back to them. "Now, strip. You have thirty seconds before I turn around."

Obviously, he was concerned about trackers. But how had he known to suspect them?

As Ella stripped and tossed her clothes on the floor, she was thankful for the jewelry and the pins in her hair. Next to her, Vivian did the same. Then they both put the bikinis on.

Turning back, Logan nodded his approval, and then walked in a circle around them.

The freaking bikini was nothing more than three tiny triangles held together with a bunch of strings. All it covered were her nipples and her mons. Everything else was on full display.

If he wanted to ensure that they had no trackers on their bodies, he had achieved his goal. Even the one she'd attached to her panties was gone, and she'd thought it would be the hardest to discover.

Except, he didn't know about the miniature ones in their jewelry and hairpins.

"Toss your shoes on top of the pile, and after that take off your earrings and your necklaces and toss them too." He glanced at Vivian's hair and smirked. "The wig has to go too. And these funky glasses you are both wearing. Now."

Crap, Ella hoped he wouldn't notice the pins in her hair. She also hoped that no camera was going to pick them up on the way. Logan wasn't the only one she had to worry about. There was more than one wolf after her.

When that was done, he pointed at the folded exercise clothes and the flip-flops. "Put these on."

To his man he said, "Collect all their belongings, put them in the duffel bag, and go. You know what to do."

"Yes, sir."

VIVIAN

*T*he Doomer was acting like the classic evil mastermind, polite and gentlemanly to a fault, and yet scary as hell.

Vivian had always found the intelligent, soft-spoken villains more frightening than the bully types, and Lokan was the scariest of them all.

The fact that Ella had thought to take someone like him on proved how naive she still was. Her daughter was no match for that devil, and a devil he was, despite his false reassurances and his concern for their dignity.

Frankly, Viv hadn't expected him to turn around and let them keep their modesty. It gave some credence to his claim that he needed them for a mission and not as sex slaves for the Doomer's island, or for his own perverted needs.

She could imagine that there were some psychos out there who entertained fantasies about having sex with both mother and daughter. Hopefully, Lokan wasn't one of those.

"Follow me," he said after they were dressed.

Lokan's man had gone in the same direction as the professor, and he was probably going to lead the Guardians on a wild goose chase around town. She wouldn't be surprised if the plan was to distribute the trackers between several Doomers and have them drive in different directions.

What she couldn't understand was how come the Guardians weren't already there. The feed from the camera inside the interview office should have alerted them to what was going on, and if the thing had malfunctioned, someone would have come in to investigate.

As they walked down the tunnel, she listened for hurried footsteps coming from behind, but the only sound echoing from the walls was the flapping of her and Ella's flip-flops.

The tunnel looked ancient, like something that had been built together with the university in the 1700s. Someone must have thought that escape tunnels were needed in case of an emergency or an invasion.

How come Turner hadn't thought to check for that?

She'd been reassured that the interview room had been thoroughly searched and that the only way in and out of it was the door to the waiting room. Had no one bothered to take a look at the building's blueprints?

Then again, the originals might have been lost, and no one knew the tunnels existed. Lokan, on the other hand, was old enough to have seen the original structure built.

Vivian wished she could share her thoughts with Ella, but her daughter was keeping the channel closed. Which was smart of her. She needed to keep her shields up against the Doomer.

Hopefully, the fear and hatred Vivian felt for Lokan was enough to block him from entering her mind as well. If the Doomer got even a glimpse, he could compel them to tell him whatever he wanted.

"You are probably wondering how I knew to avoid the trap you were setting for me," he said out of the blue, sending panic surging into Vivian's throat.

"Don't worry, I don't blame you for that. I know you had no choice but to do as you were told. I figured that you've been aided by your government in exchange for letting them use your special talents."

What the hell was he talking about?

As he glanced back at them to gauge their responses, Vivian hoped her wide peeled eyes were conveying her fear and surprise, and that he would assume they were the result of his brilliant, yet erroneous, deduction.

Satisfied with her and Ella's appropriately shocked expressions, he smirked. "I'm well aware of their secret program to collect people with paranormal abilities and use their talents in warfare. Unfortunately, I wasn't able to get close to anyone on the inside, or I would have raided their facilities a long time ago. I'm very curious about what else is out there, and if they found another dream walker. As far as I know, I'm the only one."

So, Josh had been right about the government snatching people with special abilities and keeping them locked up somewhere. God only knew what was being done to them.

Lokan cast a glance at Ella over his shoulder. "I must conclude that my compulsion doesn't work as well in dream world. Either that, or they have people who can break through it. Otherwise, you wouldn't have been able to tell them about my dream-walking ability. You were pretty convincing, but I knew that you were trying to play me when you started acting all nice and flirty. I figured out that the people holding you wanted to put their hands on me too."

As Turner and Julian had warned, Lokan had suspected Ella all along, but he had reached the wrong conclusion. The results were still the same, though. He'd managed to avoid capture and abscond with them.

At least he didn't know who was after him, which gave the Guardians an advantage. Lokan was confident in his ability to compel humans to do his bidding, but his reliance on it was his Achilles heel.

He was in for a big surprise.

"Three things confirmed my suspicions," he kept on bragging. "The first was the excellent fake identity you were supplied with. Only the government has access to such resources. The second was the hotel that you were staying at, which is a government-owned facility. And the third was the camera your people installed in the interview office. I sent my men through the tunnels to check out the room last night, and when they found it, I had the final proof that what I suspected was right." He chuckled. "Your people are probably still watching the loop my guy is feeding them. I just wonder when they are going to notice your slight body movements are repeating. By the time they figure it out, we will be up in the air and out of their reach. My idea to put on the movie was brilliant, if I say so myself."

Quite full of himself, isn't he? Ella sent.

Vivian shook her head, signaling Ella that she shouldn't talk.

Her daughter was strong enough to send thoughts directly into Vivian's head, but Vivian's ability was much more limited, and she was afraid that her response could be picked up by the Doomer.

He looked at them over his shoulder. "I apologize for keeping you silent and conducting a one-sided conversation. As soon as we are safely away, I'm going to remove the silencing compulsion and you'll be able to ask me questions."

Hopefully, by then they would get rescued.

Both she and Ella still had the hairpins in, which meant that as soon as Turner realized that he was watching a loop, the Guardians would come after them.

The problem was that the Guardians would be chasing after more than one signal, following the trackers Lokan's man had taken and most likely distributed among several of his comrades. Which meant that they would have to split up.

Vivian's gut clenched. What if Lokan had a large force with him and each tracker led the Guardians into a trap?

Supposedly, they were better trained and stronger than the Doomers, but that wouldn't help them if they found themselves vastly outnumbered.

E L L A

*E*lla felt like an idiot. She'd been naive and full of herself, and Julian had been right about her being no match for Logan. The only secret she'd managed to keep from him was the real identity of her rescuers.

So far.

She prayed that they would get rescued before he had the chance to figure that one out too.

Supposedly, Doomers weren't aware of the fact that Dormants possessed special ability in a much higher percentage than the general human population. That was what Dalhu claimed. But Logan wasn't an ordinary Doomer, and he was probably privy to information kept from the simple soldiers.

He was smart and seemed well-educated, which also differentiated him from the average Doomer. He could've figured out stuff on his own, and once he discovered that Ella and Vivian were Dormants, all his gentlemanly promises would be forgotten. He would either throw them into the Doomers' breeding program or keep them for himself. His own little harem of mother and daughter.

Talk about gross.

"You should actually thank me for freeing you from your government's clutches," Logan continued his villainous mastermind monologue. "Once you complete the mission that I need your help with, I'll set you free with new identities and enough money to last you for the rest of your life."

Right, it was just as true as the scholarship he'd promised her. Once again, he was blowing smoke up her ass, but this time she wasn't buying it.

"Naturally, it would be best if you don't return to the States and opt for settling somewhere in South America. You'll be much harder to find, and your money will buy you a more luxurious living."

As if he was ever letting them go. All his promises had one goal. To ensure their cooperation. What she wondered, though, was if he'd be satisfied with dangling the carrot in front of them or was he going to also introduce the stick?

Which would be extremely easy for him. All he would have to do is threaten to hurt one of them for the other to agree to whatever he wanted. Come to think of it, he wouldn't even need to do that. He could just compel them to do what he told them. They would be like puppets on his strings.

Glancing at Ella, Logan smirked. "Except for me, of course. I might need you to perform more services for me from time to time. You have no idea how valuable your mind-to-mind communication is. It's completely undetectable."

Damn, the guy knew how to sound convincing. She could visualize herself lazing on a beach somewhere in South America, only having to do favors for Logan from time to time to keep the money coming. From his point of view, and given what he believed Ella and Vivian's situation to be, Logan's plan seemed like a win-win.

"You are going to live like queens, and I probably won't need your special services for more than several days a year."

He smiled. "That's one hell of a compensation package for very little work."

Was he playing her again, just from a different angle?

This new Logan seemed like a completely different person from the one who'd shared her dreams, and he was treating her as if she was a tool to be used in his schemes and not someone he desired.

Evidently, Turner had been right about that too, and Logan had faked his infatuation with her the same way she'd faked hers with him.

All along, they'd been playing each other.

What she wanted to find out more than anything else, though, was whether he'd compelled her attraction to him. Would he admit to it if she asked?

They'd been walking for at least twenty minutes when they reached another fork in the tunnel.

"This way, ladies." Logan motioned for them to go ahead of him.

The short offshoot terminated in a brick wall, but as Logan grabbed one of the bricks that was sticking out and pulled, some kind of a pulley mechanism was activated and the wall started moving back.

On the other side was nothing but a staircase leading up, and Logan motioned for them to take it. Four stories later, they exited through another door and onto the roof of a parking structure.

Except, instead of a car, there was a helicopter waiting for them.

Crap. Where was he taking them? What was the helicopter's range? And more importantly, was it shorter than the trackers'?

MAGNUS

*M*agnus switched from watching the feed coming from the waiting room to the one coming from the interviewer's office. "It's taking too long."

Arwel stretched his legs in front of him. "Are they still watching the documentary?"

"The thing drags on and on. I don't know how they are not falling asleep."

"I think they already did because I'm not picking up anything. There was a brief moment when Vivian tensed, but after that nothing. The professor must have said something to upset her."

"What about Ella?"

Arwel shook his head. "I told you. She's blocking everything. I can't sense her at all."

"Is there a timer on the feed? Because the movie seems longer this time around."

"There should be. Tell Turner to check. He has the full display."

Taking a quick glance around to make sure no one was listening, Magnus tapped his earpiece. "Turner. I have a feeling that the movie has been running longer this time than during the previous interview. Can you check the timer?"

"It's just your perception," Arwel said. "What do you think could be happening in there? We are watching all the entry and exit points, and the interview room has only one door that opens to the reception area."

In his ear, Turner said, "You're right. It has been running for about two minutes longer. It might be a different version of the documentary."

"Something doesn't feel right. I'm going in."

"Stay where you are. I need the entrance to the building guarded. I'm sending Julian in."

"Okay."

The doctor wasn't a Guardian, and therefore hadn't been assigned any guard duties. He was the more logical choice.

Magnus was still watching the feed and waiting for Julian to enter when he heard him in his earpiece.

"There is no one here! The fucking movie is playing and they are not here!"

Magnus leaped up and started running. "Where the fuck are they? Who is watching the door to the reception room?"

Behind him, he heard Arwel's boots pounding on the pavement.

"I'm activating the tracking," Turner said in his ear.

Inside, all mayhem broke loose, with Guardians piling into the waiting room, and the receptionist watching them with wide, terrified eyes.

"I got this," Arwel said and walked up to her.

Rushing into the interviewer's office, Magnus joined Julian and Turner in their search for a hidden exit.

"We are wasting time. Let's follow the trackers," Julian said. "It doesn't matter how they were taken. Only that we find them before he takes them beyond the trackers' range."

"I've already dispatched the Guardians stationed closest

215

to the parking lot. The trackers are moving in four different directions."

"Fuck." Magnus kicked a chair, sending it toppling to the floor. "He was on to us the entire time."

"It would seem so." Turner removed a bunch of books off a shelf and peered inside the space he'd made. "I just hope he didn't find all of the trackers and that some are still on Ella and Vivian."

"Let's go, Turner," Julian insisted. "I know you want to find out how the bastard did it, but it's not important right now."

Ignoring Julian's suggestion, Turner kept moving books. "There is no point in us going after them until we know which direction is the right one."

Throwing his hands in the air, Julian headed for the door. "We are not going to find that out by staying in this room. I'm going to pick a direction and follow it."

"Don't be an idiot, Julian," Turner barked in a rare show of irritation. "We will get moving once it is clear which of the trackers are on Ella and Vivian. Guardians are already in pursuit and there is nothing more we can do at this point."

Groaning, Julian turned away from the door.

The damn movie was still playing in the background, and with the sound on, it was clear that it was on a loop. Except, Magnus wasn't sure he would've noticed that even if he'd been watching the feed and listening to the monotonous, droning narration.

It all sounded the same and was annoying the hell out of him, but he didn't want to waste time looking for the remote to shut it up while the Doomer was getting away with Ella and Vivian.

Magnus was losing his ever-loving shit.

Vivian had told him about putting a tracker in her underwear. If the bastard had stripped her naked, he was going to tear out the Doomer's throat with his bare fangs and watch him bleed out.

"I found it," Turner said.

Reaching into a gap he'd made between books, he pressed or pulled something. There was a subtle click of a mechanism engaging, and the bookcase started moving.

"That's how he got them out. We were watching a loop of a recording taken in the first minutes of the documentary playing, and none of us paid attention to the screen."

Magnus would have felt like a total idiot, but the fucking Doomer had outsmarted even Turner.

ELLA

$\mathcal{T}$he helicopter wasn't big, and aside from the pilot, there was only enough space for the three of them. Hopefully, that meant that its range wasn't long.

Without much preamble, Logan lifted Vivian into the chopper and then reached for Ella. There was nothing sexual in the way he handled her. Just a quick and efficient lift.

After he had them both seated inside, he got in and sat next to the pilot. Turning the chair around, he locked it in place and handed them each headphones. He then donned a pair himself. "You can talk now."

Whoop dee doo. Should she tell him how much she despised him?

Not a good idea to antagonize the enemy, especially if she wanted him to clarify some things.

As the chopper took off, Ella's stomach rose up into her throat. The feeling passed when it reached its cruising altitude.

"Can the pilot hear us?" Vivian asked.

Logan motioned for the guy to remove his headphones. "Now he can't. So what do you want to ask me?"

Before her mother had a chance to say anything, Ella

blurted the question that had been troubling her for so long. "Did you compel me to feel attracted to you?"

He smirked. "It didn't require much effort. All I had to do was to eliminate your fear of me, and the rest was all you."

Did she believe him? Ella wasn't sure. "What about compelling me to ignore other guys?"

He chuckled. "You have a poor memory, my dear Ella. Remember when I told you that you'd be sorry if you let anyone else touch you?"

Crap, he had said that.

"What did you think I meant by that?"

"I thought it was an empty threat."

"It was a simple compulsion. Every time you tried to get close to another man, you would be assailed by guilt."

Wow, that explained so much.

"I also told you that we were meant for each other, and that no one could give you what I could, making it clear that I meant sexual fulfillment. If you tried to get intimate with someone, male or female, I'm sure that it wasn't very satisfying."

Ella felt tears of relief pooling in the corners of her eyes.

This was huge. If despite Logan's compulsion she'd managed a few moments of strong desire toward Julian, it meant that her attraction to him was so powerful that it had overridden the Doomer's command. It would've been off the charts without it. They were indeed each other's true-love mates, with everything that implied.

Logan reached to wipe her tears away. "I'm sorry. I know that you hate being manipulated like this."

It was the second or third time he'd apologized, but Ella doubted Logan felt any real remorse. He was just being polite.

"But you're guilty of the same, Ella. You were pretending to warm to me, so I wouldn't suspect anything. Before you came up with the college idea, and I realized that you were orchestrating a trap for me, I had to find a way to ensure that you would want to meet me face to face."

It was a poor excuse for what he had done, but she wasn't looking for a real apology from him. However, his misinterpretation of her tears of relief for tears of frustration had given her an opening for the most important request.

"Can you please remove the compulsion? I can't stand having my mind under your control. It's a horrible feeling."

"I'm sorry to disappoint you, my dear Ella." He shook his head.

Ella's heart sank.

"We were not meant for each other," he continued. "Not that you're lacking in any way. Despite the pink, messy hair, you're still a beautiful young girl, and I even find you surprisingly intriguing, but I like my women a little more seasoned." He glanced at Vivian. "And more voluptuous."

"Thanks," her mom said. "You're not my type either. I like my men honest and law-abiding."

Logan laughed. "Touché."

At first, Ella had panicked, thinking that he wasn't going to grant her request, but then she realized that this had been his way of releasing her from that particular compulsion. Except, there were two more parts to it that he'd conveniently forgotten to address.

"What about being sorry if I let anyone touch me, and the other thing about no other man being able to give me what you can?"

"Very good, Ella." He nodded his approval. "It's important to be precise with compulsion. I still don't think anyone can give you what I can, but since I'm not going to seduce you, you are free to fornicate with whomever you please."

"Do you really need to be so rude?" Vivian asked. "What you are putting us through isn't bad enough?"

"My apologies." He bowed his head. "English is not my

native tongue, and sometimes my choice of words could be better."

He was so full of shit. Logan was very eloquent, and if Ella didn't know who he was and where he came from, she would've never suspected he wasn't a native speaker.

"Let me rephrase." He looked her straight in the eyes. "Ella, you are free to feel anything you want toward whomever you choose and enjoy it to your fullest capacity." He turned to Vivian. "Better?"

"Much. Thank you."

Ella wasn't sure. Had he really released her? She'd expected a major change, an unfurling of her metaphysical wings that would lift her up on clouds of desire, soaring toward Julian.

But none of that happened.

She still found Logan devastatingly handsome.

Except, when she imagined kissing him, nothing happened either. There was no tingling of excitement and no butterflies in her stomach. If anything, she felt slight nausea. Then she thought about kissing Julian, and everything inside her ignited as if she'd thrown a match into a puddle of gasoline.

It worked! It freaking worked! She was free!

Except, she wasn't.

As the chopper started its descent, she looked out the window and all of her excitement vanished. They were landing in an airport.

Which meant that their final destination could be as far as the Doomers' island, and there was no way the trackers would work once they reached jet plane altitude.

We are royally screwed.

The irony was that Ella recognized the place. It was the same private airport they'd arrived in.

TURNER

*J*ulian's pacing and seething were getting on Turner's nerves, and if that wasn't enough of a distraction, the waves of anxious energy he and Magnus were emitting definitely was.

"Magnus, can you take Julian out of here? I need to concentrate."

Julian plopped into a chair. "I'm not moving from here until you're ready to go after them."

For the past ten minutes, Turner had been monitoring the four different tracker groupings as they spread out and away from the city in four different directions. He was trying to figure out which of them was the odd one out. They were all moving very fast. Using the freeways, the vehicles were all exceeding the speed limit by at least thirty percent.

At some point, they would have the police stop them, which would slow them down only for as long as it took to thrall the officer and keep going, but in the meantime, they were making sure that those chasing them couldn't close the gap.

The Doomers had at least half an hour head start and were pushing the pedal to the metal.

One grouping was moving slightly faster than the others, though, and he was willing to bet this was the escape vehicle. It was either a fast sports car or maybe even a chopper. His bet was on a helicopter. It seemed to be following the freeway, but that along with the moderate speed was most likely done to make it inconspicuous.

Lokan was a smart and careful bastard, and he wasn't taking any chances.

"It's this one." He pointed at the screen. "And I think I know where it's heading."

As Magnus and Julian got behind him, Turner zoomed out and pointed at the airport they'd arrived at. "That's where he's heading. Which means that he has a plane waiting for him and he's going to take off as soon as they get there."

Julian groaned. "We are never going to make it on time."

"Not necessarily." Turner pulled out his phone. "As I've mentioned before, I have many friends in Washington who owe me favors."

"Cops can't stop a helicopter," Magnus said. "What are you going to do, call the air force base and have them send fighter jets after him?"

Turner shook his head and waited for his friend to pick up.

"Hello?"

"Hi, Fred. It's Turner. I need a favor."

ELLA

*L*ogan's private jet was very similar to the one they'd arrived on. Apparently, Navuh's son didn't enjoy the kind of luxury Gorchenco did. Was there more money in selling weapons than using them?

It seemed so.

Still, Gorchenco's legitimate business was an executive plane service, and he used the fleet's jets for his own needs.

"Are you comfortable?" Logan asked as they were seated with the safety belts on.

As usual, Ella's tongue ran faster than her brain. "What if we are not?"

He smiled. "It doesn't matter. Unless there is an emergency, and I mean the plane is on fire, don't move. If you need to use the bathroom, let my men know and they will call me. Understood?"

The two Doomers guarding them wore twin impassive expressions as they nodded their understanding, even though Logan hadn't been talking to them.

Experimentally, Ella tried to lift her hand, but the compulsion held her immobilized. "It's not comfortable to sit like that. Can you modify your command and just tell us not to get out of our seats?"

"I can do that." He smiled indulgently. "I want you to be as comfortable as possible. Don't get out of your seats. Otherwise, you are allowed to move."

"Thank you. Where are you taking us? Are we going to your homeland?"

Logan liked to talk about his brilliant plans. Maybe if she managed to engage him in a conversation, she could buy them some time.

"No, not right away. For now, I just want to get out of this country and away from your government's reach."

"What if they send fighter jets after you?"

He smirked. "You are so naive, Ella. That's not how governments work. It's not like one big machine with all the cogs working in sync. Each department is its own machine, and they don't cooperate with each other unless they are forced to by the higher-ups, and then it takes a lot of red tape. The organization in charge of paranormal abilities research is highly classified and not rich in resources. They are not going to involve other agencies in the chase."

"How do you know so much?"

"I've been hanging around Washington for a long time. I can tell you so many stories, but it will have to wait for after takeoff. We are in a bit of a rush." He winked and ducked into the cockpit, leaving them in the company of the two somber Doomers.

Ella wondered if he was going to pilot the plane himself.

Probably not.

But who knew? It didn't look like he had limitless resources at his disposal. Not that it mattered one way or another. Hopefully, he wasn't going to take off anytime soon, and the Guardians were going to catch up to them.

Except, her hopes took a nosedive when the dual jet engines roared to life. She tried to remember how long it had taken the clan's jet to warm up its engines, but she hadn't been paying attention. Bhathian had explained something about the pilot going through a pre-flight checklist, but she had no idea how long that took.

Next to her, Vivian sniffled. "You were right. We are so screwed."

Reaching over the armrests, Ella took her mother's hand and gave it a squeeze. "At least we are together."

Now that it seemed like they were not getting rescued, Ella was even more afraid to open a channel to her mother. She would have to be extra careful not to leave even the tiniest opening for Logan to dive inside her head, and she would have to keep doing that indefinitely.

Could she even maintain her reinforced shields for so long?

"Parker is going to be all alone." Tears started flowing down her mother's cheeks. "I was afraid to move forward because I didn't want to leave him. And you. You might think that you're all grown up, but you still need me."

"Of course, I need you. And I always will."

Vivian nodded. "I wish I could be as brave as you."

Fighting her own tears, Ella snorted. "I'm not brave. I'm terrified. I'm just good at fronting confidence I don't have."

Was she ever going to have the wonderful future she'd imagined with Julian? Was she ever going to experience the passion that now flowed freely from her and yearned for him?

Fate couldn't be so cruel, dangling the best life had to offer in front of her nose and then yanking it out of her reach.

"You know what I think?"

Vivian wiped her eyes with her sleeve. "What?"

"I think that Loki is real and that he is the one in charge, playing tricks on us mortals. Do you think I should pray to him? Or maybe I should flip him the finger? What would make him stop toying with us like this?"

That got a sad smile out of her mother. "Praying is a safer bet. But since we don't know who's in charge, let's just address it to whoever is listening."

"Good plan."

Ella glanced at the two Doomers, but they were acting as if they were deaf and mute. If she didn't know better, she would've suspected Logan of compelling their silence as well. But according to Dalhu, he couldn't compel other immortals.

She really hoped Dalhu was right about that. If he wasn't, she and her mother were doomed for sure.

As the plane started moving, Ella squeezed her mother's hand harder and fought to keep her tears from spilling. But as it slowed down and then stopped, it wasn't in preparation for takeoff because the engines didn't rev up. Instead, they revved down, and a moment later Logan stepped out of the cockpit.

"There is a slight delay. A foreign dignitary's jet is about to land, and there has been a terror attack warning. No one is allowed to take off or land until he's out of the airport."

It was Turner's doing. She was sure of that.

How the hell had he pulled off shutting down the entire airport?

Glancing at her mother, Ella saw the same hope she felt reflected in Vivian's eyes.

TURNER

*W*ith Magnus driving like a maniac, Turner had to remind himself that he was an immortal now, and that a car accident was not going to kill him. But it was damn hard to concentrate on making phone calls when the car was taking such sharp turns and tilting this way and that. He was clutching the phone so hard the thing was about to break even though it was clan issue and had been built with immortals in mind.

"Charlie, what do you have for me?"

He had one man at the airport, and that was the pilot. Luckily, Charlie had decided to sleep on the plane. Regrettably, he was not a Guardian, but a civilian pilot.

Except, that was what he had to work with and it was better than nothing.

"I found the Doomer's jet. After the shutdown order your guy issued, they opened the door, and I saw Lokan leave the plane and head inside the terminal. He left Vivian and Ella inside the cabin, guarded by two men. There is also the pilot, who we have to assume is a Doomer as well. Other than that I didn't see anyone else. I think that's all he has with him."

"He has other men driving away from the city with the

trackers he removed from Ella and Vivian. He might have compelled humans to do this for him, but we can't assume that. Stay at a safe distance and let me know the moment anything changes. The team that was following the right tracker should be there any moment. We are about fifteen minutes behind them."

"Got it."

Frank was preparing a hangar for their use, and he was supposed to supply them with airport security uniforms and vehicles. It was a lot to ask on such short notice, but Turner had served with Frank in Special Ops, and he knew that the guy could pull it off.

"How much longer?" Julian asked for the hundredth time.

"Five minutes or less," Magnus bit out.

Turner's phone rang again. This time it was Frank with the same question. "How much longer do you need? I'm going to eat shit for this."

"You're not. If anyone asks, direct them to me. No one wants an international incident because we allowed a foreign dignitary's wife and daughter to get kidnapped. For obvious reasons, the husband wants to keep it quiet, but if we fail to retrieve them, he's going to raise hell."

Fortunately, it wasn't the first time he'd been charged with taking care of a diplomatic mess like that, and his reputation as a private operator who dealt with such situations was well known. The story he'd told Frank was believable enough, and if his friend got in trouble for that, Turner had other friends in high places who could clear this for him.

The downside was that he would be cashing in a lot of owed favors, which meant he would have to work hard to earn more.

"You didn't answer how much longer you need me to keep the place on lockdown," Frank said.

"Give me an hour. But don't do anything until you hear from me."

"Roger that."

"We are turning into the airport right now. Do you have the airport security vehicles I asked for ready?"

"They are waiting for you by the storage hangar. Do you know where that is?"

"I do."

"Use entrance C. The guards are expecting a taxi with a bald guy sitting up front."

"I had a hair transplant."

"No kidding? I need to call them with the update."

"There are three other vehicles following behind me, and later on I expect three more. The drivers all have the code you gave me."

"I know. I was just kidding about the bald head."

"Thanks, Frank."

"Yeah, yeah. You owe me."

"I know."

Disconnecting the call, he pointed. "Turn here and then take a left."

"I can see the signs," Magnus said.

Turner tapped his earpiece. "When you reach the airport, follow the signs to entrance C." He waited for the other drivers to acknowledge the instructions. When they were done, he asked, "What's your ETA?"

ELLA

*L*ogan returned to the plane looking pissed as hell and barking orders at his men. "Airport security is looking for terrorists, and they plan on boarding every aircraft on the field. Try to look more friendly and less menacing."

Confused, the two Doomers looked at him as if he asked them to grow horns. Nevertheless, each nodded in turn and offered a yes sir.

Shaking his head, Logan waved a dismissive hand. "If anyone asks, you are my bodyguards. That will fit your expressions."

He turned to Ella. "You will say that you're my fiancée and use your fake name. I have your passports here. Vivian, you are Victoria MacBain, Kelly's mother. You will tell whoever asks that you are coming with us to meet my family in the Maldives. Understood?"

Ella nodded. "What if they ask where we met?"

It wasn't that she expected anyone to do that. Most likely the terror threat had been fabricated by Turner, and he and the Guardians were impersonating airport security personnel. But now that her mood was up, she felt like messing with Logan.

He smirked. "You can tell them that we met on the beach in San Diego, and that I swept you off your feet. You just couldn't resist my charm and good looks. You agreed to marry me on our third date. I took you with me to Washington because I had business to conduct here, and I invited your mother as a chaperone." He winked. "I'm old-fashioned and come from a traditional family who doesn't believe in premarital sex."

"Good story."

He looked smug as he took his seat across from them. "I know."

An exceptional liar, Logan was good at coming up with plausible stories. The one he invented about his whirlwind courtship would explain why she knew next to nothing about him.

Why had he bothered with it, though? If the airport security people were human, he could just compel them to walk away and say that they'd checked the plane and found nothing suspicious.

Maybe not everyone was susceptible to compulsion?

Just as not all humans could be hypnotized or thralled, some must be immune to compulsion too. Logan couldn't take the risk that he might fail to control one or more of the security people.

Therefore, he had to invent a convincing story and compel those he knew were susceptible to repeat it.

He thought he had it covered.

Ella couldn't wait to see that smug expression of his melt away when he realized who he was dealing with, and how completely wrong he'd been about the people aiding her. He thought he was so smart figuring out that the government had her. It would be one hell of a blow to his ego when he learned his mistake.

Except, that would be the least of his concerns. Logan was about to get taken, and he was never going to be free again.

Crap, as much as she resented him for kidnapping her and her mother, the thought of him losing his freedom and living the rest of his immortal life in captivity bothered her.

It shouldn't have, but it did.

She wondered when exactly he was going to realize what was really going on. Was it going to happen as soon as the Guardians climbed the stairs?

Julian had told her about the tingling alarm all immortal males were equipped with to detect the presence of unfamiliar males of their kind, but she didn't know how close they needed to be to each other for it to activate.

What would Logan do when his alarm went off?

Would he try to slam the plane's door shut and take off?

Or, would he grab her and put a knife at her throat, threatening to kill her if the Guardians didn't back off?

Damn, if she could only move, she could duck for cover as soon as it started, but she was literally a sitting duck. Heck, he could command her to put a knife to her own throat, or to her mother's.

TURNER

"Don't do this to me, Turner. I have to come with you," Julian said while buttoning up the uniform's shirt.

"You need to tuck your hair under the hat. Airport security personnel don't look like hippies."

To say that Julian didn't like getting assigned to backup was an understatement. But he was a civilian, and Turner needed to keep his mate's son safe. Besides, the kid was going to understand why Turner had to go in alone once he explained the plan to everyone.

Including Julian and Magnus, Turner had twenty Guardians with him inside the warehouse, all of them busy getting into the uniforms Fred had kindly provided for them. The others were still chasing after the decoy trackers. Those Doomers had to be captured as well. And if the drivers were compelled humans, they would have to be brought back, and Turner would have no choice but to ask Parker to release them from the compulsion.

Twenty Guardians made up a formidable force, unfortunately though, useless for what he needed them to do.

"There is a good reason for why you're coming in the

second vehicle, and Magnus is going to be there with you. I'm the only one who does not trigger the immortal alarm, and that's why I have to get inside that plane by myself. I can't even have the humans accompany me because they are too vulnerable to both thralling and compulsion. They are going to stay in the Jeep."

Julian shook his head. "You can't take on three Doomers all by yourself and at the same time ensure that Ella and Vivian don't get hurt. Worse, he can use them as hostages and take off."

"Don't worry. I have it covered."

Turner hated going in with a half-assed plan that he'd hatched on the way, but it was the best he could do.

Turning around, he clapped his hands. "Okay, people, gather around."

When he had their attention, he signaled for Arwel to cast a shroud around the group. Per his request, Frank had ordered all the employees out of the warehouse, but Turner preferred to play it safe.

"Here is how we are going to do this. We have five vehicles. I'm taking the bulletproof one, and the rest of you will have to squeeze into the remaining four."

He pulled out his iPad and showed them an aerial picture of the airport with all the grounded planes waiting for takeoff.

"This is Lokan's plane." He pointed. "And those are ours." He pointed at the two clan jets. "We don't start with him. We start with those closest to the terminal. You go in, ask the pilot, crew, and passengers to come down two at the time, check their passports, pretend to double check with headquarters, and then let them back up and ask for the next two to come down. That's what Lokan is going to observe and that's what he's going to expect."

He glanced at Julian before continuing. "When I go up, I'll

ask the pilot and Lokan to come down first, check their papers and then let them back up."

"He's going to try to compel you," Magnus said.

"I was immune as a human, and there are more like me out there. He would assume I'm one of the anomalies."

"I hope he doesn't do something stupid once he realizes that you are immune."

"He's not. After I'm done with him and the pilot, I'm going to do the same with the two Doomers, and lastly with Ella and Vivian."

Understanding dawning, Julian nodded in agreement. "He will not be alarmed because he is going to expect them to get the same treatment."

"Precisely. Except, I'm going to pretend there is a problem with their papers and ask them to come with me."

"He's not going to allow it," Magnus said.

"Not much he can do other than attacking me, but it's not going to get to that point. By the time Ella and Vivian are inside the bulletproof vehicle with the doors closed, the rest of you will have enough time to sneak into position. I'm going to go back up to explain the situation with the papers and reassure them that it's only a formality. That will solve two problems. He and his men will have no time to pull out weapons, and since I'm going to stand in the doorway, I will block the view. When their immortal alarm goes off, it's going to be too late for them to do anything but surrender."

"That's not true," Julian said. "They could kill you before anyone else makes it up there."

Smirking, Turner pulled out the gun from its holster. "I'm armed, and they are not. That gives me all the advantage I need."

54

JULIAN

*a*s Julian watched Turner climb up the stairs to the Doomers' plane, Magnus shook his head. "I don't like him going in alone. He is not a trained Guardian. But it's not as if we have any other choice."

"I trust Turner. He's the best man for the job." Julian meant every word.

Not only that, he was infinitely thankful for Turner and the huge ego that was allowing him to take on Navuh's son with his typical fearlessness and nerves of steel. No one could've pulled off this job better than Turner. Lokan wasn't going to suspect a damn thing because Turner didn't emit any scents that would've given anyone else away.

The Doomer might wonder about the strange guy he was going to mistake for a human, but he would probably assume that he was dealing with a sociopath.

They were all wearing earpieces, but, unfortunately, not the sophisticated ones that William had equipped them with. Impersonating airport security meant using their equipment, and they had those clunky old things that were at least a decade-old technology.

Still, the earpiece was functioning just fine, and they could hear Turner talking to the Doomer.

"Good afternoon, ladies and gentlemen. I apologize for the delay, but a terror threat has been made, and we take those very seriously, even though this one is probably a hoax. Are you the owner of this plane, sir?"

"Yes."

"I need you and the pilot to come down with me. And bring your passports with you. If you are not American citizens, please bring your visas as well. The rest of you please remain seated until I come back for you."

"I'm sure it is not necessary. Our papers are all in order."

That was no doubt Lokan's attempt at compelling Turner to leave.

"I'm sure they are. But I have my orders, sir. This is the standard procedure in case of a terrorist threat. Please follow me down so I can run your documents through the scanner and verify your identity."

After watching them perform the same procedure with the other planes, Lokan didn't press the issue and did as Turner asked.

Turner made a big deal out of examining the paperwork, went inside the vehicle and checked things on the attached laptop, then came out and handed the documents back.

"Everything seems fine. Thank you for your cooperation, gentlemen."

He escorted them up, and then came down with the two Doomers, repeating the same procedure.

Hopefully, Ella and Vivian were playing it cool and not doing anything to give him away. Julian trusted Ella's acting ability, but he wasn't sure about Vivian.

Waiting for the two of them to come down was nerve-wracking.

Like the pro that he was, Turner didn't act hurried, taking

his time with the two Doomers as if there was no urgency, his expression as stoic as usual and his tone bored and even. An Oscar-worthy performance.

"Balls of titanium," Magnus murmured.

As soon as he escorted the two back up, the four airport security vehicles started moving toward Lokan's jet.

"Ladies, please follow me down," Turner said.

Apparently, nothing happened because he said, "Is there a problem?"

"No, not a problem," Lokan said. "My fiancée is just a little timid. It's okay, darling. You can go with the officer. He's only going to check your papers. You too, Mom."

Magnus cursed under his breath, probably because of the mom address, but Julian let out a relieved breath. Lokan had just removed his compulsion, allowing Ella and Vivian to move.

Once on the ground, Turner repeated the same act, taking the paperwork into the Jeep and pretending to check it on his laptop. A moment later he came out.

"I'm afraid there was a problem with your papers. You need to come with me." He opened the Jeep's back door and helped Vivian in and then Ella.

Lokan appeared at the top of the stairs. "What seems to be the problem, officer?"

"Their passports don't check out. I'm sure it's just a technicality. Please step inside the plane, sir."

Ignoring Turner's order, Lokan started down.

Several things happened at once.

The Jeep sped away leaving Turner to face the Doomer alone, Turner whipped out his gun and pointed it at Lokan's head, the laser beam point blank between his eyes, and all four vehicles screeched to a stop with Guardians piling out.

"Game over, Lokan. You don't want me to splatter your brains all over your nice jet. I have perfect aim."

The Doomer leaped back.

His reflexes were fast, but not faster than a bullet. Turner nailed him in the leg, and then immediately shot the other, sending Lokan toppling down the stairs.

55

ELLA

*T*urner was putting on the act of a lifetime. Lucky for Ella and Vivian their nervousness could be attributed to other causes. Like the compulsion not to say anything about being taken against their will or disclose any information that could be harmful to Lokan in any way.

If asked about him, Ella had been instructed to say that he was a wonderful fiancé and that she was madly in love with him.

"Ladies, please follow me down." Turner motioned for them to get up.

Except, Lokan had forgotten to remove the compulsion not to move from their seats.

Turner arched a brow. "Is there a problem?"

"No, not a problem," Lokan said. "My fiancée is just a little timid. It's okay, darling. You can go with the officer. He's only going to check your papers. You too, Mom."

If looks could kill, Lokan would be dead now.

Ella's legs shook as she followed Turner down, and she felt faint as she stood by the Jeep and waited for the pretend inspection of their passports, which Lokan had handed to him.

She'd thought that the Doomer who'd taken their stuff had been driving around town with the duffel bag and leading the Guardians on a fake trail, but apparently, he'd pulled out their passports and driver licenses first and had given them to one of Lokan's bodyguards.

"I'm afraid there was a problem with your papers. You need to come with me." Turner opened the Jeep's back door and taking her mother's elbow, helped her to get inside. Ella was next.

Exchanging glances with her mother, she gave her a discreet thumbs up.

They were free.

"What seems to be the problem, officer?" Lokan asked and started getting out.

Turner shut the door behind them and blocked Ella's view of Lokan with his back. "Their passports don't check out. I'm sure it's just a technicality. Please step inside the plane, sir."

She didn't hear the answer, because the jeep's driver peeled out and sped away.

He and the other officer sitting in the back weren't Guardians. She had a feeling that they were ordinary humans. "Where are you taking us?"

"To the warehouse. Turner said to keep you there until he comes for you."

The guy sitting next to them in the back smiled reassuringly. "Everything is going to be okay, ma'am. The scumbag who was trying to kidnap you is going to be apprehended, and after you give a statement, you'll be safely returned to your father." He looked at Vivian. "Your husband must be anxious to hear from you. Would you like to call him?" He handed her his cellphone.

What kind of a story had Turner told the human authorities?

Vivian gave the phone back. "Maybe in a little while, after my heart stops racing. I'm too shaken up to talk."

"Naturally. What did the scum do to you?" He looked at Vivian and then at Ella.

Ella shook her head. "I'd rather not talk about it." All that would come out of her mouth would be that Lokan was a wonderful fiancé and that she was madly in love with him.

The guy looked disappointed, but he nodded. "I understand."

Once they reached the warehouse, the officers escorted them inside and stayed to watch over them.

Regular conversation was not possible, but with Lokan neutralized, Ella could open a channel to her mother.

I hope everyone is okay.

Her mother patted her knee. *I'm sure they are. Thirty Guardians, one Turner, and one Julian can handle three Doomers no matter how powerful.*

Stupidly, Ella hoped they didn't hurt Lokan too badly either. He wasn't a good guy, but he wasn't as bad as she initially believed him to be.

She'd seen real evil, and it had been all human. Romeo, Stefano, the two druggies in the hotel that Julian was turning into a halfway house, and all of those men who'd violated and abused the girls in the sanctuary. Those people had no redeeming qualities, or rather nothing that could redeem the evil they'd perpetrated.

Gorchenco and Lokan were different than that scum. They weren't good people, but they both had redeeming qualities. Or at least she believed they had.

Less than fifteen minutes later, Turner entered the warehouse alone.

"Thank you for your help, gentleman," he addressed the officers. "My associate is waiting for you outside for debriefing."

Which probably meant thralling. After their talk with the

associate, they were not going to remember any details from the rescue operation.

"Glad to be of assistance. Is the airport cleared for take-offs and landings?"

"Yes, it is."

When the men left, Turner lifted his hand to stop Ella and Vivian's barrage of questions. "No one got hurt, except for Lokan and his men, but nothing fatal. Their injuries are going to heal in no time."

"Thank God. Or rather, thank Turner." Ella ran up to him and wrapped her arms around his neck. "Thank you." She kissed his cheek. "Thank you so much. You were amazing. You should get an Oscar for that performance, and I mean it. Totally believable."

"Let the man be." Her mother tapped her shoulder. "You're smothering him."

"Sorry." Ella let go, realizing too late that Turner had been like a stiff broom in her arms, waiting for her assault to be over.

She needed to remember that her future father-in-law was not a hugger.

56

JULIAN

*J*ulian couldn't wait to hold Ella in his arms, but there was a lot of cleanup work to do.

His job was to patch up Lokan and the other two Doomers, while the Guardians conducted *interviews* with everyone on the field, erasing memories and planting a story that Turner had prepared.

Reluctantly, Julian headed toward the bigger of the two clan's jets, where the injured Doomers had been stowed.

There was only one Guardian with them, but it seemed the three were neutralized.

"I already knocked them out with sedative shots," Liam said.

"If he were awake I would have knocked him out with a punch to his smug face." Even injured and knocked out, that expression was still there. "I'm going to wash my hands."

After scrubbing up the best he could in the small bathroom, Julian wiped his hands with a paper towel because that was all there was.

Immortal bodies would not get infected, but washing before touching a wound was so ingrained in him that he hadn't stopped to think that he didn't need to scrub so hard.

When he came out, he looked for the med kit, finding it in one of the overhead compartments. "Did he ask any questions before you put him to sleep?"

"I knocked him out before he regained consciousness after hitting his head falling down the jet's stairs."

"That's a shame." Julian opened the kit and pulled out a pair of scissors. "I would've paid to see the expression on his face." He started cutting the pants off to expose the wound.

Seeing the defeat in the Doomer's eyes would have been so satisfying.

He wasn't a vindictive kind of guy, but that scumbag had almost gotten away with stealing Ella, the most important person in Julian's life, and that was unforgivable.

After tearing the rest of that pant leg off, Julian went to work on the other one.

The wounds weren't serious. Apparently, in addition to all his other talents, Turner was also an excellent sharpshooter. Somehow he managed not to hit any major artery or shatter a bone. Was it a fluke? Or had he been careful not to damage the important Doomer?

They needed to interrogate the son of a bitch, but that didn't mean that he had to be delivered in pristine condition. The types of injuries he'd sustained were going to heal by the time they returned to Los Angeles.

"Was he disbelieving, raging, anything?"

Liam shook his head. "Sorry to disappoint you, mate, but the dude was as cool as a cucumber. The only emotions I picked up from him were sadness and resignation. He probably expects us to kill him or torture him."

"The second one is going to happen for sure. Kian wants to get information out of him, and he's not going to volunteer it."

"Who knows?" Liam shrugged. "I wouldn't be surprised if he has daddy issues. Can you imagine being Navuh's son?"

"Could be worse. The bastard is not a loving father, that's

246

for sure, but he puts his sons in positions of power. That's a better fate than that of the other Doomers."

After digging out the first bullet, Julian sutured the wound closed and bandaged the leg.

"We don't know that. Sometimes it's better to be an invisible speck than a diamond under the microscope of evil."

Shaking his head, Julian started on the other leg. "Where did you hear that saying?"

"I made it up."

Ignoring his hatred for the Doomer and treating him as he would any other patient, Julian did a good job. That was what decent doctors did. He could always beat Lokan up later when they got home.

The guy wasn't going anywhere.

Once Julian was done with the other two Doomers as well, he went to the bathroom and washed his hands again.

"I'm heading out. Are you okay here by yourself with the three of them?"

Liam smiled and lifted a case full of syringes. "No one wakes up without me allowing it."

"I'll see you back in the village."

"Say hello to Ella and Vivian for me and tell them welcome back."

"I will."

Now that he was done with his duties, Julian was going to take Ella into his arms and never let her go.

Turner had said that he was going to keep her and Vivian in the warehouse until the cleanup was done. That was about a mile and a half away, and the vehicles had been returned already, which meant that Julian was going on a run.

57

ELLA

*W*hen Turner left Ella and Vivian alone in the warehouse, it was somewhat anticlimactic, especially after the movie Ella had created in her mind.

In that scene, Julian was running up to her in slow motion like the hero of a romantic movie, sweeping her into his arms and swinging her around.

In real life, she was sitting on a dusty crate beside her mother, both of them waiting for their men to be done.

Julian had been tasked with tending to the wounded Doomers, while Magnus and other Guardians were busy thralling memories out of the minds of humans.

Still, it was so much better than the alternative.

"What do you think they are going to do with Lokan's jet?" Vivian asked. "They can't just leave it like that. Someone has to take it away."

"I don't know, but I'm sure Turner has a plan. He thinks of everything."

"I wonder what Navuh will think? Is he going to worry about his son? Does he care about him?"

"What I wonder about is whether Turner is going to make it look like Lokan had deserted."

Vivian chuckled. "I'm glad that it's no longer our concern. We did our parts and are now free to live our lives. The only thorn in that beautiful future is Gorchenco."

It wasn't the only one. Her mother still had to transition without incident, and so did Ella.

As she thought about Julian ushering her on that journey, a flutter of excitement started in her belly. There was no more reason for waiting. No more worrying about Lokan, and no more compulsion preventing her desire for Julian from manifesting in its full intensity. Ella wanted him with every fiber of her body and soul.

Was he in for a big surprise.

As the warehouse doors screeched and started to open, the butterflies in Ella's stomach took flight, their wings flapping in a mad frenzy. And when Julian entered and started running toward her, Ella jumped off the crate and ran into his waiting arms.

It was just as she'd imagined.

With a face-splitting grin, his arms closed around her, and he swung her up and around.

"Ella," he whispered her name like a prayer. "My sweet, beautiful Ella."

Despite her mother watching, Ella tightened her arms around Julian's neck and pulled his head down for a kiss.

He groaned as she licked inside his mouth, finding his tongue and caressing it with hers. In no time, she felt his fangs grow longer, and knowing what it did to him, she licked around one and then the other.

They were so absorbed in the kiss that they didn't notice Magnus come in until he cleared his throat. "I hate to interrupt the reunion, but we need to return the uniforms and clear the premises."

As he spoke, more Guardians entered the warehouse, all wearing airport security uniforms.

"Later," Julian whispered in her ear as he put her down.

"You bet," she whispered back.

Climbing to stand on the crate, Vivian clapped her hands to get everyone's attention. "Thank you all for coming to our rescue, and I think Turner deserves a big round of applause for orchestrating yet another flawless mission."

Without hesitation, everyone clapped, making Turner visibly uncomfortable. His expression didn't change much, the only thing giving him away was a slight thinning of his lips.

"That's not necessary, people. I was just doing my job. But thank you. Go change out of the uniforms so we can all get out of here."

"Shouldn't we give them some privacy?" Vivian asked.

Magnus kissed her cheek. "It doesn't bother them, love. But if you're uncomfortable, I can take you to the plane."

Her mother grimaced. "I don't want to be alone with the Doomers."

Magnus tightened his arm around her and kissed the top of her head. "You won't be. They were taken to the big jet, and you're going in the small one. Besides, they are all sedated."

Julian growled. "Tell me what they did to you."

Crap. He'd interpreted her mother's grimace to mean that they'd been mistreated.

"Nothing. Logan is a wonderful fiancé and I'm madly in love with him." Ella slapped a hand over her mouth and shook her head.

Julian's eyes were blazing as he asked, "Did he compel you to say that?"

She nodded.

He turned to Magnus. "We need to call Parker."

Magnus looked at Vivian. "Did Lokan compel you too?"

"Yes. What Ella said is the only thing I can say about him."

Pulling out his phone, Magnus made the call. "Parker. Your mother and sister are safe, but we need your help to override the Doomer's compulsion again. He ordered Ella and Vivian to say only nice things about him. I'm putting you on speakerphone."

Ella shook her head. "I don't think hearing his voice alone will work, but let's give it a try."

Over the speaker, Parker commanded, "Ella, say something nasty about Lokan."

"Lokan is a wonderful…crap. It didn't work."

Turner handed Magnus his tablet. "Try putting him on a video chat."

"Give me a moment," Parker said. "I'm going to my computer. You'll be able to see me better."

When he was ready, Magnus handed Ella the tablet. "Good luck."

On the screen, Parker smirked at her. "I told you that you should've taken me. I bet you're sorry now."

"Terribly. Get on with it, Parker. I hate having no control over my mouth."

"You never do."

"Parker!"

"Fine. Ella, tell me something nasty about Lokan."

"He's a liar." Ella jumped up and down. "It worked! Parker, you are a lifesaver. I love you. I'm going to give the tablet to Mom now. You need to tell her to do the same thing."

When Parker was done with Vivian, she had a few more choice words to say about the Doomer.

Taking Ella's hand, Julian turned her toward him. "I'm surprised that all you have to say about him is that he's a liar."

"A liar, a manipulator, a kidnapper, and probably many other things. But other than compelling us to say nice things about him and not to talk or to move, he treated us with respect." She looked at Vivian. "Right, Mom?"

Her mother waved a dismissive hand. "He was manipulating us, that's all. It was all fake. I'm sure all of his lofty promises were lies."

"What did he promise you?" Julian asked.

"Later." Turner clapped his back. "We will go through a full debriefing on the plane home. Right now I want you to change out of the uniform and then escort Ella to the smaller jet." He looked at Magnus. "You too."

"What about our things?" Ella asked. "We have stuff in the hotel."

"Kri is on her way with your things. She packed up for everyone who's going home today."

"That's good. I would like to change out of this freaking bikini."

Julian frowned. "What bikini?"

"I'll tell you on the plane."

JULIAN

"There goes our romantic weekend in Washington," Ella said as they entered the smaller of the two clan jets.

"I'm just thankful that everything ended well and that none of ours got hurt." Julian motioned for Ella to take the window seat and then sat next to her. "So far."

She frowned. "What do you mean, so far? Isn't it all over?"

"Did you forget about the Doomers with the trackers? The idiots are still driving away like maniacs. We have Guardians chasing them."

"How many were there?"

"Three cars are being followed. We don't know how many Doomers are in each."

"Don't worry about it," Magnus said as he helped Vivian into a seat. "That's child's play compared to what we pulled off here. We all owe Turner big time. If not for his friend grounding Lokan's plane, we would have never made it on time."

Following Magnus's statement, there was a long moment of silence, as each of them imagined the ramifications.

"I vote for throwing him a party," Ella said. "What does he like to eat?"

Julian scratched his head. "I will have to ask my mother. Which reminds me."

He pulled out his phone and texted Turner. *A friendly reminder. If you didn't do so already, please call Bridget asap. She's mad that you didn't yet.*

"Is he coming home with us?" Ella asked.

"He's waiting for the other Doomers to get captured and delivered to the larger jet. He will fly home with them."

"I see." She turned to the window.

Reaching for her hand, he clasped it between his. "Talk to me."

"I can't." She slanted her eyes toward Magnus. "When we get back home, there are a lot of things I need to tell you."

Julian tensed. "Good or bad?"

Her smile was sly. "Very good." She waggled her eyebrows.

And if that was not enough to grab his shaft's attention, her feminine scent suddenly intensified, causing it to punch out against his zipper in an instant.

"Whose home are we going back to?"

Ella cast a quick glance at Vivian, who smiled and nodded.

"Yours. I'm moving in with you. If you don't mind, that is."

"Mind? Are you nuts? I love you. I never want to be apart from you again."

He pulled out his phone, hesitated, leaned to kiss her cheek, then went back to the phone. "I'm texting Ray. He needs to find someone else to share a house with."

"He can move in with my former roommates," Magnus said. "They still didn't find anyone to take my place."

"I'll suggest it."

He tried to phrase the text to Ray as politely as possible,

254

but it was still offensive. There was no nice way to boot someone out of his house within a five-hour notice.

I'm coming back with Ella, and she is moving in with me. I would very much appreciate it if you could find another place to stay before we arrive. Magnus suggests that you check with his former roommates.

A few minutes passed before Ray replied.

Congratulations. I'll find someplace to crash tonight, but I'll have to come back for my things tomorrow. Also, you'll need to help me move the piano.

Julian didn't want Ray to come back the next day. He wanted Ella all to himself.

How about you pack up your stuff and leave it by the front door. Once you find a place, I'll bring your things over, including the piano.

This time Ray responded right away. *I appreciate the free of charge moving service, but you have to be extra careful with my baby. She's irreplaceable.*

Julian smiled. *I'll wear white gloves and treat her as if she's made from eggshells.*

You'd better. One scratch on her and I'll make you pay.

The guy was such an asshole, but so was Julian for throwing him out. *I promise there will be no new scratches on her*. Before moving the fucking grand piano, he was going to take pictures from all angles and document all the existing scratches.

Pocketing the phone, he smiled at Ella. "All done."

"When is he moving out?"

"Before we get back."

Her eyes widened. "You told him to just pack up and leave tonight? That's terrible."

"Don't worry about him. Once he finds a permanent place, he's getting a free moving service from me, and that includes his piano."

"It's still rude. But I have an idea how you can make it up to him."

Julian arched a brow. He didn't owe Ray a thing, and if the situation were reversed, Ray would have had no qualms about booting Julian out.

"He invited my mother and me to a concert he's giving. How about you come with us? It will mean a lot to Ray."

"Of course, I'll come." Not as a gesture of goodwill toward his ex-roommate, but to make sure that the guy didn't flirt with Ella, which was most likely the reason he'd given her the invitations in the first place.

Ella smiled happily. "We can all go together. Magnus? Will you come too?"

"Sure. I like classical music."

Footsteps on the stairs announced someone coming up, and a moment later Kri appeared at the door with duffel bags slung over each shoulder and a suitcase in each hand. "Hello, everyone."

Magnus jumped up to take the luggage from her. "Why didn't you give me a shout? I could've carried all of this up."

She waved a dismissive hand. "I told you to stop treating me like a girl. I'm a Guardian, and a goddamned good one even if I'm relegated to the least exciting jobs. Like packing stuff." She grinned at Ella and then Vivian. "You can't imagine how glad I am to see you two. I had a few moments of panic there, and I didn't like it at all."

"Thank you for bringing our things," Ella said. "Are you coming with us?"

"I'm going on the other plane." She winked. "It's much more interesting over there. See you back at the village, people." She saluted them and turned around.

Magnus closed the door behind her and then knocked on the pilot's door. "Morris, we are ready to go."

They all buckled up, but it took another ten minutes or so until the plane started moving.

Ella looked up at the overhead compartment. "If I remember right, there is a blanket and a pillow up there."

"I'll get it for you." Julian released the buckle and got up. "Anyone else want a blanket?"

"Is there another one?" Vivian asked.

"There are plenty."

"Then sure." She cuddled closer to Magnus. "There is nothing I like better than snuggling with my guy."

"Same here," Ella murmured.

Magnus opened the fridge compartment and pulled out four bottles of Snake's Venom. "Champagne would have been better, but since this is the only alcohol here, we will have to make a toast with beer." He popped the caps off the bottles and handed them out.

"To mission accomplished and a long and happy future for us all." Magnus raised his bottle, clinked it with the other three, and then took a long swig.

"Amen," Vivian said and took a small sip. "God, this stuff is potent."

"Julian? Do you want to make a toast?" Ella asked.

He raised his bottle and clinked it with hers. "To us."

"To us," she repeated.

VIVIAN

"I'm going to carry Ella home," Julian whispered as the limo stopped at the village's underground parking.

Vivian looked at her daughter's peaceful sleeping face and smiled. Ella hadn't looked so relaxed since before her ordeal.

She'd fallen asleep on the plane, then had woken up when they'd landed, and fallen asleep again in the car. Julian had been holding her the entire time as if afraid to let go of her even for a moment.

Love was in the air, and it smelled fantastic.

Vivian patted his bicep and whispered, "When you wake up tomorrow, come by our house. We can have a late breakfast or early lunch together."

"Will do." Julian maneuvered himself and his precious cargo out of the car. "Good night."

"You too."

The chances of them actually showing up for breakfast or lunch were slim. Maybe they would come for dinner.

Listening to the conversation between Lokan and Ella during the helicopter ride had explained so much.

Ella's attraction to Julian had been suppressed by Lokan's compulsion, which had caused her to doubt their relationship.

Fated mates were supposed to crave each other with overwhelming intensity, and Vivian could attest to the veracity of that claim.

Her craving for Magnus had been so intense and so immediate that it had overpowered her feeling of anxiety and despair. In the midst of a crisis, with her daughter taken by traffickers and sold to a Russian mobster, she couldn't keep her hands off him.

It was still just as powerful, and tonight, for the first time since the very beginning of their relationship, she was going to enjoy him without any barriers between them.

It was going to be epic.

Magnus slung his duffle bag over his shoulder and reached for Vivian's suitcase which Okidu was holding on to. "Thank you for getting us home, Okidu."

The butler bowed. "It was my pleasure, master. But my service is not done. I will carry the luggage to your home."

"That won't be necessary." Magnus took the suitcase from his hand. "Good night, Okidu."

Looking offended, the butler bowed again. "Good night, master." He bowed to Vivian. "Good night, madam."

She still found it hard to believe that Okidu was a sophisticated robot. Maybe that's what he had been originally, but in her opinion, he had everyone fooled. At some point he had become a sentient being. After all, he was supposed to be ancient, like in tens of thousands of years old. The amount of information he'd accumulated over the years should have been enough to facilitate self-awareness.

But she wasn't a scientist, and her information came mainly from watching and reading science fiction. If the butler was sentient, William would have known that.

Outside the pavilion, they parted ways with Okidu, and Magnus transferred her suitcase to his other hand. "What's that sly smile about?" He wrapped his arm around her shoulders.

"You know what is happening tonight, right?"

He smirked. "I've been entertaining a few ideas. If you're not tired, that is. You didn't sleep on the plane."

"I wonder why?"

As soon as Ella and Julian had fallen asleep in each other's arms, Magnus and Vivian had started kissing and hadn't stopped until the young couple woke up.

"No regrets here."

"Nor here, and I'm not tired. Well, not too tired. But other than that, what else is happening tonight?"

"A foot massage?"

"Hmm, why not. I would love one. But aside from that too."

He shook his head. "Just tell me, or I'll keep guessing all the way home."

Should she?

Now she was considering surprising him. But was it too late to back off?

"I think I'll wait until we get home to tell you."

"Why is that?"

She looked at the heavy suitcase he was schlepping. "You might drop the luggage on your foot, and then I'll feel guilty for causing you injury."

"Easily solved." He stopped walking, put the suitcase down, and the duffel bag on top of it.

"Come here." He pulled her into his arms. "Now tell me what you're planning, or I'll have to kiss it out of you."

"That's not a threat, silly. But fine." She stretched on her toes and whispered in his ear. "Tonight, we are throwing away the condoms."

Magnus lifted his face to the sky. "Thank the merciful Fates."

Cupping his cheeks, she brought his face down and kissed his lips. "Let's go home, my love."

E L L A

*S*nuggled against Julian's chest, Ella was warm and cozy despite how chilly the village got at night. "What about our luggage?" she murmured into his neck.

"I got it."

Her eyes popped open. "You are carrying me and the luggage? Put me down!"

He nuzzled her cheek. "We are almost there. Besides, how else am I going to prove that I'm a worthy mate for you? Strong and capable?"

"I can think of a much more pleasant way you can prove it to me."

He looked puzzled. "Are you uncomfortable? Am I squeezing you too hard?"

She laughed. "No, silly. I'm very comfortable. I was just thinking how nice and warm I am in your arms, despite how cold it is here at night."

He climbed the stairs to the front porch and dropped her suitcase to open the door. "Is there something I'm supposed to say as I carry you over the threshold?"

"Welcome home?"

"That works. Welcome home, my love." He entered the

dark house and continued straight to the bedroom. "Do you want to grab a shower? Or do you want to go straight to bed?"

"Shower first."

"I'll bring in the luggage."

Should she suggest that they shower together?

Until now they'd only kissed, except for that one time that Julian had gotten carried away, but that had been so brief, and she'd reacted so badly to it, that it didn't count.

Ella didn't know how to initiate, or how to tell him that she was ready. Heck, should she just tell him about the compulsion and be done with it?

Let him figure the rest out?

In any case, it was better that she shower alone. It would give her time to come up with a plan. Their first time together should be special. She didn't want to half-ass it.

Sexy lingerie would have been helpful, but she had none. The closest thing was the string bikini Lokan had forced her to put on, but nothing of his was going to taint her time with Julian.

As he returned with her suitcase, Julian laid it on top of the dresser. "I'll shower in Ray's room and then make us coffee. You said that there are things you need to tell me when we get home."

"Yeah." She'd forgotten about her promise.

So that's how this was going to happen.

She was going to tell Julian about the compulsion and its removal. Then she was going to tell him that the moment it had been lifted, her desire for him ignited like an inferno.

Or, she could hurry up with the shower, be done with it before he was back, and wait for him naked in bed.

That should do it.

Because frankly, she didn't want to talk. What she wanted was to join with the man she loved and become one in every possible way.

Which included a venom bite.

God, she didn't know if she craved it or feared it. A little bit of both, probably. Oh, heck, she was such a liar. She definitely craved it, and the little fear that came with it only added to the excitement.

So, she was a little weird that way. Or maybe not. Maybe it was natural for a Dormant to crave her immortal lover's bite.

Yeah, that totally made sense. Survival of the species and all that.

As she stepped under the spray, Ella chuckled to herself. She was nervous, which usually made her ramble on and on, and now she was doing it inside her own head.

Except, what reason did she have to be anxious?

She and Julian were in love, and they wanted each other passionately. These were just wedding-night type jitters.

She'd never had voluntary sex before.

Was she going to be any good at it?

Lockstep with her desire was fear, entwined together with performance anxiety. A combustible mixture, that was for sure.

JULIAN

*J*ulian moved with immortal speed as he set up the coffeemaker and then rushed into the shower. The plan was to be done before Ella finished her shower and wait for her in bed.

Something had changed after her second rescue. Ella seemed different. Perhaps the prospect of never seeing him again had been so traumatic that it had burned away the last vestiges of her previous ordeal?

Given her subtle clues and the not so subtle scent of her desire, he had a feeling she was ready to be his, but as he had promised, she was in the driver seat and he wasn't going to assume anything.

She'd had this done to her enough times.

The first time they made love, it would be entirely by her choice and without any pressure or even coaxing from him.

That didn't mean, though, that he couldn't tempt her, and waiting for her in bed with his naked torso on display was fair play. In case he'd misinterpreted, the boxer shorts had to stay on. Besides, he didn't want to appear presumptuous.

Ella might interpret it as him pressuring her into sex before she was absolutely sure she was ready.

Still slightly damp from his quick shower, Julian poured them both coffee and sped to the bedroom. The water was still running in the bathroom, so he had a few moments to prepare.

After putting down the mugs on the nightstands, he went into the closet and pulled on a pair of boxer shorts, then opened a new bottle of cologne and sprayed himself with it.

Hopping in bed, he sat propped against a pile of pillows, pulled the comforter over his lower half, and reached for the coffee mug. When Ella got out of the bathroom, she was going to find him sipping coffee in bed, looking as nonchalant as could be. Lucky for him, she wasn't an immortal, so she wouldn't smell the scent of his excitement and arousal.

Except, his pretend nonchalance was blown away as soon as Ella stepped out of the bathroom with nothing but a towel wrapped around her delectable body.

His fangs didn't elongate gradually, they just punched out over his lower lip.

Holding the towel clutched in her fist, she looked at him with hooded eyes, the scent of her arousal perfuming the air.

"Hi," she whispered.

"Hi to you too, gorgeous."

But even though his words came out sounding like a cross between a hiss and a growl, Ella didn't seem frightened. Just shy and hesitant.

Perhaps she needed a little encouragement?

"I wish I had X-ray vision. I can't wait to see your stunning body."

She chuckled. "You don't? With that glow, I was sure you could see right through this towel. But since you can't…" She let it drop.

"Dear sweet Fates." He hissed in a breath. "Gorgeous."

Her breasts were perfectly shaped, round and yet upturned, with small rosy nipples that were hardening right before his eyes. Her narrow waist flared into generous hips, not too large, just rounded and feminine, and her legs were long and shapely.

She was perfection, all creamy paleness and feminine softness, rendering him thunderstruck.

Blushing, she lifted her arms, but instead of shyly covering her breasts like he'd expected, she spread her palms over her belly. "I could lose a few pounds."

That was it, he couldn't stay in bed a second longer. Leaping out, Julian was in front of her before she had a chance to suck in a breath.

"You are perfect." He peeled her hands away from her beautiful belly. "I love it that you're soft all over."

She lifted her face to him and smiled. "I'm not perfect, but you are. You would make any mortal insecure with that six pack of yours and everything else." She waved a hand over his mostly bare body.

"To me, you are a goddess. Always and forever." He wrapped his arms around her and lifted her to him. "Can I take you to bed?"

Ella lifted her hands and threaded her finger into his hair. "Yes."

E L L A

*J*ulian's voice must have dropped a full octave, making him sound different. If Ella hadn't known him as well as she did, that would have been enough to scare her, let alone the inch and a half long fangs and glowing eyes.

Except, she'd had plenty of time to mentally prepare for this. At first the idea of getting bitten had seemed so foreign and frightening, but after spending weeks with immortals she was more intrigued than scared. Besides, this was Julian, the man she loved and trusted with her very life. Which meant that before they took this major step, he should be aware of all the facts.

As he laid her on the bed, she took his hand and kissed it. "I have to tell you something."

"What is it?"

While in the shower, she'd prepared what she wanted to say to him and how, but for fear of spoiling the mood, she'd planned on doing it after and not before they made love. Except, it didn't feel right to hold off. Julian deserved to know that he'd been right about them being fated for each other from the very start.

"Lokan admitted to compelling my attraction to him and to blocking me from feeling it for anyone else. He also made me feel guilty whenever I was getting close to you. I interpreted that feeling of guilt as not being worthy of you, and of having darkness in me, but it was all artificial. Once he removed the compulsion, it was like a smothering blanket was lifted off me, and I felt an intense desire for you. I knew then that I was not only ready but eager to make love, and that we were fated for each other. My desire for you has been muted by his compulsion, but even as strong as his hold over me was, he couldn't kill it completely because my need for you managed to overpower it."

Throughout her monologue, Julian gazed at her, his glowing eyes not straying for a moment from hers. "I'm going to kill him," he said when she was done.

He'd get over it. Once they made love, Julian would find it in his heart to forgive Lokan. Especially since he couldn't kill him even if he really meant it.

Reaching for him, she smiled. "You'll have to wait for Kian and Turner to be done with him first. Now I want you to make love to me, and I don't want you to hold anything back. I want to experience the real Julian, not a watered down version of you."

A sly smirk lifted one corner of his mouth, which looked really funny because of his fangs. "Are you sure? I can get pretty intense."

God, hearing him say that ignited her libido as if he'd flipped the override switch, cranking the dial all the way into the red zone.

"No holds barred," she husked.

Talk about a switch.

If he'd looked feral before, it had been because of the fangs, but now his entire expression was changed. Gone was the softness in his eyes, replaced by a burning desire.

Ella was in for the ride of a lifetime and she couldn't wait.

In a heartbeat, he covered her body with his and pulled her arms over her head, threading their fingers.

"Am I too heavy for you?"

"You are perfect." She loved feeling his weight, the hard contours of his chest pressed against her breasts.

Her man was magnificent.

He took her lips, kissing her softly at first, and then possessing her mouth. His tongue went dueling with hers, then retreated and thrust again in an unmistakable imitation of what he intended to do to her next.

She was panting by the time he let go.

Lifting his head, he looked into her eyes. "Still okay?"

"Perfect."

"Your skin is so soft all over." He nuzzled her ear, his hot breath sending shivers through her body.

Her nipples tightened.

"You like this, don't you?" He nipped her earlobe, then sucked it into his mouth.

She arched up. "Yes."

Unthreading their fingers, he left her hands over her head and propped himself on his forearm. Looking at her with those intense glowing eyes of his, he cupped her breast, then swirled a finger around her areola. "Lovely, soft and hard." He lightly pinched her nipple.

Biting down on her lower lip, she stifled a moan as he did the same with the other one. If he kept this up, she was going to climax just from that.

As he pinched her nipple harder, a bolt of lightning shot straight to her throbbing center. "Your moans belong to me. Don't hide them. I'm greedy for every sound you make."

Bossy Julian was sexy, she just needed to make sure that this new facet of him didn't leave the bedroom or wherever else they were making love. He could boss her around all he wanted in bed, but not anywhere else.

Skimming his hand down her belly, he looked into her eyes, gauging her response.

Touch me, she said in her head, hoping he could hear her, and as his fingers brushed over her mons, she thought he had. But then he stopped, and returned them to her nipple, pinching it lightly again.

His gaze rapt on her breasts, he murmured, "I love how responsive your nipples are." Then he dipped his head and sucked one into his mouth.

"Yes." She arched up. "More."

His fingers skimmed over her belly again, but this time, he didn't stop, and as they reached her throbbing clit, Ella almost jumped out of her skin.

Two seconds of this and she was going to come all over those magic fingers. Spreading her legs lewdly, she invited more. Could he bring his other hand into play and push two inside her? She was aching to be filled, but still too embarrassed to ask for what she needed.

Maybe next time she would, but not their first. She just couldn't.

"You're so wet," he murmured against her nipple.

"I need you," she whimpered, hoping it would be enough.

"Need me to do what, this?" He swirled his finger around her clitoris without touching it directly.

"Yes. More."

Without warning, his finger left the top of her slit and pushed inside her.

Ella hadn't expected to climax so soon, and as the orgasm exploded out of her, she arched her back like a bow, impaling herself on that magic finger as deep as it could go.

JULIAN

*A*s Ella climaxed, Julian had to call on every bit of restraint he could muster not to mount her and take her right there and then. After nearly two months of abstinence, it was mission impossible.

Except, he would make it possible because he wasn't done preparing her. She was small and he was a big guy, and unless she was sopping wet as he entered her, it would be painful.

Not acceptable. The only pain she would suffer tonight would be the momentary one of his fangs piercing her flesh.

The orgasm was a fluke. Ella hadn't been supposed to climax after so little foreplay, but it seemed that she hadn't been exaggerating when she'd claimed her desire for him was intense.

Planting a soft kiss on her parted lips, he stroked the damp hair off her forehead. "That was just the appetizer to the appetizer."

"You're going to kill me with too much pleasure."

"Not a chance. There could never be too much pleasure for my mate." Sliding down on the bed, he pressed his engorged erection to the mattress and implored it to hold off for just a few minutes longer. As turned on as Ella was, it wouldn't take long to bring her up again and have her explode all over his tongue.

She didn't protest, which meant that she wasn't a stranger to oral pleasuring. On the one hand it enraged him that the Russian had stolen even that from them, but on the other hand he was glad that the bastard had given some consideration to her pleasure.

Lifting his head, he looked into her eyes. "I hope I don't come in my shorts the instant I get your taste on my tongue."

Smirking, she reached down and cupped his cheek. "I've heard that immortal males need no recovery time, so that shouldn't be a problem."

He pretended to frown. "Who told you that?"

"Carol. Why, isn't it true?"

She seemed worried, which made him chuckle. "I can go all night long, but you're not ready for that. Once you are immortal, though…"

"Oh, God. I can't wait."

Applying gentle pressure to her thighs, he coaxed them to part a little wider. Her little clit was swollen, and she was slick from her earlier release, her lower lips plumped and parted, exposing her inner sheath.

And yet, Ella didn't shy away from his touch or his eyes, which was the best indication of how ready she was. Or maybe of how much she loved him.

Or both.

Fates, it was so inviting. He could extend his tongue and thrust it into that welcoming heat, but there was more to making love than going straight for the target, and the longer the buildup the better it was going to be for her.

He was going to die in the process, but it was a worthy sacrifice. Trailing his lips up one thigh, he resisted the urge to hurry, kissing his way up and stopping just before the gates of heaven to kiss the inside of her other thigh.

"Julian," she hissed. "Don't tease me."

He lifted his head. "Are you in a hurry to go somewhere?"

Cranking her neck, she looked at where his head was and smirked. "I have all night. But do you?"

"Imp." He nipped her thigh.

She was right, though. He wanted to believe that his will was invincible and that he could carry on for as long as he pleased, but the reality was a painfully hard shaft that he was subduing into obedience by pressing it as hard as he could into the mattress. Except, the thing was too soft to provide enough pressure. A granite altar would have worked much better.

It would have been appropriate too.

After all, he was about to worship his goddess with his tongue, which required an altar.

She rocked her hips. "Kiss me, Julian."

He liked that she asked for what she wanted. It was the best proof that she was more than ready to make love for the first time. What had been done to her before didn't count as such.

Pressing a soft kiss to her puffy lips, he inhaled her sweet scent, his eyes rolling back in his head from pleasure. "I think I'm already addicted to your scent. From now on, I'm going to do this every night." He flicked his tongue over her engorged bud.

Ella's hips jerked and she hissed. "Good, because I'll never get enough of this."

Unable to wait any longer, he speared his tongue into her drenched sheath, scooping her juices and groaning as they coated his mouth.

She let out a moan. "Oh, Julian. I'm getting close again."

"Not yet." He nipped her thigh. "Try to hold it off for a little bit longer."

"I can't. I need to come."

Lusty imp. He'd never expected her to be so orgasmic. Was he a lucky guy or what?

Next time, he was going to prolong her pleasure. But this time he was going to give her what she wanted. After all, he'd promised her that she would have all the control. And even though she'd given it back to him, he wasn't going to push her just yet. Not on their first time.

With a growl, he cupped her ass cheeks and pushed his tongue inside her again, going as deep as he could and nuzzling her clitoris at the same time. Not the most elegant cunnilingus, but it seemed to please her nonetheless.

"Yes!" Her sheath tightened around his tongue, and her fingers threaded into his hair, pulling hard. "Yes!" She threw her head back and uttered the most delectable sound. A moan that had started as a whimper and ended as a groan.

He'd never heard a woman make a sound like that. It was the sexiest thing ever. Snarling, he lapped up her copious juices, the taste and smell and her gyrating hips finally snapping his resolve.

Practically tearing his shorts off, he pushed up and settled between her thighs, aligning his loaded gun with her entrance.

E L L A

*A*s Ella gazed into Julian's lust-infused eyes, her heart swelled with love for him.

"My mate," she whispered. "Make us one."

Grasping his shaft, he ran the tip up and down her wet folds, coating it in her juices, then nudged her entrance.

She arched up, encouraging him to press forward. "I'm ready, Julian. Don't make me wait any longer."

But he didn't ram into her as she'd expected. Instead, he eased inside her an inch at a time, stretching her impossibly wide but painlessly. Watching his beautiful face straining with the effort to go slow, she followed a drop of sweat as it detached from his forehead and landed on her chest.

"I love you," he whispered and took her mouth before she could say it back.

Sweet, sweet Julian, so considerate, so selfless, but she was done waiting, and she wasn't as fragile as he thought her to be. Wrapping her arms around him, she reached as far as she could, dug her fingers into the tight muscles of his buttocks, and pushed up, impaling herself on his length.

For a brief moment it stung, but not enough to take away from the intense pleasure of being filled by him.

Joined at last.

With a groan, Julian rested his damp forehead against hers. "Impatient girl."

"Very." She arched up again, getting him even deeper inside.

It was on the tip of her tongue to ask him to fuck her hard, but that kind of language didn't belong between them. It was what she'd heard in movies and read in books, but it wasn't how she wanted to communicate with her mate.

"Make love to me, Julian," she said instead.

And the words felt right, settling between them like a soft cloud, contrasting with the hard length pulsating within her. But the beauty of it was that both were about passion and love.

As he pulled out and surged inside her again, her inner walls clamped around him, wresting a strangled groan from his throat.

As Julian's thrusts got harder and faster, she knew he wasn't going to last, but that was fine. They were in no hurry, and the night was still young.

Well, not really, it was probably two in the morning, but time was irrelevant. She'd had a good rest and he was an immortal. They could keep going for hours.

Letting go of his ass cheeks, she lifted her hands to his back and wrapped her legs around the back of his thighs, clinging to him and readying for the wild ride he was about to give her.

Muscles tight, he rammed into her, hitting the end of her channel, again and again, the glow in his eyes so bright that she could feel the heat of it on her skin.

Or was she imagining it?

It was hard to tell with all the sensations bombarding her at once. And yet, she could feel him swelling impossibly big inside her, and as his ragged breaths turned into growls, she instinctively turned her head and offered him her neck.

As his hands clamped on her head, immobilizing it, she experienced a moment of fear, but instead of the bite she'd braced for, she felt his tongue laving the soft spot where her neck met her shoulder.

Even as wild as he was, Julian retained the presence of mind to prepare her, and as his fangs sank into her flesh, it was more erotic than painful. Her sheath convulsing around him, Ella's eyes rolled back in her head as she orgasmed again.

It was too much.

And yet when his shaft kicked inside her, filling her with his semen, another climax rocked through her.

Then his venom hit her system and she floated away on a cloud of euphoria.

65

JULIAN

*A*s Ella drifted off, Julian retracted his fangs, licked the puncture wounds closed, and buried his face in the hollow of her neck, still slowly thrusting inside her and riding out his orgasm.

He wasn't nearly done, and if Ella were an immortal he would have waited a moment for her to float down and started over again. But she was still human, and as it was, this had been the best sex of his life, and he shouldn't be greedy for more. Instead, he breathed in her scent, feeling grateful beyond measure for the gift of her.

Fates, the intensity with which he loved this incredible girl was overwhelming. She'd blown his mind, changed him from the inside out, and he was never going to be the same again. But it was all good. She'd made him a better man. She'd given him purpose, and he was going to spend the rest of his immortal life worshiping at her feet.

Right now, though, he needed to clean her up and tuck her under the blanket because she was wiped out and was probably going to keep sleeping till morning.

Sliding out of her as gently as he could, he winced as their combined issue spilled onto the sheets. There was nothing he could do about it without waking Ella up, other than maybe pushing a towel under her.

With that in mind, he tiptoed to the bathroom, grabbed a clean towel and several washcloths and tiptoed back, only to realize that he should probably soak the washcloths in warm water.

He was a novice at this, but he was going to learn and be the best mate possible to Ella. A gold medalist at taking care of his girl.

He chuckled softly as he headed back to the bathroom. His competitive streak had kicked in, and as with everything else, he needed to be the best at being a mate too.

It was a worthy goal, though. Probably more important than all the others combined.

Padding back with the wet washcloths in hand, he sat on the bed and cleaned his beauty as best he could, then gently pushed a dry towel under her tush, and covered her with the blanket.

After disposing of the washcloths, he lifted the comforter and joined his love in bed. Snuggling up to her, he kissed her temple. "Good night, my precious," he murmured.

Lying on his side, he watched her gorgeous face. She looked happy, relaxed, and a small smile was lifting the corners of her lush lips. A wave of pure satisfaction washed over him because he was responsible for that expression.

A happy wife meant a happy life. He'd read or heard it somewhere. And if that was true for humans, it was even truer for immortals.

A happy true-love mate meant an eternity of bliss.

66

KIAN

"And I thought Turner was paranoid," William said as he finished preparing the third cuff. "I understand that he is Navuh's son, but he's not Houdini. And if he can open one cuff, he can open all four. But he can't. I guarantee it."

"It's for the psychological effect." Pushing away from the desk he'd been leaning against, Kian dusted off the back of his pants.

Even though William still used his old lab from time to time, it looked like it hadn't been cleaned since he'd moved to the new one in the village. He hadn't used it for cuff making, though. The last one William had made had been for Robert. That was why he hadn't brought the components to the new location.

Nevertheless, he'd been working on a new design, and Lokan would be the first one to have the displeasure of being a test subject.

Waving with the caliper, William huffed. "If you want a psychological effect, you shouldn't put him in the nice cell apartment. Stick him in the smallest one and have him ponder the torture he's about to suffer."

He clamped the tool on the completed cuff and compared the measurement to the one Turner had provided. It was important that the cuffs fit snugly but not so tightly as to cause injury.

"Turner's plan to extract information from Lokan consists of several stages, and in the first one he's going to be treated as well as a guest would."

"I don't see how that would work." William buffed the cuff with a cloth and then placed it next to the other two.

"Neither do I." Impatient for the Doomer prince's arrival, Kian started pacing. "But I trust Turner. He hasn't failed us yet. The guy is a fucking genius, and I'm not saying it lightly. Sometimes I feel as if he's taken over my job as the clan's strategist."

"If you ask me, that's a good thing. You can focus on drumming up more business." William removed his glasses, replaced them with protective goggles, and then reached for his earphones. "I'm about to use the whiny power sander."

The thing should have been called a head drill because that was what Kian felt every time William turned it on.

"I'm going to be out in the corridor."

William nodded, waiting for Kian to leave the lab before turning the tool on.

Glancing at his watch, Kian checked the time. Turner's plane should be landing soon, and since traffic was not a problem this late at night, the Doomers should be arriving within an hour. Not that he was interested in Lokan's men, they were already in stasis and heading for storage in the catacombs, just in their leader.

He still couldn't believe how lucky they'd gotten. It seemed like the Fates had been working overtime to bring this about. So many things had to happen to bring Lokan into his hands.

If Julian hadn't gone to the psychic convention, he wouldn't have met Vivian and fallen for her daughter's picture. But if he had acted upon it right away and started dating the girl, she wouldn't have fallen victim to traffickers, wouldn't have been sold to the Russian mobster, and would have never met Lokan, who'd become obsessed with her too.

Then there was Turner. If not for him and his connections in Washington, Lokan would have absconded with Vivian and Ella and they would have been lost forever to the clan.

The question that occupied his mind now was what he wished Navuh to believe happened to his son.

One option was to rig the plane to explode somewhere in the middle of the ocean and have Navuh believe that Lokan was dead.

The other option was to hide the plane somewhere and make him think that Lokan had deserted.

Kian preferred the first choice, but in case Navuh actually cared for his son, Lokan could be used as a future bargaining chip.

Until that was decided, though, they had to make sure that Navuh didn't suspect the clan's involvement in Lokan's disappearance. Even if he cared nothing for his son, it would be a matter of pride for him to retaliate against the clan and he would go to great lengths to do that, including hurting humans who he suspected of association with them.

That's why they were going to hide Lokan's executive jet in Mexico. Once again, a friend of Turner's was taking care of that. Evidently, making planes disappear was a service that the private operator was providing for governments as well as individuals.

It would buy them time to interrogate Lokan.

What they would learn from him would influence which option was best.

ELLA

*E*lla woke up with a smile on her face, which hadn't happened in a long time. Being snuggled in Julian's arms might have something to do with that, as well as a good night's sleep without expecting a visitor.

Julian had assured her that with the strong sedative Lokan had been given, he couldn't dream actively. Which meant no dream sharing.

The question was what would happen later. Once Lokan was locked up in a cell, Kian wasn't going to keep him sedated. Could they threaten him with bodily harm if he dared to intrude on her dreams again?

She would have to suggest it to Kian. After what she'd gone through to help him capture Navuh's son, he owed her at least that. But that was all the mind bandwidth she was going to dedicate to the Doomer.

This was a new day and a new beginning for her, and Ella didn't want to dwell on the past if she could avoid it.

"Good morning, gorgeous." Julian nuzzled her neck. "Did you sleep well?"

"Fantastic." In fact, she'd never felt better.

Was it the effect of the incredible lovemaking? Or had it been the venom? She felt vital, invigorated, happy.

"That's good to hear." He kissed her lips.

She kept them tightly closed. "I need to brush. And pee."

"Then go." He lifted the blanket, exposing her nude body.

Her first instinct was to snatch it from him and cover up, but she didn't.

She was starting this new day with a bang, and that meant confidence in her body, which Julian was practically devouring with a pair of hungry, glowing eyes.

"You'd better hurry, love, or you won't make it to the bathroom."

As she swung her legs over the side of the bed, Julian held on to her with his arm around her middle.

She glanced at the towel he must have put under her last night. "That won't help much if you don't let me go, and I pee on your bed."

"Our bed." He removed his arm from her waist. "I need to go too." He flung the comforter off him.

Oh, boy. Ella stopped and gawked. He was fully erect, his shaft standing up like a mast. "Is that your morning wood or is it for me?"

"Both." Smiling, he slapped her bottom. "Go. Before I change my mind."

If she didn't need to pee so bad, she would've stayed and taunted him some more. He wasn't the only one ready for round two.

Julian allowed her about a minute of privacy before coming in, and then he joined her in the shower.

She ended up very clean and very satisfied, and then he toweled her dry and carried her back to bed.

"I could get used to that," Ella said as he put her down.

"Me too." He leaned and kissed her nose. "I'm going to make coffee."

Hey, she could get used to that too, especially since Julian hadn't bothered to put anything on, and she delighted in the sight of his beautifully muscled backside as he headed for the kitchen.

When he returned holding a tray with two coffee mugs and a plate of chocolates, she also got an eyeful of his glorious front.

"These will have to do for breakfast. We are out of everything else." He put the tray on the nightstand.

"We could go grocery shopping." She grinned. "This will be my first time buying stuff for my own kitchen."

"Do you have your special glasses with you?"

Her smile wilted. "No, Lokan took them from us, together with the trackers and everything else we had on. We were lucky that he didn't think that the hairpins could have trackers in them."

"Thank the merciful Fates." Julian rubbed a hand over his face. "I don't know what I would have done if I had lost you. I would have spent every moment of my life searching for that fucking island."

"Don't." She reached for his hand and brought it to her cheek. "It doesn't make sense to get angry over what ifs. I'm here, and we are together, and Lokan is locked in a cell."

"What if he enters your dreams again?"

"I give you permission to beat him up if he does."

That got an evil smile out of him. "I'm looking forward to it. I don't want him anywhere near you ever again. That evil son of a bitch is handsome. Takes after his monster of a father."

Ella leaned and kissed Julian's lips. "He can't hold a candle to you. You are a god even among immortals."

The smile got even wider. "I think I just grew an inch."

She glanced down. "I'd say."

"Lusty wench." He picked up a chocolate and put it in her mouth. "I would happily join you in bed for round three, but I need to feed you something healthier than chocolates, and the house is empty of food. We have to either go shopping or hit the café."

She grimaced. "I don't want to go to the café. We won't have a moment's peace there, with everyone wanting details of what went down. But I can't go grocery shopping without my glasses. I think we have no choice but to go to my parents' house."

"Your mom invited us for brunch."

"I know. I heard her. I just didn't want to open my eyes." She sighed. "I wish I were truly free, and that includes the Russian giving up on finding me."

"You should have let the Guardians kill him."

She waved a dismissive hand. "I'm glad I didn't. The road-block operation was much safer for everyone than the fake fire Turner planned to set on the Russian's estate. No one got hurt, and I'm grateful for that. Besides, it's not a big deal. I don't plan on leaving the village often."

"What about college? You said you were going to find one in the area and commute."

"I found an even better solution. An online university."

He arched a brow. "Since when do they teach nursing online? It's a hands-on occupation."

"I decided to study something else. I wanted to be a nurse to help people, but I can help more by organizing charity. My mom and I checked, and we found an accredited online bachelor's degree in nonprofit management. I can do that while running the charity. Which reminds me." She jumped out of bed. "I want to check how it's doing."

She opened the suitcase, which was still on the floor where Julian had put it last night, pulled out her laptop, and hopped back in bed.

Sitting cross-legged even though she was nude, which was a testament to how comfortable she was with Julian, Ella booted it up. Hopefully, it had enough charge left for a short session.

"Oh, wow. It keeps on growing. No major donations, but tons of small ones. We've collected close to thirty thousand."

"That's great news." Julian didn't sound overly enthusiastic.

"I know it's a drop in the bucket, but we've just started. It will grow exponentially, you'll see."

"Fates willing."

"Oh, they are."

As his phone started buzzing, Ella remembered that hers was gone. "I hope the Guardians captured the Doomers who had our purses. The clan phones are in there. If they fall into the wrong hands, they can be reverse-engineered."

Julian snatched the phone. "Hi, Vivian." A long pause. "Sure. I'll tell Ella. See you later."

"Was it about lunch? Because I'm starting to feel hungry."

"Yes, and also about a party. Callie and Wonder are organizing a barbecue on Sunday to celebrate your safe return."

"Awesome. I'm glad they are doing it on the weekend and not right away. Now let's get dressed and go to my parents to eat. I also need to give Parker a big hug for his help."

As she said the words, it dawned on her that she'd been referring to Magnus as her parent, and that it hadn't been the first time she'd done it.

In part, it was because saying she was going to her mother's house didn't sound right, and neither did going to her mother and Magnus's house. But the truth was that she was starting to think of him as a father figure, mainly because in every way that counted he was.

Her real father would always be in her heart, she was never going to forget him, not even for one day, but she had room in there for Magnus too. He'd certainly earned the right.

The heart was a funny thing.

Its capacity had no limit, and there was always room for more people to love.

The end...for now...

COMING UP NEXT
THE CHILDREN OF THE GODS BOOK 29
Dark Prince's Enigma

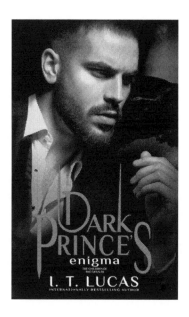

FOR EXCLUSIVE PEEKS AT UPCOMING RELEASES
JOIN MY *VIP CLUB* AND GAIN ACCESS TO THE **VIP** PORTAL AT
ITLUCAS.COM
CLICK HERE TO JOIN
(If you're already a subscriber and forgot the password to the VIP portal, you can find it at

the bottom of each of my emails. Or click **HERE** to retrieve it. You can also email me at

isabell@itlucas.com)

Dear reader,

Thank you for joining me on the continuing adventures of the ***Children of the Gods***.

As an independent author, I rely on your support to

spread the word. So if you enjoyed the story, please share your experience, and if it isn't too much trouble, I would greatly appreciate a brief review on Amazon.

Click here to leave a review

Love & happy reading,

Isabell

DON'T MISS OUT ON

THE CHILDREN OF THE GODS ORIGINS SERIES

1: GODDESS'S CHOICE

2: GODDESS'S HOPE

THE PERFECT MATCH SERIES

PERFECT MATCH 1: VAMPIRE'S CONSORT

PERFECT MATCH 2: KING'S CHOSEN

(READ THE ENCLOSED EXCERPT)

PERFECT MATCH 3: CAPTAIN'S CONQUEST

THE CHILDREN OF THE GODS ORIGINS

1: GODDESS'S CHOICE

When gods and immortals still ruled the ancient world, one young goddess risked everything for love.

2: GODDESS'S HOPE

Hungry for power and infatuated with the beautiful Areana, Navuh plots his father's demise. After all, by getting rid of the insane god he would be doing the world a favor. Except, when gods and immortals conspire against each other, humanity pays the price.

But things are not what they seem, and prophecies should not to be trusted...

THE CHILDREN OF THE GODS

1: DARK STRANGER THE DREAM

Syssi's paranormal foresight lands her a job at Dr. Amanda Dokani's neuroscience lab, but it fails to predict the thrilling yet terrifying turn her life will take. Syssi has no clue that her boss is an immortal who'll drag her into a secret, millennia-old battle over humanity's future. Nor does she realize that the professor's imposing brother is the mysterious stranger who's been starring in her dreams.

Since the dawn of human civilization, two warring factions of immortals—the descendants of the gods of old—have been secretly shaping its destiny. Leading the clandestine battle from his luxurious Los Angeles high-rise, Kian is surrounded by his clan, yet alone. Descending from a single goddess, clan members are forbidden to each other. And as the only other immortals are their hated enemies, Kian and his kin have been long resigned to a lonely existence of fleeting trysts with human partners. That is, until his sister makes a game-changing discovery—a mortal seeress who she believes is a dormant carrier of their genes. Ever the realist, Kian is skeptical and refuses Amanda's plea to attempt Syssi's activation.

But when his enemies learn of the Dormant's existence, he's forced to rush her to the safety of his keep. Inexorably drawn to Syssi, Kian wrestles with his conscience as he is tempted to explore her budding interest in the darker shades of sensuality.

2: DARK STRANGER REVEALED

While sheltered in the clan's stronghold, Syssi is unaware that Kian and Amanda are not human, and neither are the supposedly religious fanatics that are after her. She feels a powerful connection to Kian, and as he introduces her to a world of pleasure she never dared imagine, his dominant sexuality is a revelation. Considering that she's completely out of her element, Syssi feels comfortable and safe letting go with him. That is, until she begins to suspect that all is not as it seems. Piecing the puzzle together, she draws a scary, yet wrong conclusion...

3: DARK STRANGER IMMORTAL

When Kian confesses his true nature, Syssi is not as much shocked by the revelation as she is wounded by what she perceives as his callous plans for her.

If she doesn't turn, he'll be forced to erase her memories and let her go. His family's safety demands secrecy – no one in the mortal world is allowed to know that immortals exist.

Resigned to the cruel reality that even if she stays on to never again leave the keep, she'll get old while Kian won't, Syssi is determined to enjoy what little time she has with him, one day at a time.

Can Kian let go of the mortal woman he loves? Will Syssi turn? And if she does, will she survive the dangerous transition?

4: DARK ENEMY TAKEN

Dalhu can't believe his luck when he stumbles upon the beautiful immortal professor. Presented with a once in a lifetime opportunity to grab an immortal female for himself, he kidnaps her and runs. If he ever gets caught, either by her people or his, his life is forfeit. But for a chance of a loving mate and a family of his own, Dalhu is prepared to do everything in his power to win Amanda's heart, and that includes leaving the Doom brotherhood and his old life behind.

Amanda soon discovers that there is more to the handsome Doomer than his dark past and a hulking, sexy body. But succumbing to her enemy's seduction, or worse, developing feelings for a ruthless killer is out of the question. No man is worth life on the run, not even the one and only immortal male she could claim as her own...

Her clan and her research must come first...

5: DARK ENEMY CAPTIVE

When the rescue team returns with Amanda and the chained Dalhu to the keep, Amanda is not as thrilled to be back as she thought she'd be. Between Kian's contempt for her and Dalhu's imprisonment, Amanda's budding relationship with Dalhu seems doomed. Things start to look up when Annani offers her help, and together with Syssi they resolve to find a way for Amanda to be with Dalhu. But will she still want him when she realizes that he is responsible for her nephew's murder? Could she? Will she take the easy way out and choose Andrew instead?

6: DARK ENEMY REDEEMED

Amanda suspects that something fishy is going on onboard the Anna. But when her investigation of the peculiar all-female Russian crew fails to uncover anything other than more speculation, she decides it's time to stop playing detective and face her real problem —a man she shouldn't want but can't live without.

6.5: MY DARK AMAZON

When Michael and Kri fight off a gang of humans, Michael gets stabbed. The injury to his immortal body recovers fast, but the one to his ego takes longer, putting a strain on his relationship with Kri.

7: DARK WARRIOR MINE

When Andrew is forced to retire from active duty, he believes that all he has to look forward to is a boring desk job. His glory days in special ops are over. But as it turns out, his thrill ride has just begun. Andrew discovers not only that immortals exist and have been manipulating global affairs since antiquity, but that he and his sister are rare possessors of the immortal genes.

Problem is, Andrew might be too old to attempt the activation process. His sister, who is fourteen years his junior, barely made it through the transition, so the odds of him coming out of it alive, let alone immortal, are slim.

But fate may force his hand.

Helping a friend find his long-lost daughter, Andrew finds a woman who's worth taking the risk for. Nathalie might be a Dormant, but the only way to find out for sure requires fangs and venom.

8: DARK WARRIOR'S PROMISE

Andrew and Nathalie's love flourishes, but the secrets they keep from each other taint their relationship with doubts and suspicions. In the meantime, Sebastian and his men are getting bolder, and the storm that's brewing will shift the balance of power in the millennia-old conflict between Annani's clan and its enemies.

9: DARK WARRIOR'S DESTINY

The new ghost in Nathalie's head remembers who he was in life, providing Andrew and her with indisputable proof that he is real and not a figment of her imagination.

Convinced that she is a Dormant, Andrew decides to go forward with his transition immediately after the rescue mission at the Doomers' HQ.

Fearing for his life, Nathalie pleads with him to reconsider. She'd rather spend the rest of her mortal days with Andrew than risk what they have for the fickle promise of immortality.

While the clan gets ready for battle, Carol gets help from an unlikely ally. Sebastian's second-in-command can no longer ignore the torment she suffers at the hands of his commander and offers to help her, but only if she agrees to his terms.

10: DARK WARRIOR'S LEGACY

Andrew's acclimation to his post-transition body isn't easy. His senses are sharper, he's bigger, stronger, and hungrier. Nathalie fears that the changes in the man she loves are more than physical. Measuring up to this new version of him is going to be a challenge.

Carol and Robert are disillusioned with each other. They are not destined mates, and love is not on the horizon. When Robert's three months are up, he might be left with nothing to show for his sacrifice.

Lana contacts Anandur with disturbing news; the yacht and its human cargo are in Mexico. Kian must find a way to apprehend

Alex and rescue the women on board without causing an
international incident.

11: Dark Guardian Found

What would you do if you stopped aging?

Eva runs. The ex-DEA agent doesn't know what caused her strange
mutation, only that if discovered, she'll be dissected like a lab rat.
What Eva doesn't know, though, is that she's a descendant of the
gods, and that she is not alone. The man who rocked her world in
one life-changing encounter over thirty years ago is an immortal as
well.

To keep his people's existence secret, Bhathian was forced to turn
his back on the only woman who ever captured his heart, but
he's never forgotten and never stopped looking for her.

12: Dark Guardian Craved

Cautious after a lifetime of disappointments, Eva is mistrustful of
Bhathian's professed feelings of love. She accepts him as a lover and
a confidant but not as a life partner.

Jackson suspects that Tessa is his true love mate, but unless she
overcomes her fears, he might never find out.

Carol gets an offer she can't refuse—a chance to prove that there is
more to her than meets the eye. Robert believes she's about to
commit a deadly mistake, but when he tries to dissuade her, she tells
him to leave.

13: Dark Guardian's Mate

Prepare for the heart-warming culmination of Eva and Bhathian's
story!

14: Dark Angel's Obsession

The cold and stoic warrior is an enigma even to those closest to
him. His secrets are about to unravel...

15: Dark Angel's Seduction

Brundar is fighting a losing battle. Calypso is slowly chipping away
his icy armor from the outside, while his need for her is melting it
from the inside.

He can't allow it to happen. Calypso is a human with none of the

Dormant indicators. There is no way he can keep her for more than a few weeks.

16: Dark Angel's Surrender

Get ready for the heart pounding conclusion to Brundar and Calypso's story.

Callie still couldn't wrap her head around it, nor could she summon even a smidgen of sorrow or regret. After all, she had some memories with him that weren't horrible. She should've felt something. But there was nothing, not even shock. Not even horror at what had transpired over the last couple of hours.

Maybe it was a typical response for survivors--feeling euphoric for the simple reason that they were alive. Especially when that survival was nothing short of miraculous.

Brundar's cold hand closed around hers, reminding her that they weren't out of the woods yet. Her injuries were superficial, and the most she had to worry about was some scarring. But, despite his and Anandur's reassurances, Brundar might never walk again.

If he ended up crippled because of her, she would never forgive herself for getting him involved in her crap.

"Are you okay, sweetling? Are you in pain?" Brundar asked.

Her injuries were nothing compared to his, and yet he was concerned about her. God, she loved this man. The thing was, if she told him that, he would run off, or crawl away as was the case.

Hey, maybe this was the perfect opportunity to spring it on him.

17: Dark Operative: A Shadow of Death

As a brilliant strategist and the only human entrusted with the secret of immortals' existence, Turner is both an asset and a liability to the clan. His request to attempt transition into immortality as an alternative to cancer treatments cannot be denied without risking the clan's exposure. On the other hand, approving it means risking his premature death. In both scenarios, the clan will lose a valuable ally.

When the decision is left to the clan's physician, Turner makes plans to manipulate her by taking advantage of her interest in him.

Will Bridget fall for the cold, calculated operative? Or will Turner fall into his own trap?

18: Dark Operative: A Glimmer of Hope

As Turner and Bridget's relationship deepens, living together seems like the right move, but to make it work both need to make concessions.

Bridget is realistic and keeps her expectations low. Turner could never be the truelove mate she yearns for, but he is as good as she's going to get. Other than his emotional limitations, he's perfect in every way.

Turner's hard shell is starting to show cracks. He wants immortality, he wants to be part of the clan, and he wants Bridget, but he doesn't want to cause her pain.

His options are either abandon his quest for immortality and give Bridget his few remaining decades, or abandon Bridget by going for the transition and most likely dying. His rational mind dictates that he chooses the former, but his gut pulls him toward the latter.
Which one is he going to trust?

19: Dark Operative: The Dawn of Love

Get ready for the exciting finale of Bridget and Turner's story!

20: Dark Survivor Awakened

This was a strange new world she had awakened to.

Her memory loss must have been catastrophic because almost nothing was familiar. The language was foreign to her, with only a few words bearing some similarity to the language she thought in. Still, a full moon cycle had passed since her awakening, and little by little she was gaining basic understanding of it--only a few words and phrases, but she was learning more each day.

A week or so ago, a little girl on the street had tugged on her mother's sleeve and pointed at her. "Look, Mama, Wonder Woman!"

The mother smiled apologetically, saying something in the language these people spoke, then scurried away with the child looking behind her shoulder and grinning.

When it happened again with another child on the same day, it was settled.

Wonder Woman must have been the name of someone important in this strange world she had awoken to, and since both times it had been said with a smile it must have been a good one.

Wonder had a nice ring to it.

She just wished she knew what it meant.

21: Dark Survivor Echoes of Love

Wonder's journey continues in *Dark Survivor Echoes of Love*.

22: Dark Survivor Reunited

The exciting finale of Wonder and Anandur's story.

23: Dark Widow's Secret

Vivian and her daughter share a powerful telepathic connection, so when Ella can't be reached by conventional or psychic means, her mother fears the worst.

Help arrives from an unexpected source when Vivian gets a call from the young doctor she met at a psychic convention. Turns out Julian belongs to a private organization specializing in retrieving missing girls.

As Julian's clan mobilizes its considerable resources to rescue the daughter, Magnus is charged with keeping the gorgeous young mother safe.

Worry for Ella and the secrets Vivian and Magnus keep from each other should be enough to prevent the sparks of attraction from kindling a blaze of desire. Except, these pesky sparks have a mind of their own.

24: Dark Widow's Curse

A simple rescue operation turns into mission impossible when the Russian mafia gets involved. Bad things are supposed to come in threes, but in Vivian's case, it seems like there is no limit to bad luck. Her family and everyone who gets close to her is affected by her curse.

Will Magnus and his people prove her wrong?

25: Dark Widow's Blessing

The thrilling finale of the Dark Widow trilogy!

26: Dark Dream's Temptation

Julian has known Ella is the one for him from the moment he saw her picture, but when he finally frees her from captivity, she seems indifferent to him. Could he have been mistaken?

Ella's rescue should've ended that chapter in her life, but it seems like the road back to normalcy has just begun and it's full of obstacles. Between the pitying looks she gets and her mother's attempts to get her into therapy, Ella feels like she's typecast as a victim, when nothing could be further from the truth. She's a tough survivor, and she's going to prove it.

Strangely, the only one who seems to understand is Logan, who keeps popping up in her dreams. But then, he's a figment of her imagination—or is he?

27: Dark Dream's Unraveling

While trying to figure out a way around Logan's silencing compulsion, Ella concocts an ambitious plan. What if instead of trying to keep him out of her dreams, she could pretend to like him and lure him into a trap?

Catching Navuh's son would be a major boon for the clan, as well as for Ella. She will have her revenge, turning the tables on another scumbag out to get her.

28: Dark Dream's Trap

The trap is set, but who is the hunter and who is the prey? Find out in this heart-pounding conclusion to the *Dark Dream* trilogy.

29: Dark Prince's Enigma

As the son of the most dangerous male on the planet, Lokan lives by three rules:

Don't trust a soul.

Don't show emotions.

And don't get attached.

Will one extraordinary woman make him break all three?

30: Dark Prince's Dilemma

Will Kian decide that the benefits of trusting Lokan outweigh the risks?

Will Lokan betray his father and brothers for the greater good of his people?

Are Carol and Lokan true-love mates, or is one of them playing the other?

So many questions, the path ahead is anything but clear.

31: DARK PRINCE'S AGENDA

While Turner and Kian work out the details of Areana's rescue plan, Carol and Lokan's tumultuous relationship hits another snag. Is it a sign of things to come?

32 : DARK QUEEN'S QUEST

A former beauty queen, a retired undercover agent, and a successful model, Mey is not the typical damsel in distress. But when her sister drops off the radar and then someone starts following her around, she panics.

Following a vague clue that Kalugal might be in New York, Kian sends a team headed by Yamanu to search for him.

As Mey and Yamanu's paths cross, he offers her his help and protection, but will that be all?

33: DARK QUEEN'S KNIGHT

As the only member of his clan with a godlike power over human minds, Yamanu has been shielding his people for centuries, but that power comes at a steep price. When Mey enters his life, he's faced with the most difficult choice.

The safety of his clan or a future with his fated mate.

34: DARK QUEEN'S ARMY

As Mey anxiously waits for her transition to begin and for Yamanu to test whether his godlike powers are gone, the clan sets out to solve two mysteries:

Where is Jin, and is she there voluntarily?

Where is Kalugal, and what is he up to?

35: DARK SPY CONSCRIPTED

Jin possesses a unique paranormal ability. Just by touching someone, she can insert a mental hook into their psyche and tie a string of her consciousness to it, creating a tether. That doesn't make her a spy, though, not unless her talent is discovered by those seeking to exploit it.

36: DARK SPY'S MISSION

Jin's first spying mission is supposed to be easy. Walk into the club, touch Kalugal to tether her consciousness to him, and walk out.

Except, they should have known better.

37: DARK SPY'S RESOLUTION

The best-laid plans often go awry...

38: DARK OVERLORD NEW HORIZON

Jacki has two talents that set her apart from the rest of the human race.

She has unpredictable glimpses of other people's futures, and she is immune to mind manipulation.

Unfortunately, both talents are pretty useless for finding a job other than the one she had in the government's paranormal division.

It seemed like a sweet deal, until she found out that the director planned on producing super babies by compelling the recruits into pairing up. When an opportunity to escape the program presented itself, she took it, only to find out that humans are not at the top of the food chain.

Immortals are real, and at the very top of the hierarchy is Kalugal, the most powerful, arrogant, and sexiest male she has ever met.

With one look, he sets her blood on fire, but Jacki is not a fool. A man like him will never think of her as anything more than a tasty snack, while she will never settle for anything less than his heart.

39: DARK OVERLORD'S WIFE

Jacki is still clinging to her all-or-nothing policy, but Kalugal is chipping away at her resistance. Perhaps it's time to ease up on her convictions. A little less than all is still much better than nothing, and a couple of decades with a demigod is probably worth more than a lifetime with a mere mortal.

40: DARK OVERLORD'S CLAN

As Jacki and Kalugal prepare to celebrate their union, Kian takes every precaution to safeguard his people. Except, Kalugal and his men are not his only potential adversaries, and compulsion is not the only power he should fear.

41: Dark Choices The Quandary

When Rufsur and Edna meet, the attraction is as unexpected as it is undeniable. Except, she's the clan's judge and councilwoman, and he's Kalugal's second-in-command. Will loyalty and duty to their people keep them apart?

42: Dark Choices Paradigm Shift

Edna and Rufsur are miserable without each other, and their two-week separation seems like an eternity. Long-distance relationships are difficult, but for immortal couples they are impossible. Unless one of them is willing to leave everything behind for the other, things are just going to get worse. Except, the cost of compromise is far greater than giving up their comfortable lives and hard-earned positions. The future of their people is on the line.

43: Dark Choices The Accord

The winds of change blowing over the village demand hard choices. For better or worse, Kian's decisions will alter the trajectory of the clan's future, and he is not ready to take the plunge. But as Edna and Rufsur's plight gains widespread support, his resistance slowly begins to erode.

44: Dark Secrets Resurgence

On a sabbatical from his Stanford teaching position, Professor David Levinson finally has time to write the sci-fi novel he's been thinking about for years.

The phenomena of past life memories and near-death experiences are too controversial to include in his formal psychiatric research, while fiction is the perfect outlet for his esoteric ideas.

Hoping that a change of pace will provide the inspiration he needs, David accepts a friend's invitation to an old Scottish castle.

45: Dark Secrets Unveiled

When Professor David Levinson accepts a friend's invitation to an old Scottish castle, what he finds there is more fantastical than his most outlandish theories. The castle is home to a clan of immortals, their leader is a stunning demigoddess, and even more shockingly, it might be precisely where he belongs.

Except, the clan founder is hiding a secret that might cast a dark shadow on David's relationship with her daughter.

Nevertheless, when offered a chance at immortality, he agrees to undergo the dangerous induction process.

Will David survive his transition into immortality? And if he does, will his relationship with Sari survive the unveiling of her mother's secret?

46: Dark Secrets Absolved

Absolution.

David had given and received it.

The few short hours since he'd emerged from the coma had felt incredible. He'd finally been free of the guilt and pain, and for the first time since Jonah's death, he had felt truly happy and optimistic about the future.

He'd survived the transition into immortality, had been accepted into the clan, and was about to marry the best woman on the face of the planet, his true love mate, his salvation, his everything.

What could have possibly gone wrong?

Just about everything.

47: Dark haven Illusion

Welcome to Safe Haven, where not everything is what it seems.

On a quest to process personal pain, Anastasia joins the Safe Haven Spiritual Retreat.

Through meditation, self-reflection, and hard work, she hopes to make peace with the voices in her head.

This is where she belongs.

Except, membership comes with a hefty price, doubts are sacrilege, and leaving is not as easy as walking out the front gate.

Is living in utopia worth the sacrifice?

Anastasia believes so until the arrival of a new acolyte changes everything.

Apparently, the gods of old were not a myth, their immortal descendants share the planet with humans, and she might be a carrier of their genes.

48: Dark Haven Unmasked

As Anastasia leaves Safe Haven for a week-long romantic vacation with Leon, she hopes to explore her newly discovered passionate side, their budding relationship, and perhaps also solve the mystery of the voices in her head. What she discovers exceeds her wildest expectations.

In the meantime, Eleanor and Peter hope to solve another mystery. Who is Emmett Haderech, and what is he up to?

For a **FREE Audiobook, Preview chapters, And other goodies offered only to my VIPs,**

JOIN THE VIP CLUB AT ITLUCAS.COM

TRY THE SERIES ON

AUDIBLE

2 FREE audiobooks with your new Audible subscription!

THE PERFECT MATCH SERIES

PERFECT MATCH 1: VAMPIRE'S CONSORT

When Gabriel's company is ready to start beta testing, he invites his old crush to inspect its medical safety protocol.

Curious about the revolutionary technology of the *Perfect Match Virtual Fantasy-Fulfillment studios*, Brenna agrees.

Neither expects to end up partnering for its first fully immersive test run.

PERFECT MATCH 2: KING'S CHOSEN

When Lisa's nutty friends get her a gift certificate to *Perfect Match Virtual Fantasy Studios*, she has no intentions of using it. But since the only way to get a refund is if no partner can be found for her, she makes sure to request a fantasy so girly and over the top that no sane guy will pick it up.

Except, someone does.

Warning: This fantasy contains a hot, domineering crown prince, sweet insta-love, steamy love scenes painted with light shades of gray, a wedding, and a HEA in both the virtual and real worlds.

Intended for mature audience.

Perfect Match 3: Captain's Conquest

Working as a Starbucks barista, Alicia fends off flirting all day long, but none of the guys are as charming and sexy as Gregg. His frequent visits are the highlight of her day, but since he's never asked her out, she assumes he's taken. Besides, between a day job and a budding music career, she has no time to start a new relationship.

That is until Gregg makes her an offer she can't refuse—a gift certificate to the virtual fantasy fulfillment service everyone is talking about. As a huge Star Trek fan, Alicia has a perfect match in mind—the captain of the Starship Enterprise.

King's Chosen

When Lisa's nutty friends get her a gift certificate to *Perfect Match Virtual Fantasy Studios*, she has no intentions of using it. But since the only way to get a refund is if no partner can be found for her, she makes sure to request a fantasy so girly and over the top that no sane guy will pick it up.

Except, someone does.

Warning: This fantasy contains a hot, domineering crown prince, sweet insta-love, steamy love scenes painted with light shades of gray, a wedding, and a HEA in both the virtual and real worlds.

EXCERPT

Lisa eyed the large blue envelope. "Thank you. You guys are the best."

If it was a gift certificate, which it probably was, Lisa hoped it was to a department store. Getting older meant that it was time to start taking better care of her skin, and good moisturizers were pricey.

"You're welcome." Bridget thrust it into Lisa's hands. "Now open it already."

The gleam in Bridget's eyes didn't bode well for something as mundane as a department store gift card.

Unfortunately, her besties weren't into practical gifts.

What had they gotten her? A gift certificate to an adult toy store? A ticket to a male strip show?

Ann lifted her Margarita in a salute. "A quarter of a century is a milestone birthday, and we decided to splurge on something special for you." She waggled her brows.

"Thanks a lot. Way to make me feel ancient."

Ann shrugged. "It's just a number."

Turning the envelope around, Lisa searched for clues. If it was something embarrassing, she would just stick it in her purse and open it when she got home.

Charlotte, who was bristling with excitement, waved an impatient hand. "Open it already."

"Do I have to?"

"Absolutely."

At least it wasn't a box or a gift bag. That precluded something like the vibrator they had gotten Linda for her birthday. But if it was a gift certificate for a private male striptease like the one they'd gotten Rachel, she was just going to thank them, put it away, and forget about it. It was a waste, but gifting it to someone else was out of the question.

Lisa wasn't as nuts as her friends. They were the best, but they constantly pushed her limits. To be frank, though, she needed that.

The seven of them had started the birthday tradition in college. Everyone would pitch in for the gift, and the idea that got most votes won. Obviously, Lisa's never had. According to her friends, her ideas were no fun.

That's what happened when an accounting major shared

an apartment with a bunch of art and theater majors. Practical had never been part of their vocabulary, and every little thing led to a drama. Nevertheless, she wouldn't have traded any of them for someone else, and not only because they made her seem less boring by association.

Sharon, Rachel, and Bridget had moved out of their shared rental house years ago, but Lisa, Charlotte, Ann, and Linda were still there. The only difference was that each had her own room now. With the insane cost of housing in Santa Monica, moving out of a rent-controlled house would have been foolish, and for once her financial acumen had not been ignored.

New rents had doubled over the last seven years.

Taking a deep breath, Lisa tore the envelope open and pulled out a cream-colored card. The title "Perfect Match" was embossed on one side, and there was a web address and an access code on the other. That was it. No instructions, no brochure to explain what the heck it was. Nothing.

Except, the name said it all.

"Do you guys really think that I'm so desperate that I need a matchmaking service?"

True, she hadn't had a boyfriend in forever, but it wasn't as if she was sitting home alone, eating ice cream and watching the dumb box.

Not every day, anyway.

Lisa had been on plenty of dates. The problem was that all of those guys had been meh, and her impressive list of first dates had translated into a very few seconds and almost no thirds.

Perhaps the problem was that most of those dates had been arranged by her well-meaning friends, and it was quite obvious that Lisa didn't share their taste in guys.

Ann giggled. "It's not that kind of matchmaking service."

"What is it then?"

From across the table, Charlotte smirked. "They promise

to find you a perfect sexual match and then arrange a virtual hookup."

Horrified, Lisa glanced around the busy restaurant, but it didn't seem as if anyone had heard Charlotte's explanation. "Keep it down. And are you guys nuts? You know me better than that. I don't do hookups."

Her friend leaned closer and whispered. Loudly. "Yeah, and that's what so great about this service. A virtual hookup is not the same as a real one. None of your many prudish objections apply. You can't catch a disease, there is no morning-after walk of shame, and you don't even have to wax."

True. Except, having sex with a stranger, even virtually, wasn't Lisa's thing. She wanted romance, she wanted intimacy, and she wanted love.

Was that too much to ask for?

Charlotte kept going. "It's new. They've been beta-testing it for over a year and only opened it officially a couple of months ago, but there is a waiting list already. I put your name down as soon as I heard about it. It's perfect for you."

Lisa shook her head. Out of all the crazy ideas her friends had come up with, that one took the gold medal. "Please explain how it works, and what am I supposed to do with it. I'm not saying I will, but just out of curiosity."

Bridget crossed her arms over her chest. "Don't you dare waste it. We spent a fortune on this, and it's nonrefundable. Not unless you go through it and then claim you were unhappy with it and ask for your money back. There is a satisfaction guaranteed clause."

At least, there was that. She could pretend to do it and then ask for a refund. "Okay, I'm listening."

"So it goes like this," Charlotte started. "You fill out a questionnaire. It asks you about your perfect type of guy, your sexual fantasies, and that sort of stuff. It's supposedly very thorough. The computer compiles the data and matches it against what it has collected from guys who filled out the same thing. It finds you the perfect match, schedules an appointment for both of you at the same time, but you don't get to see each other. You get hooked up to a virtual machine in one room, and the guy in another. The machines could be in the same facility or across the globe, and you wouldn't know. You get to experience your craziest sexual fantasy in complete anonymity."

Lisa chuckled. "I can just imagine the kinds of guys who purchase the services. Perverts, geeks, old men… you get the picture. "

"What do you care?" Charlotte waved a dismissive hand. "All you see is the avatar the guy creates for himself, and he's sure going to look like a hunk. This is totally cerebral, and, personally, I think it's beautiful. Freedom from body issues, insecurities, hang-ups, social conventions, etc. You can be whoever you want to be and do whatever with whomever."

"What if it turns out gross and I want out?"

"There are safeguards. A certain word you can use that freezes the program. It's all on their website. You can read it all online. Any question you can imagine is answered."

"I'm sure I can think of a few new ones. Like, what if I like the guy and want to meet him? Not that it's a possibility, but hypothetically."

"You can put in a request, and if the guy agrees, information can be exchanged, like email addresses or phone numbers. And the other way around. But they don't recommend it, precisely because of what you said before. There might be a huge age difference, or he might be on another continent. Currently, they only have the two offices in the States—one is in Los Angeles and the other one in New York, but they plan on opening branches in the UK, Canada and Australia."

"Another possibility is that he is married," Ann said.

"The perfect way to cheat on one's spouse without actually cheating. Does virtual sex count as infidelity?" Lisa wasn't sure.

"I don't think so," Ann said. "It's like watching porn with a twist. Although I don't think I would be okay with my boyfriend doing that."

"Just think of the possibilities." Charlotte lifted her hands in the air. "It's a great way to experiment. If I want to check out sex with another chick, I don't think Ron would mind."

"Pfft." Ann crossed her arms over her chest. "Knowing your pervy boyfriend, he would want to watch. But would you allow him to do the same with another guy?"

"Sure. It's not real. It's a fantasy, so why not?"

Thinking of it objectively, it really was just a step beyond porn, and supposedly everyone was doing it.

Except for Lisa. "I wonder if I can request to be paired with single guys only."

Linda shook her head. "A single man can still have a girl-friend or lie on the questionnaire. It's not like they are doing background checks for virtual hookups, which is another reason not to meet the guy face to face. He can be an ax murderer for all you know."

"Stop analyzing this to death." Charlotte clapped Lisa on the back. "You're looking to be matched with someone who'll fulfill your most secret, filthiest fantasies, not a future husband. When was the last time you had sex? And I mean a good one. Memorable. "

Never.

Lisa had had a total of two steady boyfriends, and neither had been particularly memorable in that department. And as for her numerous dates, none had inspired even a tiny spark of desire, let alone hopping in bed and doing the horizontal mambo.

It was pathetic.

There was only one man she'd ever felt physically

attracted to, like in weak in the knees attracted, and he barely acknowledged her existence.

Lisa didn't even know his name.

They worked in the same building and shared an elevator ride from time to time. Sometimes he would nod at her, and she would smile back.

That was the extent of their contact.

He looked to be in his mid-thirties, had smart eyes, and filled his fancy business suits very nicely. He also smelled fantastic. She hadn't seen a wedding ring on his finger, but that didn't mean he wasn't married. No way a man like him hadn't been snatched up a long time ago. He probably had kids too.

Her attraction to the mystery guy baffled her. Lisa had met guys who were just as good-looking or more, but none had had the same effect on her. There was something about him, some inner strength that she found enticing. And it didn't matter that he never smiled, never acknowledged anyone's presence even though he'd been riding the elevators with the same people day in and day out.

Perhaps it was the suit. Or the slight nod she was the only recipient of.

Maybe she had a weakness for men in suits. Or maybe it was his severe demeanor. It should've repelled her, but for some reason, it had the opposite effect.

Her office was on the third floor, and his was higher up. It seemed so easy to just stay in the elevator, ride it up to where he got out, follow him to his office, and find out his name. But she didn't have the guts to do it. Even though he'd never done more than nod in greeting, he must've noticed that she'd always gotten out before him. There was no reason for her to go any farther than that.

Her intentions would've been transparent.

Finally, some peace and quiet.

With a sigh, Samuel leaned back in his chair and looked out the windows of his twelfth-floor corner office. The sun had set hours ago, and since the smog was not too bad the stars were visible.

Not that Sam was into stargazing, but he needed to take a moment to wind down before tackling the stack of proposals he had to go over. His cyber security business was booming, which was good, but he was running out of steam, which was bad.

At least now that everyone had gone home, Sam could concentrate on the task without being bothered by phone calls and people coming in and out of his office. Or so he thought until Gregg opened the door and walked in, his flip-flops slapping against the floor.

As usual, his partner's idea of appropriate office attire was baggy shorts, a button down shirt that was never ironed, and either sandals or flip-flops.

Gregg planted his butt in a chair across from Sam. "Why are you still here?"

"I can ask you the same question."

"I forgot something in my office. What's your excuse?"

"I have work to finish."

"Don't we all. Go home, Sam. "

"What for? So I can take the proposals home and finish going over them there? I prefer not to. It's not like I have someone waiting for me."

"And whose fault is that?"

"Fuck off, Gregg. I'm not in the mood for one of your philosophical lectures."

"Not all women are nasty, self-centered, manipulative, gold-diggers."

No, just the ones Sam had had the misfortune of dating.

He was done with that.

Maybe he should get himself a mail-order bride from

Ukraine, or some other shit-hole that happened to produce hotties who wanted American husbands. But with his luck, he'd get stuck with another nasty viper. The only difference would be the Russian accent. Or Ukrainian. Was there a difference?

"You know what your problem is?" Gregg stretched his legs out and crossed his arms over his chest.

"No. But I'm sure you're gonna tell me."

"You have a weakness for the glitzy model types. Why do you think they put so much effort into their looks? It's a bait to lure horny guys like you. You should look for a nice, ordinary girl."

As if that was going to happen while Sam worked hundred-hour weeks and interacted socially only during charity events, which were also work-related.

In the world of big business, Samuel was the face of the cyber security firm that he and Gregg had founded a decade ago. Participating in those events was not optional, and it wasn't fun. Supposedly, their purpose was to raise support for charity, but for him, as well as for many of the other attendees, the main purpose was drumming up new business. Mingling and schmoozing with the CEOs and decision makers of big corporations meant connecting with potential new clients.

That was where he'd met Alexandra. Or rather where she'd first sunk her claws into him. And before her, it had been Natasha, and before that, Tiffany.

They could've been clones. Beautiful, elegant, charming, attentive, and single-mindedly dedicated to achieving one goal—snagging a wealthy husband.

With each one, Sam had hoped this time it would be different. After all, some of the women attending those events were CEOs of companies and top-tier executives, but he'd never been lucky enough to be approached by one of them. The ones who gravitated toward him had only one thing in mind, and contrary to their sales pitch, it wasn't sex, it was matrimony.

As the saying went, lunacy was doing the same thing over and over and expecting different results. Since the last breakup, Sam was doing his damnedest to ignore attractive women in general. He was tired of the drama, and he needed a break to clear his head.

It wasn't easy. Temptation was everywhere. Like that pretty accountant in the elevator, with her glasses and her sensible shoes and her guileless eyes. It was all fake. Underneath the unassuming, nice girl façade there was probably just another viper. After all, she was a junior partner in a large CPA firm, which meant that she was smart, calculating, and interested in money.

A nice girl. Right. Not in his world. Maybe they existed in fairy tales.

"Don't you have anything better to do than harass me?" Sam glared at his partner. "I'm not sitting here and scratching my balls. I have work to do."

Gregg grinned. "Actually, I need to get back to my office and pick up one of those gift certificates the guys from Perfect Match gave us. I'm going to take it home and schedule myself a virtual hookup."

"Have fun. Just remember that those gift certificates represent half of our compensation." The other half was in the company's stock.

The job they'd done for Perfect Match wasn't one of Sam's better deals. The company was young, and all their investment capital had gone into developing their sophisticated hardware and software. In addition, it had been a cyber security nightmare that had taken months to implement. The main reason Sam had agreed to take it on at that price was that the CEO was an old buddy of his and Gregg's from Caltech.

Besides, he believed the company had promise, and if it

succeeded, their stock would one day be worth a lot more. Not only that, in the long run they would become a well-paying client. With plans to expand their services globally, they would need a lot more cyber protection and Sam's company would be the natural choice.

Given the glowing reviews of the beta testers, the service had great potential. Especially once they reached a volume that would allow them to lower their prices. Currently, it was out of reach for most.

"Oh, I will." Gregg waggled his brows.

"You really enjoyed the test run."

When they'd been approached, Gregg had volunteered to check it out before they committed to a complicated job that initially wasn't going to bring in any money.

"It was all they'd promised and more. You should try it."

"I will, just after you tell me all the details of your fun-ride." Which wasn't going to happen. Gregg, who had no problem butting into Sam's love life, was very tight-lipped about his own. Real or virtual.

"Let me tell you one thing, Sam. Women are just as horny as men. Perhaps more so because they have better imaginations. Give a woman a safe environment to explore her sexuality, and she'll blow your mind." With that, Gregg pushed to his feet, pulled out a folded envelope and dropped it on the desk. "Here, your perfect, custom-made girlfriend awaits."

Sam arched a brow. "I thought you forgot to pick up the gift certificate and that's why you were back."

"I did. I forgot to pick one up for you. That one was mine."

PERFECT MATCH 2: KING'S CHOSEN
IS AVAILABLE ON AMAZON

Also by I. T. Lucas

Dark Haven
47: Dark haven Illusion
48: Dark Haven Unmasked

PERFECT MATCH
Perfect Match 1: Vampire's Consort
Perfect Match 2: King's Chosen
Perfect Match 3: Captain's Conquest

The Children of the Gods Series Sets

Books 1-3: Dark Stranger trilogy—Includes a bonus short story: The Fates take a Vacation

Books 4-6: Dark Enemy Trilogy —Includes a bonus short story—The Fates' Post-Wedding Celebration

Books 7-10: Dark Warrior Tetralogy

Books 11-13: Dark Guardian Trilogy

Books 14-16: Dark Angel Trilogy

Books 17-19: Dark Operative Trilogy

Books 20-22: Dark Survivor Trilogy

Books 23-25: Dark Widow Trilogy

Books 26-28: Dark Dream Trilogy

Books 29-31: Dark Prince Trilogy

Books 32-34: Dark Queen Trilogy

Books 35-37: Dark Spy Trilogy

Books 38-40: Dark Overlord Trilogy

Books 41-43: Dark Choices Trilogy

Books 44-46: Dark Secrets Trilogy

MEGA SETS

The Children of the Gods: Books 1-6—includes character lists

The Children of the Gods: Books 6.5-10—includes character lists

---

TRY THE CHILDREN OF THE GODS SERIES ON AUDIBLE
2 FREE audiobooks with your new Audible subscription!

FOR EXCLUSIVE PEEKS AT UPCOMING RELEASES & A FREE COMPANION BOOK

Join my *VIP Club* and gain access to the VIP portal at

ITLUCAS.COM

CLICK HERE TO JOIN

(OR GO TO: http://eepurl.com/blMTpD)

INCLUDED IN YOUR FREE MEMBERSHIP:

- **FREE** CHILDREN OF THE GODS COMPANION BOOK 1
- **FREE** NARRATION OF GODDESS'S CHOICE—BOOK 1 IN THE CHILDREN OF THE GODS ORIGINS SERIES.
- PREVIEW CHAPTERS OF UPCOMING RELEASES.
- AND OTHER EXCLUSIVE CONTENT OFFERED ONLY TO MY VIPS.

Printed in Great Britain
by Amazon

57520486R00185